The Signal Tree

Mike E. Hughes

Signal Tree Books

For information, contact:

Mike E. Hughes

Website: www.mikeehughes.com

mikehughesee@outlook.com

ISBN (print): 979-8-9942688-0-3

First Edition February 2026

Dedication

Grandpa John

a kindred spirit across time

Contents

Acknowledgments

To my wife, Betty: Your unwavering support and patient understanding made the long hours of writing possible and joyful. Thank you for your inspiration and encouragement every step of the way.

To my daughter, son-in-law, and grandkids: Your love, enthusiasm, and constant cheering lifted my spirits throughout this journey. I am grateful for every moment of support and every reminder of why stories matter.

To my editor, Rita Halter Thomas: Your keen eye, thoughtful feedback, and dedication sharpened this story at every turn. I am deeply grateful for your editorial expertise and partnership in shaping these pages.

To Jerry Jenkins and his support team at Leverage Brands: Your wisdom, practical teaching, and the Your Novel Blueprint program provided the foundation for my craft. Your guidance and resources shaped my creative journey in immeasurable ways.

To Laurence O'Bryan and the BooksGoSocial team: Thank you for your comprehensive support in formatting and launching this book. Your professionalism, encouragement, and help with publishing logistics, website design, marketing, and early reader outreach made the final step from polished draft to publication possible.

I am forever thankful to each of you for being an essential part of this book and this dream.

Rooted in reverence, with heartfelt embrace,
Guided by the signal tree's ancient trace.
Forever the bond between us unbroken,
Ancestry honored, their stories awoken.

Chapter 1
Chicago—Last Look

If Dad were here, things would be different.

Finnwick Shepperd stood on the fourteenth-floor balcony of their Oak Brook condo, one hand wrapped around a stainless-steel travel mug, eyes tracing the distant skyline's sprawl. Early September air, a mix of exhaust and fresh-mown grass—Chicago waking, crisp and bright.

Far below, Interstate 88 stitched its way through the city, a river of cars streaming east. He could almost convince himself this was just another morning out for air, not his last look.

A heavy duffle hung from his shoulder, packed with more than clothes: an odd collection of things he couldn't store, wouldn't dare ship, and probably shouldn't need—his wrestling medal, a photo booth strip of him and Latesha pulling faces at Grant Park, and the coin Dad used to press into his palm for luck.

His phone buzzed. Latesha: "Call me when you get there—and get back before we miss another Grant Park day!" A second buzz—Rick, his Montini teammate: "Bro, hurry back before practice fr. Congrats on snagging captain!"

Wick exhaled, something caught between a sigh and a laugh. Captain. It felt good—if he didn't lose the honor before senior year started. He thumbed Latesha's text, hesitating. There wasn't anything he could say that wouldn't come off as a promise he wasn't sure he could keep.

Inside, the condo was a hollow shell, boxes lined up like dominoes—kitchen, books, Mom's shoes—waiting for a moving truck that should never have come. The couch was gone, leaving deep dents in the carpet—just like the ones where Dad's "command post" chair always sat for Bulls games. Wick wiped his eyes, shook himself, and stepped into the hallway, intent on one last look before Chicago disappeared.

The elevator dinged. Trey, their building's maintenance supervisor, stepped off, wielding a "For Sale or Lease" sign. He gave Wick a quick once-over and grinned.

"Morning, champ. Made us proud at the Montini Spring Invitational."

"Thanks, Mr. Trey." Wick offered a smile he didn't quite feel.

Trey's smile softened. "Hard to believe you're leaving. I remember when your folks brought you home swaddled like a burrito. Now look at you. Growing up, winning medals, ready to take on the world."

Wick tried to respond, but all that came out was, "Yeah."

Wick eyed the "For Sale or Lease" sign in Trey's hands, the words landing harder than he'd expected. "Your mom said to put this up today. Painters come tomorrow. Place won't look the same without your dad's running medals."

Wick kicked at the worn carpet, desperate not to say goodbye. "You think I could use the basement bunk room, if Mom lets me come back to finish school?"

Trey's face lit up. "You can bet on it. Heck, help me deliver packages or groceries to the neighbors if you want to make a few bucks. Montini needs its champ."

On impulse, Wick hugged him—one fast squeeze, awkward but real.

In the parking lot, Mom's SUV was packed tight with duffle bags, backpacks, and a cooler stuffed with sandwiches and whatever cereal she declared travel ready. Nora—her mouth already set for teasing—slouched in the back seat, headphones on, fixing Wick with the kind of stare that usually meant she wanted the last word, even if nothing had been said yet.

"I can drive," Wick offered.

"Next time," Mom said, setting her purse between the seats and tapping the ignition button. "Traffic's thick."

He slid into the passenger seat. The air felt different—empty, somehow—like everything that mattered had failed to fit in the boxes.

The building fell away in the mirror as they pulled out, and Chicago faded behind them. Buildings turned to trees; expressways thinned to highways, then winding roads. Wick pressed his forehead against the window, counting down familiar landmarks— lakefront, school, park sign—until there were none left.

A blue sign streaked past: Welcome to Arkansas—The Natural State.

Wick heard his mom let out a breath as she pulled into the Mountain View Medical Center parking lot—no endless search in some multi-story deck, just a wide-open lot and a low, brick building. Nothing like the maze of glass-and-steel towers back home.

"We promised Gram and Gramps we'd stop," Mom said, shifting the car into park. "Uncle Billy's here."

Wick scratched his eyebrow, searching his memory for a face. "I hardly remember him."

"You used to love playing outdoors with Billy," Mom said, sighing as she sank back into her seat, closing her eyes for a moment and letting her hands rest at her sides.

"That was before I grew up." His words sounded final, even to him.

Mom nodded, eyes still closed for a moment as she drew a long breath before speaking. "He's in Room 214. Wait there while Nora and I check in with the nurse, okay? Don't wander."

The hallway was muted beige and smelled faintly of lemon cleaner—unmistakably hospital. Wick found Room 214 and slipped inside.

Billy—looking older and asleep—didn't stir as Wick crept past to look out the window. Wick's elbow bumped a glass, knocking it onto the floor with a crash.

Billy jolted awake—eyes unfocused and confused, still caught in a dream.

He lurched upright, planted himself between Wick and the door, and in a single, terrifying instant, grabbed for something Wick couldn't make out. The glint of a blade caught the cold hospital light.

Wick stiffened, suddenly aware that Billy was blocking his exit.

Chapter 2
The Signal Tree

Wick backed toward the window, his eyes darting between his escape route and Billy, his ninety-five-year-old great-great-uncle, standing in a hospital gown, holding a knife in one hand and gripping the rail of the hospital bed with the other. This was nothing like high school wrestling, where defeat ended with walking off the mat. He missed that certainty: the rules, the mats, the way Dad would clap his back after every match, win or lose. But now, everything felt like another crisis. He snatched an aluminum chair and hefted it between them, ready to fend off a charge. He glanced out the window. Two floors up—the tree limb would break his fall. He grimaced at the thought of missing. A broken leg still beat getting stabbed. The chair rattled in one hand while he fumbled at the latch with the other, never breaking eye contact with Billy.

Panic spiked as he realized the window was stuck. A more profound dread followed. *Mom and Nora could walk through that door any second.* He hesitated, picturing the three of them squished into the kitchen of their high-rise Chicago apartment, Dad humming behind the Sunday paper. He was never supposed to be the one protecting the family. He couldn't leave them. He abandoned any thought of escape, fingers biting into the cold aluminum frame until his knuckles whitened. He braced his feet, stance unyielding. "Billy. Stop." His voice was shaking but resolute. "Drop the knife."

Uncle Billy blinked rapidly, mumbling incoherent words under his breath. Wick took a step closer, gripping the chair like a shield.

"Stop muttering, Billy. I can't—" Wick hesitated, straining to catch meaning in the broken words. "I can't understand you."

Billy's wild eyes brightened with sudden recognition. "Finnwick. Can't believe you're here. Missed you."

"Great. I'm here," Wick said, cautiously keeping the chair between them. "Just put the knife down."

Billy didn't seem to hear him. "I got it back—it took everything, but I got it. They're watching. Always watching. The doctor, the nurse—" He sucked in a sharp breath and his gaze darted toward the door. "Take it. Crystal. Knife. Hide them."

Billy stumbled, hands trembling, glancing toward the door.

"Billy—set it down." Wick's heart slammed against his ribs, his skin prickling despite the lingering warmth of the room. He didn't dare look away from Billy.

"Guard them with your life, Wick," he whispered. "Like we used to. You and I, together."

Wick swallowed hard, his confusion deepening. "Together? Billy, what are you—"

"No—no time to catch up." His eyes darted to the door. "Tomorrow. Come tomorrow. Alone." Billy hunched at the edge of the bed, clutching the blanket. He jolted upright, panic rising in his voice. "They can't see."

Wick slid the knife into its leather sheath and shoved it into his pocket, along with the small crystal Billy pressed into his hand. Keeping his eyes on Billy, Wick edged toward the door. "I've got them. Stay back." He tightened his grip on the chair, steel in his voice now. "If you rush me, I'll slam you."

Wick's heart raced. He stumbled into the hallway beneath the buzz of a flickering fluorescent light casting harsh shadows that pulsed around him. He nearly jumped—then relief flooded him when he spotted his mom and Nora approaching from down the hall. Every step amplified sounds—his shoes squeaked, and distant doors creaked closed. Only now did he realize how tense he'd been; it was like the whole hospital had been closing in on him until that moment.

Nora's brow furrowed, as it often did when she was confused. "Whatcha doing with that chair? Stealing it?"

Mom paused, pinching the bridge of her nose. "Wick, what's happening?"

"Uncle Billy—he's not okay." Adrenaline still coursed through him.

Mom glanced at Billy's door. "Wick, stop fooling around. The nurse said he's out cold."

Wick tensed and grabbed her arm. "Seriously, Mom. Don't go in."

She shook him off with a smile. "Wick, honey, I don't have time for games." She peeked through the small window and chuckled softly. "See? He's snoring. Told you—he's fine."

Wick bit back a protest, his pulse racing. "We should go."

Mom herded them to the stairwell. "Come on, kids. Let's get to your grandparents. They'll be glad we're moving to Mountain View."

A man stepped into their path. "Mrs. Shepperd?"

Mom blinked, her confusion evident. "Yes? Have we met?"

"I'm Vilnius Whitmore." He extended his hand. "George and I played football in high school. He always talked about you."

"Oh—George. Do you know him well?"

"We were part of the '98 state championship team." Vilnius's tone softened. "It truly saddens me to hear about his disappearance. Is there any news?"

Mom's expression tightened slightly. "Three months now—nothing new."

Vilnius shook his head solemnly. "That's a shame. I admire George. If anyone can survive, it's him. He's resourceful."

Mom forced a tight smile—one she used when she was done talking. "Thank you, Mr. Whitmore. Excuse us. My parents are waiting."

As they walked by, Wick sensed Vilnius's gaze. "Sorry about your dad," Vilnius said. "By the way—did Billy tell you anything?"

Wick froze mid-step, his heart racing at the question. Had he been watching? "No—nothing. Billy was out."

Vilnius gestured down the hall, where a young woman in a hospital gown slowly paced while holding an IV stand. "That's my daughter, Abby. She likes to check on Billy during her treatment."

Wick forced a nod, his fingers brushing the pocket where the knife and crystal were tucked away. "Nice to meet you." What did he know about Billy? He pushed past Vilnius and hurried toward the stairwell.

"Reach out if you need anything," Vilnius called after him. Vilnius's words lingered, gnawing at him. *Reach out? No way.* The knife and crystal weighed heavily in his pocket, a reminder of the uncertainty pressing down on him.

He could hardly focus as his mom talked about Gram and Gramps, the farm, and something about s'mores waiting for them. Delectable treats couldn't bring Dad home.

Pulling away from the hospital, Wick sank into his seat. Passing the Stone County courthouse in downtown Mountain View, the buff-colored stone walls caught his attention, glowing softly in the afternoon sun. The stones resembled nature's time capsule—rough, grainy, and weathered. The warm, earthy tones lent the courthouse a timeless quality. Nearby buildings appeared stuck in time; their storefronts closed, as though evening had settled early. They passed an old gas station, its rusted pump beneath a faded Coca-Cola sign—relics of a forgotten era.

Wick's focus drifted. *Should I tell them? About Billy, Vilnius, the crystal—the sheer insanity of it all?* But Mom looked so worn, fragile. How would she handle it? He pressed his forehead to the window, closing his eyes for a second.

Tomorrow—he decided. Sort the puzzle out first.

Wick stared out the window as trees blurred past, wishing for something—anything—familiar.

Nora's voice sliced through the tension. "This road feels like a rollercoaster. Do you miss Chicago yet, Wick?"

He grunted. "Yeah. It's just trees here."

Nora nudged Wick. "Did you call Latesha?"

Wick shook his head, glancing at his phone. "Not yet."

"Didn't you promise to call when we got here?" Mom asked.

"I will. It's been—a lot," Wick muttered, not sure how to explain the knot in his chest.

They turned onto a dusty, unpaved road that led through an old iron gate at the end of the road. Mom eased off the gas, letting the car slow. "We're here."

Wick's voice dripped with disbelief. "Here? We can't live here."

"It's better than you realize. Gram and Gramps put a lot into the place."

The tires crunched over loose gravel. The 1930s home stood ahead, its siding not wood but weathered, faded asphalt shingles, old and seemingly forgotten by time. Nothing about it looked like their high-rise apartment in Chicago. Wick turned to estimate the expanse of land. White oak trees appeared to stretch on indefinitely. Yet his eyes kept drifting back to the house. The windows were framed by chipped whitewash over weathered wooden panes, the paint flaking off in small, brittle pieces, like bark shedding from a birch tree. The past had latched onto every corner of this place, filling the entire structure with years of untold stories.

"How big is this place?" Wick said.

"It's over three thousand acres," Mom said with a lift in her voice.

Nora stared out the window. "What's the big deal?"

Mom tapped the brake. "You'll understand in time." She hesitated before continuing. "There's more to learn—about who you are."

Wick glanced at her, curiosity sparking. "What do you mean?"

Mom smiled as if she had been expecting this. "You and your sister have Cherokee blood from your gramps. This land has been in our family for generations."

Wick blinked. "So—we're Cherokee?"

She chuckled softly. "Technically, it's part of who we are, but we haven't been immersed in the culture for quite some time. Our family history stretches back much farther than I can explain."

Wick put his hand on his head, unsure how to process it.

"You'll understand more when you talk to Gramps. Our heritage is more than just blood, Wick. It's about a connection, respect for the land, and respect for traditions. Gramps feels that deeply. Trust me, he can explain it better."

Wick stared again at the towering lines of trees, Mom's words tumbling through his mind.

He tried to envision this forest as something more—something he was meant to feel connected to—but the idea seemed distant, like a story he hadn't yet learned. As they neared their destination, his attention wandered. A white picket fence framed the house, but it wasn't the house that captivated him the most.

It stood out sharply against the towering oaks lining the forest as though it had secrets to share.

"What's with that bent tree?"

"Oh, that's a signal tree," Mom said. "The Cherokee used them to point to important places—like water sources, caves, or hunting areas."

Wick stared at it, intrigued despite his longing for Chicago—and Dad. The tree looked old—like it had been shaped that way on purpose.

Gram and Gramps walked out, grinning and waving.

"Nora, Wick, hop out and hug Gram and Gramps," Mom said.

Gram stood by the fence, tall and slender in a wide-brimmed sun hat, her long brunette hair tucked behind her ears. Her reading glasses dangled from a string around her neck, same as always. She waved with both hands, smiling wide. Gramps was beside her—muscular, balding under a worn cap, his overalls dusty, hands thick and calloused. They looked older than Wick remembered—more weathered. He used to run straight into their arms, but now, at seventeen, he found himself half-heartedly returning their hug, self-conscious about not being a little kid anymore.

"Laura. You must be exhausted." Gram hugged her tightly. "Come inside, dear. You need a nap."

The screen door spring released a distinctive creak as it closed behind his mom and Gram.

Wick let out a breath when Gram ushered Mom into the house, leaving him and Nora alone with Gramps.

They rounded the side of the house, their steps crunching softly on the gravel path. Wick and Nora found themselves beneath a canopy of towering oak trees as they approached a garden. A circular fire ring was surrounded by six time-worn wooden chairs, each with simple cushions tied to the seats. The earthy scent of charred wood lingered in the air. Wick paused, the scene tugging at a half-buried memory—he'd sat here before, maybe seven years old, legs too short to touch the ground, watching Gramps coax flames from kindling. He hadn't thought about that for years. Now the chairs looked smaller. It felt like stepping into a moment that had waited for him to return.

Gramps grinned, gesturing toward the fire ring. "I'll teach you how to start a fire," he said. "You need to learn survival skills. You never know when they might come in handy."

As Gramps went to gather wood, Wick pulled out his phone and scrolled aimlessly. His signal bars flickered between one and none. "Nora, listen. I can't stay here."

Nora's eyes widened. "What do you mean? You just got here."

"I need to head back." Wick glanced at the fire ring before turning to his sister. "Getting captain of the Montini wrestling team is a great honor. If I don't go back, they'll pick someone else. I've worked too hard to let this slip away."

"You promised to stay." Nora's voice broke. "I'll be all alone—" She hesitated, then added more softly, "And what about Dad? We still need to find him."

"You'll be fine," Wick said, his expression firm yet gentle. "Gram and Gramps will be here, and so will Mom."

"And what about Dad?" Her voice trembled.

Wick sighed deeply. He had been dreading this conversation. "Sis, think about it. Would Mom have moved us here if she thought Dad was coming back?" He paused before voicing the thoughts that had been clawing at his mind for weeks. "No one is even searching anymore."

"Don't you dare say that." Nora's eyes brimmed with tears, and her voice echoed through the trees. "Dad's not gone. He's not."

"We all love Dad, Nora," Wick said, quieting his tone. "But it's been three months."

She shook her head, choking back a sob. "Then why won't you stay? If you love him, why are you leaving?"

Wick hesitated. To Nora, staying meant searching—meant hope. But to him, it felt like standing still while everything he'd worked for slipped away.

"I need that scholarship. You know how much my Olympic dream means to me. This is my chance, and I can't throw it away—"

"Who cares about scholarships or the Olympics at a time like this? Dad's more important." Nora crossed her arms, glaring at him.

"Look, I know Dad is important." Wick ran a hand through his hair. "We'll see how things go tomorrow. Let's relax and visit Gram and Gramps."

Nora wiped her eyes and turned away. Wick kicked the dirt, letting the conversation end there, wishing he hadn't said anything.

Gramps returned with kindling. "See, kids? You need sticks of different sizes. Small ones, like matchsticks, some the size of pencils, and finally, ones as thick as your arm. That's how you build a fire."

Wick gave a thumbs-up. "Sure, Gramps."

Gramps stacked the wood in a teepee, then headed into the house. "I'll be right back, kids."

Eager to change the subject, Wick pulled out his phone and typed into the search bar. His signal wavered—one bar, then none—but the page finally loaded. "Hey, check this out. I found a quick way to start a fire."

"How?"

"Gasoline. I saw a can by the shed."

"Are you sure about that?" Nora shook her head. "I'm standing back."

Wick poured gasoline over the woodpile.

"Wick, don't," Nora said.

He struck the match, and Gramps appeared in the back porch doorway. "Don't—" But it was too late. The fumes from the gasoline had already risen to meet the match flame. A deafening whoosh rang out, and the woodpile exploded into a blazing fireball. The blast hurled Wick backward. Nora's scream pierced the air. The world spun in chaotic flashes of fire and sky before everything went black.

Chapter 3
Lost

When Wick opened his eyes, the world spun. Gramps was above him, calling his name, but the sound was drowned out by the persistent, sharp ringing in Wick's head. Slowly, the ringing faded, and Gramps's voice broke through. "Finnwick. Are you okay? Can you hear me?"

Wick coughed, bit by bit returning to reality. He barely nodded. "Yeah—I'm fine." *Did that just happen?*

"That's my boy," Gramps said, clearly relieved. "Stay seated. Take it easy."

As Mom leaned in to scold Wick, Gramps held up his hand to defuse the situation. "Now, he's okay. Let's enjoy the fire and roast hot dogs."

The fire still blazed nearby, casting a warm glow, calming and eerie all at once. The danger had passed, but this new life's strange and unfamiliar environment and what had happened with Uncle Billy still loomed large in Wick's mind. *I can't believe I did that. What was I thinking—gasoline?*

Gram brought out hot dogs and marshmallows as they sat by the fire. Wick and Nora skewered hot dogs and made s'mores.

Wick saw Gramps whittling a stick and reached into his pocket to retrieve the knife Billy had given him. Gramps asked to see the knife and, chuckling, leaned over to demonstrate how to pass it properly. "Spine of the blade, son. Don't want to cut yourself."

Wick wanted to tell Gramps about Billy, the knife, and the crystal, but Gramps seemed to enjoy the moment too much for Wick to spoil it. "This is rusty. How about I sharpen it and give it back to you tomorrow?"

"Sure."

After dinner, when the fire was dying and everyone was enjoying the evening breeze, Gramps leaned over and carefully handed Wick a small, plastic-covered object. "Here, before I forget—it's yours."

Wick blinked as he took the coin. "What is this?"

"An 1855 Seated Liberty Silver Dollar. This one's proof grade—it's worth near $20,000. I've been saving it for you. You can do what you want with it—car, college, it's up to you."

Wick was stunned. "Gramps, this is unbelievable."

Gramps smiled. "We can't give you much, boy, but this—this should help you get a start. You'll be going to college soon. If you need funding, you can sell it. It's your call."

Wick pocketed it carefully, grateful but distracted. He stared at the towering tree past the house, noticing its odd shape. "What's up with that tree?"

Gramps glanced at it with a smile. "That, my boy, is a signal tree. Native Americans used them as signposts to point toward water sources or hunting grounds."

Wick listened but barely concentrated. There was too much to process—Billy's cryptic warnings, Vilnius, this new land, and the history Gramps had mentioned.

Gramps shook his head and continued. "Our land is rich in resources—timber, rocks, and minerals. I've turned down offers, even one from a company named Crystalis Vitalis, offering to buy it for $10 million."

"You're kidding—why do they want the land?"

"Couldn't say, but I don't trust what anyone else might do to it—sell off the trees, build houses, strip mine. People think we own the land. The county says we own the land. On paper, we own the land. The truth is, we belong to the land. Can we carry the land with us? No. We return to dust, but the land, rocks, and trees will remain long after we're gone. I want to honor those who came before me. I've done my part to preserve the land, and when I'm gone, I hope you and Nora will do the same."

Wick heard Gramps talking, but his mind went elsewhere. *Wow. I'd sell. I wonder how much the penthouse costs.* He imagined the opulence of viewing Lake Michigan from the twentieth floor as he reached for his phone. Wick walked to the other side of the campfire, faced away, and began searching.

His thoughts were interrupted by Gramps resting a hand on his shoulder. "Wick, you seem preoccupied—can I help with anything?"

"Well, I was wondering if you have Wi-Fi—you know, in case Nora and I need it for school."

"No, we don't have it yet. Your mom asked us to check last month. Yelcot said they could put it in. It should be ready before school starts. Do you need Wi-Fi before school starts?"

Rats. Embarrassed, Wick put the phone in his pocket. "No, sir, I was just wondering."

"Alright," Gramps said, patting Wick on the back. "There are a few hours of daylight left—you could explore a little. Start near that signal tree. I think you'll find it interesting."

Wick hesitated. "I'm not the outdoor type, Gramps. I don't want to get lost like Dad."

Gramps laughed. "Your dad couldn't get lost. He knows the land too well."

"Well, maybe a bear got him," Wick said half-jokingly.

"Not likely." Gramps chuckled. "These aren't grizzly bears like you see in the movies—these are black bears. I've lived here my whole life and have only seen bears twice—they ran away. Black bears avoid humans. Nothing's gonna hurt you out there." He pointed toward the signal tree. "Look, we're on a hill. How about you start at the signal tree and walk a short distance? When you're ready, retrace your steps. Whatever you do, don't cross a creek. Remember, walk uphill to get back. You'll see the house or the road. Even if it gets dark, you can see the house lights or the blinking lights on the radio tower. Call if you need help. You're here now, and you need to learn the property. Have fun exploring."

Wick hesitated, staring at the dense forest ahead. He'd never explored anywhere except Chicago's Grant Park, and that was always with friends and family. There were trees in Grant Park, but nothing like this—nothing so dense and looming. There were no sidewalks here, just uneven ground and paths that seemed to vanish into shadow. As Wick neared the signal tree, he looked back. Gramps smiled and gave a thumbs-up, but the warmth of his gesture faded quickly as the forest swallowed Wick's frame. Downhill, a large boulder, the size of an elephant, loomed, adding to the sense of foreboding. He turned in the direction the signal tree pointed, his breath tight in his chest. Every sound—every rustle of leaves—seemed amplified in the stillness.

As he stepped forward, unease crept over him, but the thought of disappointing Gramps nudged him onward. The path ahead was dim, shrouded by a thick canopy overhead. The shadows deepened with every step. The forest didn't just surround him—it pressed in. Each step felt like a journey beyond the point of no return. Gramps said it was safe, but something in the evening air whispered otherwise.

Here goes.

Wick pushed farther along the faint path, the trees leaning in as though they were keeping whispered secrets from him. His steps echoed softly against the ground, the crackle of twigs and leaves beneath his feet the only sound—until an insistent knock broke the silence.

Tap. Tap. Tap.

Wick froze mid-step and turned his head toward the noise. Perched high on a towering oak was a woodpecker, easily the size of a crow. Its crimson crest stood out against the dull bark, flaring like the tip of a matchstick. Each strike of its beak sent a rhythmic thud reverberating through the forest—unnaturally loud in the quiet, like the bird was hammering directly into his chest, almost too powerful for a bird.

The tapping bird looked more at home than Wick felt. He drew a slow breath as the tension in his muscles eased. He watched it hop along the tree, trying to shake the feeling of being out of place. The sight reminded him of slow days in Grant Park, watching pigeons strut fearlessly between tourists' feet, back when things were normal and safe. *I miss home. It feels like a lifetime ago.*

Wick turned and glanced behind him, where tangled vegetation thinned just enough for the roof of Gramps's house to peek through. Barely visible, the house clung to the horizon like a lifeline, its red metal roofing a reminder he wasn't completely lost. *I could head back now.* He shifted uneasily, aware that Gramps probably thought he'd gone farther by now, deep into the woods. A grin tugged at his lips. *No sense going far. I can explore later.*

He circled back, feeling the tension in his shoulders ease as he returned to the signal tree's crooked trunk. Wick slid down with his back against the rough bark, catching his breath. Staring up at the sky, he saw jet contrails streaking toward Chicago.

Wick's hand brushed his pocket. The coin. *Twenty thousand dollars. Bronco or red Camaro? I still can't believe it.* Holding it, feeling its cool, heavy surface, grounded him. He pulled out the crystal Uncle Billy had given him, admiring its glassy, smooth, pointed surface.

What was Billy trying to warn about? He turned the crystal over in his hand, cold and smooth against his skin. *If Billy is crazy, why does this feel important?*

He leaned his head against the tree and closed his eyes, both the coin and crystal clasped tight.

At that moment, the world seemed to lurch beneath him. His vision tilted. He tried to steady himself, but the ground shifted, spinning beneath his feet in dizzying circles. He swayed, gripping the coin and crystal tighter as though they could keep him grounded, but the unsteadiness worsened.

The shift was fast. He fell.

The expected impact never came. When the dizziness faded and he blinked the blur from his eyes, the world around him had transformed.

He sat up slowly as the strange reality presented itself. The ground had been solid and warm before; now, it was soft and cold.

Snow?

His heart skipped. Deep white blankets stretched across the ground, so thick his hands almost vanished as they plunged into it. He blinked, scrambling to stand, his breath coming in shallow gasps as his sneakers squeaked against the frosty ground.

His mind raced, confusion blooming into panic.

"What?" he hollered, his voice thin against the frigid air. The cold bit his face brutally, attacking the skin on his arms and legs that had been warm just moments ago. *It's summer. I swear!*

He'd been walking not five minutes earlier, under the hot sun filtering lazily through green leaves. Now, the sun was a pale orange disk, hanging low and angled in the wrong direction. Before, when he'd looked downhill, the sun had been off to his right. Now, facing the same way, it slanted off to his left—as though the world had quietly spun out of place. And the sky—clear now, with no contrails like before—made it even stranger. Everything seemed off. *Am I losing my mind?*

Wick's breath turned to white clouds as he took in his icy, breath-heavy surroundings—the skeletal trees, bare and brittle under a layer of frost. The oppressive canopy that pressed in from above was gone, leaving emptiness and an open sky behind. The boulder was still downhill. The signal tree loomed overhead, its twisted branches unmistakable, pointed toward something unseen. This was the same place.

But time—the trees, the snow—everything told him that time had shifted.

How long was I out?

Panic surged, his pulse racing as confusion morphed into a strange mix of dread and disbelief. He'd spent countless winters in Chicago. The snow wasn't foreign. Nor was the chill biting at his bare skin. But this—this was different. This wasn't Grant Park where you could duck into a museum or café and thaw out.

Wick's thoughts jumped to Nora, masking the fear momentarily. His sister loved the snow, holidays, and winter breaks—the excitement of sledding downhill. *She will love this. I've got to tell her!*

But as he looked for the red roof, there was no house. No Nora.

The wind shifted, colder this time, punishing him for standing still. Wick looked around for a sign of warmth or comfort. But optimism had vanished along with summer.

He pulled out his phone, hoping the small screen would offer some explanation—or connection.

Nothing.

Full battery when we got here, he thought. *What the heck?*

He pressed the power button repeatedly, shaking it like that would do anything.

"Come on!" he snapped, feeling helpless. *How is it dead?*

Wick scanned the area, the wind seeping through the fabric of his lightweight shirt, cutting deep. All around him was nothing but frost-bitten land and disturbingly bare trees. *It's too cold for this.* Where the house stood, the land stretched desolately on. There was no home. There was no road.

Where are they? I can't just stand here.

Reluctantly, he pocketed the dead phone and tried to think logically. *How did I end up here? Wish Gramps were here.* Gramps had told him to avoid crossing the creek. The logic must still apply. Wick pushed back his fear, cleared his throat, and turned downhill. *I have to go. I have to survive.*

His sneakers, meant for pavement, weren't made for trekking through snow. Each step was carefully negotiated over hidden rocks, roots, and ice. He stumbled more than once, his hands flying out for balance. *I can retrace my steps*, he reminded himself. The tracks he left behind in the fresh snowfall glistened as his safety line.

By the time he reached the creek, the cold had sunk deep into his bones. The wind whistled, gnawing at his ears and cheeks despite his constant movement. His arms grew tired from crossing them against his chest for warmth. The shallow stream gurgled, the sound small against the oppressive silence as if even the water were too cold to roar.

Wick paused. *Don't cross it*, he reminded himself. Gramps's calm but firm voice hovered in his mind. Instead of stepping over the rocks and moving to the wrong side, he turned and followed it upstream.

Then, Wick saw a peculiar and out-of-place shape through the trees. His heartbeat quickened. His eyes widened as two horses, pulling what looked like a wagon, materialized near the water's edge. A man knelt beside one rear wheel, fiddling with it, seemingly lost in focus.

Wick's heart leaped—hope against reason. He ran toward the man, snow crunching underfoot, barely noticing the man's old-fashioned attire, the thick winter coat, leather gloves, and trim hat more reminiscent of—a period movie. But that didn't matter. Help was help.

"Hey! Hey!" Wick waved his hand, his voice echoing across the empty forest. Out of breath, he stumbled to a stop by the wagon. "Can you help me? I'm lost. I—I need to use your phone."

Startled, the man jerked upright and grabbed a rifle resting against the wagon. His eyes narrowed as he looked at Wick, uncertainty clouding his features. Seeing Wick's distressed state, he slowly lowered the rifle but kept it within reach, his gaze still cautious. The man appeared to be in his late thirties or early forties, his brown beard flecked with snow.

"Phone, you say?" he asked, his voice carrying a hint of suspicion.

"Yeah, a phone, a telephone. Can I use it, please? I need to get a message to my mom."

The man straightened up, brushing snow off his gloves. "Well, Sonny, if you want to send a message, you need a telegraph. But ain't no telegraph out here." The man glanced at the horizon; his gaze searching for something. "Saw one up in Springfield, though. That's upstate, Missouri—a long way off." He smiled to himself without explanation. "Wired my sister in Oregon last time I was there. I sure miss my little sis."

I've landed where telephones are as foreign as a spaceship. The thought of never seeing his sister again hit Wick. *Nora.* His mouth went dry, remembering the playful conversations and the jealous teasing about who got Dad's attention more. A tear pooled at the corner of Wick's eye. He blinked before it could fall. He straightened, clearing his throat sharply, trying to pull himself together.

"Tain't no phones or telegraphs here, lad," the man continued, lowering his voice. "Only thing you got here is distance." He winked, then gestured to the wagon. "You help me with this wheel; maybe we can get somewhere."

"Mountain View?" Wick asked, hoping to get back to town to make sense of all this.

"Yes, I also like this view of the mountains."

"No, I mean the town of Mountain View?"

"Tain't no place called that around here. We're headed to Riggsville."

Wick blinked; nothing looked right. No power lines, no phones, no roads. No Mountain View. It was like he had gone back in time.

Chapter 4
Frozen

Wick considered his options as they repaired the wagon wheel, standing in the strange, snowy landscape that felt both unfamiliar and grimly real. He could retrace his steps to the elephant-sized boulder, hoping the world would right itself, or explore downstream alone and possibly freeze. At that moment, his only viable choice seemed to be going to Riggsville.

He exhaled a shaky breath, and his decision was made as he settled into the bench seat beside the driver. His thoughts were as scattered as the snowflakes swirling in the chilly air. Everything about this world felt simultaneously vivid and surreal, a dream he couldn't shake, no matter how hard he tried. *How is this possible?* The question echoed through his mind like a haunting refrain.

He couldn't wrap his head around it—one moment, he was in the forest during summer, and now, he was somewhere he could only describe as a history book come to life. His mind raced back to the bizarre events with the crystal and coin. Could they have caused this? This was beyond anything he could have prepared for. The world had shifted under his feet, making him feel like a pawn on a giant chessboard.

Harsh reality settled in, like the cold creeping through his clothes. He needed to survive—wherever he was. *What am I supposed to do?* An edge of desperation tinged his inner voice, fueled by the biting wind and the enormity of his predicament.

"I need clothes." Wick's teeth chattered, his lips barely able to form the words as the wagon bumped along the rough trail. "Boots. A jacket. I'm freezing." Each word slurred as the cold seeped through his soaked sneakers and jeans, the wind slicing into him like icy knives. The wagon's creaking was the only sound in the vast wilderness around him, and with each jostle, the isolation pressed harder, reminding him he was stranded—not just geographically, but in time itself.

The wagon driver, whose name Wick still hadn't caught or maybe just hadn't been listening for, cast a sideways glance at him as he softly called to the horses, gently urging them onward with light flicks of the reins. The flurrying snow shadowed the driver's face, but his voice rasped good-humoredly beneath his thick beard. "Ain't you got warmer things?"

"No, apparently, they're a bit short on North Face jackets in whatever century this is," Wick replied, half-joking, wrapping his arms tighter. Not funny, he realized—he was freezing.

The man eyed Wick's attire—jeans, sneakers, and a T-shirt—with a bemused chuckle. "Don't know what kinda mess you fell into, son, but we'll fix you up proper soon as we reach Riggsville. I reckon it'll take another hour—and that's if the horses don't decide to lie down and make snow angels. We're slogging along slower than a man could walk up these snowy roads. Reckon we'll be there about noon."

Wick was caught off guard. He thought it was still late afternoon. Morning! He hadn't just lost track of a few minutes or even hours. He'd somehow missed an entire night without noticing. And all the while, the world had shifted under him, as if someone hit fast-forward and left him behind.

Their conversation faded into silence as the miles of rough, rocky terrain stretched before them. Wick wished he could somehow leap through time again, bypassing freezing uncertainty. He couldn't help but scan the vast, snow-smothered hills rising in the distance, looking for anything that might make sense of his impossible situation.

None of this is real, Wick thought, rubbing his hands together in a futile attempt at warmth. It couldn't be. This had to be some elaborate practical joke.

Yet, the bite of the cold and the aching numbness in his feet argued otherwise.

The wagon driver cleared his throat and reined in the horses as if sensing the young man's discomfort. "Tell you what," he said, leaning over to unfasten two blankets from the horses. His bushy mustache twitched with amusement. "I'll loan you the horse blankets—the beasts'll manage for a while. You, though, look 'bout ready to freeze solid."

"You sure?" Wick asked, pulling the coarse woolen blanket around his back, his frozen body desperate for warmth.

As he wrapped thick blankets around his shoulders, warmth slowly returned to his chilled limbs. Wick let out a heavy breath, slumping in relief. He didn't mind the smell of horsehair and sweat clinging to the wool—right now, it was the best thing he'd ever felt.

"Thanks," he mumbled, unable to hide his gratitude. If not for this guy, he'd probably be a popsicle when they reached Riggsville.

"Well, you're welcome," the driver grunted. "Can't have you keelin' over. You'll have to carry the wagon if we lose the horses."

Wick cracked a weak smile in response. "Good thing I've been hitting the gym."

Bumping along in the wagon, snowflakes drifted lazily down, covering the rough road around them. Wick closed his eyes for a moment, trying to process everything. He tried piecing it together. One minute, he was in modern-day Arkansas, thumbing through his phone and considering his wrestling scholarship—and the next, he was thrown back into a snowy wilderness without warning: the signal tree—the spinning and falling sensation.

Was that it? Some—time warp?

Wick's brain was racing—wild with disoriented thoughts. Suddenly, Wick pictured his dad. *Dad! That's it. It has to be! Is this what happened to Dad?* The idea struck like a gut punch, and for a brief, heart-clenching moment, he allowed himself to entertain the possibility.

Maybe Dad hadn't gone missing or gotten lost after all. Perhaps he'd been transported somewhere too—in the same way, to this place, or another time entirely.

His breath hitched. *What if Dad's here somewhere?* The notion made Wick's pulse quicken, anxiety and hope colliding in a confusing mix. *Dad will know what to do.* The thought calmed him, even as it brought up feelings he'd buried long ago. *Dad can fix this. Dad will get us back to Mom, Nora, Gram, and Gramps.* Wick swallowed hard, closed his eyes briefly, and then looked at the driver.

"Hey, um—do you know anyone named George Shepperd?" Wick asked, trying to sound casual, disguising his angst and hopeful edge. *Please—please let Dad be in town.*

The driver's brow furrowed, and he shook his head. "George? Nah—can't say as I rightfully know anybody by that name. Sorry, lad."

Wick's heart sank. He bit down on the inside of his cheek, nodding. Of course, it wasn't going to be that easy. *But Dad could be here—somewhere. Right?*

Wick tried to shove the disappointment aside. It wasn't like the driver knew for sure. His dad could still be out there, somewhere. *Maybe Riggsville?* If luck was on his side. If this wasn't a dead end.

The wagon hit a big rut, and Wick grabbed the side rail to avoid being thrown off.

The driver laughed. "Rougher than a wild bronc, eh?"

Wick felt every bump as the wagon clambered over boulders and ruts that seemed impossible to cross. He knew he could walk faster than the wagon, but he was glad to have the ride.

He opened his eyes in time to see something on the horizon—a plume of smoke curling up beyond the next hill. More buildings, maybe? Civilization? Riggsville?

"That it?" Wick asked. His voice sounded hopeful, almost pleading.

The wagon driver leaned forward, shading his eyes against the falling snow. "Yep. Home sweet home. Riggsville ain't much, but she's warm. It'll do for now."

They crested the hill, and the town revealed itself in the valley below: a scattering of wooden buildings and horse-dotted fields. In the soft light, it looked picturesque—like something out of a movie set for an old western, complete with wooden porches, horse troughs, and smoke trailing lazily upward from chimneys.

The sight only stirred unease in Wick's gut. How long would it take to find a way back to his time?

He couldn't think about that now—not without losing it entirely. Instead, he concentrated on the approaching town, mentally listing what he'd need to survive. Warmer clothes. A decent meal. A place to sleep that didn't involve sharing a blanket with livestock.

***

As the wagon halted near the entrance to Riggsville, Wick hopped down, shaking the stiffness from his frozen legs.

"Best head over to the general store," the driver suggested, nodding toward a building with a wide, sagging porch. Signs painted in faded white letters read Tailor, Dry Goods & Sundries. "Jed will fix you up."

"Right," Wick said, nerves jangling as he eyed the front door. What were the chances that a guy named Jed stocked Patagonia jackets and Arc'teryx pants?

Stepping inside, Wick was assaulted by the smell of burning pine and—*potatoes?* The general store appeared to be a catch-all for every necessity, with shelves stacked high with canned goods, kitchenware, farm supplies, and bundles of clothes. The place looked like a Cracker Barrel with hanging pots and lanterns, and coal oil lamps with flames dancing behind glass.

"Noon, son," said the portly clerk behind the counter, sparing a glance as he fiddled with a worn ledger. "What can I get ya?"

"I need—everything," Wick said, bracing himself against the sudden rush of heat from the potbelly stove in the center of the store. He stepped up to the counter, his feet still feeling frozen despite the warmth in the room. "I need a coat, boots, hat, gloves—food and bottled water."

The clerk turned, grabbed a bottle from the shelf, and plopped it on the counter before Wick. "Got bottled elixir. Got bottled oil. If you want water, there's a well out back, or you can grab a drink from that bucket."

Wick turned to see the wagon driver take a long drink after picking up a ladle and scooping water from a bucket. Then Wick watched in wonder as the driver grabbed a second scoop and splashed his face, water dripping to the wooden floor with wide cracks.

Wick turned and looked around, trying not to show how much he wanted another option. He hesitated as he picked up the ladle, scooped some water, and took a small drink.

The clerk's bushy mustache twitched. "How you plannin' on payin', son?"

Wick leaned forward and spoke softly, as if speaking loudly would invite someone to rob him. "I have this rare coin worth a lot of money; thousands, but I don't want to sell it. Could you hold it until I bring you the money?" Wick pulled out the coin.

The man tilted his head back, then tossed his head into a laugh. "Worth what now?" He tipped his money box open wide to reveal handfuls of shiny coins identical to Wick's and, chuckling, placed his hands on his hips. "Looks like you're sittin' on a fortune, eh?"

Wick's face burned with frustration. "No, this one's—special."

The clerk raised an eyebrow and laughed harder. "If they were worth that much, I could retire, buy riverfront bottomland, and live the good life. No, shiny shoes and a fancy coin won't buy much here, son. We run on food and firewood." He finally caught his breath. "Look, tell ya what—gloves and a hot meal I can do for that coin, but that jacket and boots you want? More than you've got, I'd say."

Frustrated, Wick looked around the store as if some help would swoop in and get him out of this precarious situation. "Well, how about credit?"

The man gave a sharp glance that landed just shy of offended.

"Credit? Last I let that happen, ol' Jim moved off without paying. I'd like to get my hands on that guy." He slid the coin back across the counter. "Eh, lad. I like yer spirit. For now, if'n you want gloves and a scarf—that'll be one dollar. But I'm sorry, the coat and boots are more'n what you've got there."

Wick turned away, defeated. Searching for any money he might have overlooked, he emptied his pockets.

The clerk eyed the crystal, his eyebrow lifting with interest. "Is that—one of them healin' crystals from the mountain?"

Wick shrugged. "Maybe. I don't know."

The man's gaze fixed intently on the crystal, like a hawk zeroing in on its prey. His left hand flexed, as if testing an unseen pain. "Might be good for rheumatism! Can I hold it?"

"Okay, just don't drop it."

The clerk gently closed the crystal in his hand, his face softening as he twisted his wrist and tested the tightness in his joints. "Tell you what," he said slowly. "Trade this li'l gem, and I'll throw in the jacket, boots, and food you're askin' about."

Wick hesitated, his mind racing. *Could I part with Billy's crystal?* The decision gnawed at him.

Before Wick could decide, something on the counter caught his eye—a folded newspaper, its edges yellowed and frayed. *Crimean War rages on. Treaty of Neah Bay signed.* Wick blinked. He remembered the Crimean War from eleventh-grade history.

Impossible.

Snatching it, he scanned the top in disbelief. "1855!"

His voice broke, filled with its sheer absurdity. His heart thumped wildly now, each beat louder than the last.

The clerk glanced over, hardly impressed. "Oh, that? It's old, maybe two weeks or so. News don't travel fast out here."

But Wick barely heard him. His mind spun. The room in front of him blurred—oil lamps, woodstove, shelves lined with unfamiliar products, all far too real now.

The air seemed to close in, everything fading into a low, numbing hum. Wick's hands trembled as the magnitude of it all hit.

1855.

He wasn't just lost—*he was lost in time.*

Chapter 5
Howls in the Night

The clerk still held the crystal in his hand, his eyes gleaming slightly as he regarded it, but Wick wasn't ready to part with it—yet.

"I need a minute," Wick muttered. "I—I need to step outside."

The clerk raised an eyebrow, giving a sharp glance. "Sure, kid, but don't be long. Weather's blowin' in, and I don't wait forever for business to be done." He handed the crystal back gently, watching as Wick clutched it and stepped out.

The cold air hit fast as Wick stepped onto the porch. The frigid wind whipped through Riggsville, biting his face. His shoes crunched softly against the snow-covered planks beneath him.

He shivered—though the chill in the air was nothing compared to the cold realization wedged in his chest: *I'm in 1855. I need that coat.*

A hundred and seventy years. Gone.

Nora, Mom, all of it separated from everyone, stuck in a time far removed from the life he had known. Dad was nowhere to be found. He clenched his jaw. The world around him was eerily quiet—no hum of a distant plane, no traffic, nothing modern. Just the snow and the steady wind whispering through the trees, utterly indifferent to his plight.

I'll freeze out here.

Wick tightened his grip on the crystal Billy had shoved into his hand, but it couldn't keep him warm. The choice gnawed at him—trade the crystal and survive—or hold onto it and freeze. Wick turned the crystal over in his palm, the slick, glassy surface cool against his skin. Each rotation brought back Billy's warning from the hospital, a tumble of desperate words and wild eyes. What had he said—*guard it?* Or was that part of Billy's delusion? Wick's grip tightened, his breath steaming up around him. *Sorry, Billy,* he thought, forcing himself to focus on the here and now.

He instinctively pulled out his phone. He pressed the power button again, hoping it would come to life.

Nothing.

The blank screen might as well have been an abyss swallowing his last connection to the world he knew. He exhaled sharply, shoving the worthless blob of plastic back into his pocket. *No signal. No phone. Just 1855—and no family.* His pulse quickened. He didn't have a choice.

Wick took one last glance at the narrow street coated in snow, the wind whipping across it like something alive, and then straightened his shoulders.

He walked back inside the general store with stiff legs, inhaling deeply as the wood smoke clung like a blanket to the thick air. It felt warm and oppressive, the sudden heat almost suffocating after being outside. Everything inside was still strangely out of time—

lanterns flickering, wood stove crackling, pots and utensils hanging like relics. *How could this be real?*

The clerk's gaze darted upward when Wick entered. "You ready to deal?"

Wick nodded sharply, his stomach knotting. His fingers twitched, the knot in his stomach sinking deeper, like a stone slipping out of reach beneath dark water. "Okay. The coat, boots, gloves, hat, and food, but if I'm trading, you need to throw in the knife and matches."

The clerk gave him a nod and smiled before folding his arms. "Deal, but it ain't easy to get matches 'round here. Afraid a flint will have to do."

Wick frowned. "Flint? How do you use a flint?"

The clerk's eyes appeared to gleam with satisfaction. He guided Wick outside and ran through the motions. "It's easy, kid. Hit the flint with the back of the knife blade. Sparks hit your dry leaves or grass and blow to ignite the flame." Tiny sparks flickered before dissipating.

Wick forced a smile. "Thanks."

Back inside, Wick set the crystal on the counter. There was no hesitation.

"Good choice, kid."

Gathering his goods, Wick bundled the heavier coat against his chest and sighed. It won't fix things, he reminded himself before stepping out the door. *At least I can survive.*

***

Stepping onto the front porch, Wick considered exploring Riggsville, but realized he might lose his trail back to the homestead if he didn't backtrack soon. *Better get back before dark.*

Wick trudged through the snow, his new boots crunching soundly beneath him. He reached a slow trot downhill, making better time than the loaded wagon had made uphill in the snow. The loss of the crystal lingered, though he tried to shake it off. *It's about surviving. That's all that matters—for now.*

The woods were quiet except for the faint creak of trees swaying in the wind, the same woods Wick had first stumbled through when everything—changed. With food in his pack and warmth enveloping him, he had a fighting chance. The falling snow lightened but hadn't stopped—the tracks from the wagon he'd ridden in were already starting to blur and fade, making them difficult to follow. By the time he reached the creek, the sky had shifted from dull gray to a paler orange as the sun inched lazily toward the horizon. The babble of the small stream broke the eerie silence. Peering through the twilight, he spotted a raccoon crouching near the water's edge, its tiny hands pawing at the icy stream. For a moment, the animal met his gaze—unconcerned by him, more focused on survival, just like he was. Then, it meandered off, disappearing into the forest. The sun wouldn't wait. It was already slipping behind the hills, and long shadows stretched before him, making the landscape look anything but friendly. Wick adjusted his backpack, feeling the weight of the supplies he'd gathered. He followed what remained of the tracks, thankful for the warmth of his new boots.

Still, the air out here felt different. Silence used to be comforting. Now, it gnawed at him like something out of place. He trudged onward through the growing dusk. Within a few hundred yards, the trees thinned, and he found himself back where it all began—where time had unraveled. Hope flared in his gut when he reached the familiar area near the large rock. *Maybe—just maybe— I'll see home.*

His heart dropped. There was nothing. No house. No Nora. Just the same silent, snow-covered trees and the lifeless sky above him.

I'm stuck here.

Almost mechanically, Wick collected firewood, focused on survival. The food in his pack could wait until the fire blazed. His muscles ached with the cold as he knelt beneath the cedar branches, sheltering from the snow that continued to fall lightly around him. The snowy landscape offered no dry leaves or grass. Without easily ignitable material, getting a fire going would be difficult, if not impossible. He followed the clerk's instructions, striking the knife blade against the flint. Once, then twice—tiny sparks, but nothing. No flame. Again, and again.

Frustration ate away each time the fire refused to catch. His hands shook as the cold seeped into his bones again. *Why isn't this working?* Exasperated and ready to give up, he plopped down and shoved his hands into his coat pockets. *Lint!* He quickly combed his pockets, gathering fuzz balls, tiny threads, and lint. *It's worth a shot.* He balled it up and set it beneath the twigs.

Please—

When he sparked the flint, the lint ball caught fire, flaring orange and spreading into the sticks. Wick sat back, releasing a breath he hadn't realized he'd been holding. Though the warmth rose slowly, the assurance of light and heat immediately comforted.

He could survive the night—at least for now.

Wick hugged his knees to his chest, staring at the fire. He almost wished Latesha were there—she'd know how to crack a joke or make him forget how lost he felt.

***

Wick shoveled in the potatoes the clerk had handed him, curling closer to the fire for warmth. The snow drifted ahead, shrouding the forest in a muffled blanket of white. The campfire and potatoes—plain but essential—were everything: the warmth, the nourishment, and some sense of normalcy, however fleeting.

As twilight faded into night, he cinched his coat and leaned in to feed the fire. The embers popped softly, and with every flicker of flame, Wick felt the slightest sense of safety amid the chasing shadows. He was alive. He would make it.

Or so he thought.

***

The first howl cut through the silence—sharp and distant, rolling with the wind through the trees. Wick stiffened, breath catching in his throat.

Wolves?

The woods were thick, but the sound carried, threading through the hollows. Wick swallowed hard; the pack felt closer than he wanted to admit.

Another howl rose, then another—higher tones intertwining with deeper ones, creating a feral harmony that drifted through the night—ghostly echoes. The wolves weren't here, but their voices pressed the shadows tighter. He wasn't alone. The fire was his only ally.

Wick backed up to the boulder, keeping the fire between him and the woods. He tossed in another branch, fueling its light. *Stay out there.*

Crack.

He flinched at the snap of a branch, gaze snapping toward the tree line. *Not too close. Please.* Or was it just his nerves? He gripped his knife, fingers whitening on the hilt, his heart thrumming in his chest.

The night ebbed and flowed with the sound—quiet for a while, then pierced by a series of howls, answering one another across the distance. Never closer, never louder, just cyclic. It was a reminder. It was a warning.

For the first time, Wick leaned back, allowing himself to relax as he gazed at the sky. It was like seeing the universe anew, breathtaking and endless. It contrasted sharply with Chicago, where city lights swallowed the stars.

By now, his body had settled into a pattern: make a fire, guard it like a priceless treasure, and always listen for anything moving in the silence. He could explore the area tomorrow—there must be a way back. But as the flames blazed brightly, distant howls pierced the night, a chilling reminder that more than just the cold was present. Tonight, his focus was on listening—and surviving whatever might be prowling in the darkness.

Chapter 6
The Bluff

Wick startled awake, amazed he had slept at all. He listened intently to the dead quiet. *Wow! Distant howls might be better than eerie silence.* He must have slept a while because the fire had simmered to a bed of glowing coals. Wick pulled his coat tighter and pushed the last sticks into the embers, hoping they would quickly catch flame. He marveled at the starry sky. Looking around, he saw a silvery glow on the horizon, barely perceptible yet unmistakable. It was a subtle hint of light, a whisper of the morning, gently breaking through the darkness. *Dawn! I survived.*

Instinctively, he pulled out his phone to check the time and temperature and to call Gramps—still, nothing.

Wick had been taught how to pray by his mom and in Sunday school but had seldom prayed earnestly. He had learned to repeat the Lord's Prayer, dinner, and nightly prayers, but this felt different. *God, I know I don't often pray, but please lead me home.* The irony was not lost on him. Yesterday, he didn't think of Gramps's house as *home*, but now, he could accept any place with family as home.

He thought about staying put, in hopes Gramps or his dad might, by some miracle, find and rescue him. He considered returning to Riggsville, but what could he hope to find there? He thought about leaving—just picking a direction and walking without looking back. Finally, he thought about using the rock as a base of operations, fanning out in different directions and returning each time he came up empty.

Whether by inspiration from God or blind hope, Wick stood with intent to explore. He shouldered his backpack and readied for travel. Inky blackness turned to pale blue, hinting at the promise of a new day. Wick headed away from the rock, away from the comfort of the fire, and further away from his only confirmed hint of civilization, Riggsville. Still close to freezing, the temperature must have broken overnight as the snow was melting. He could no longer rely on tracks in the snow to find his way back. Every twenty steps, he broke a limb and laid it in the direction he was going, marking his trail. He would estimate an hour for each direction, then turn around and return to the rock as his base of operation.

Angling downhill, he eventually reached the creek. Each time he neared it, the briars became thicker, leaving their mark on his arms and legs. Hesitant to cross, he retraced his trail to the rock and started again.

This time, he decided to stay level, not going up or down. He walked what he thought was an hour and stopped. He looked around. Nothing but trees and rocks. Uphill, he could see a ridge or a mountain, but he would need to return to the base and start that exploration as a new path. Downhill, there would or should be a creek. At least fewer briars were on this "bench," a level stretch of ground between a ridge and the creek.

For his next pass, he wanted to reach higher ground. He picked what he thought was the direction. At first, the ground went slightly lower, leveled out, and then rose to higher ground. He walked for about an hour and stopped. He was on higher ground, but the ridge still loomed ahead. *I want to see the top of that hill. Something must be there. I just know it.* Careful to mark his trail, he trudged on.

Reaching the top of the hill, he noticed a change in scenery: fewer trees, with moss-covered rocky outcrops, flat with the ground, almost like large patios ranging in size from a backyard patio to a tennis court. The combination of green moss with gray rock gave the plateau an ancient feel, as though nature had been quietly painting the rocks for centuries. The sun had melted the snow and warmed the rock. He took a break and sat in the middle of a large outcrop. The moss was soft and fine. *Hey, this is dry! I could use this to start my next campfire.* He found several dry clumps and stuffed them in his backpack.

After a brief rest, he wanted to see the edge of the ridge. As he neared it, he spotted a grand cedar. Its base vanished into the rocky bluff, roots finding no visible soil, while its crown thrust up and out over the rim. The tree was no taller than Wick, which could have meant youth, but its thick, gnarled, tangled base and wind-beaten crown hinted at another truth: this cedar might be centuries old. *How can it survive?* Its survival in this hostile environment gave Wick hope that he, too, could survive.

Wick sat, admiring the view. Below the bluff were large rocks, standing tall and proud like ancient sentinels, having broken away from the bluff eons ago. The monolithic formations, as tall as the bluffs themselves, dominated the landscape with their imposing presence. Their weathered surfaces were etched with the marks of countless seasons, covered in patches of lichen and moss that added a touch of green to their rugged, gray faces. He could hear the soft babble of a creek beyond the rocks.

Wick was in awe, but even more so when a hawk glided in and landed on the cedar. He had seen a hawk at the Lincoln Park Zoo in Chicago, but never in the wild. Yet here he was, almost close enough to touch this majestic creature. The whole scene felt magical and sacred. Then, out of nowhere, the realization struck him. *The signal tree! The signal tree pointed somewhere. Could it point here? Could it be that simple? Had he overlooked the most obvious solution—the signal tree?*

Wick was flooded with a sense of urgency. *I have to get back to the signal tree!* He felt a strange sense of completeness and calm, yet urgency. It was as if the hawk had spoken to him and even understood his new resolve to return to the signal tree. Wick stood and headed back, silently thanking the hawk, hope restored at this new plan.

Chapter 7

Condemned

As Wick neared the signal tree, he stopped to reflect. *What if this doesn't work?* Would he be stuck there forever? What if it took him further back in time, making his situation worse? If it did work, how freaked out would his family be, and how could he even try to explain what had happened to him?

His pulse spiked as the idea latched onto him, sudden hope sparking under his skin. Every moment since arriving—since falling into this impossible world—had started *here*, next to the signal tree. If this strange whirlwind of time had a beginning, maybe it also had an end—it had to.

Wick stood just feet from the massive oak's distinctive S-shaped curve, breathless and wild-eyed. *No more waiting!* His heart pounded against his ribs, hammering as the trees seemed to join in behind his heartbeat. Thud, thud, thud. It was practically vibrating through him. Without thinking, he placed both trembling hands squarely on the trunk, feeling instantly the gnarled, cool ridges of its bark.

Before he registered the shift, it began—the careless swoop of nausea, the dizzying whirl of the ground beneath him pulling out like a loose thread. His vision spun and twisted, color draining into shadows and light—time rolled backward and forward all at once. The tree's branches seemed to curl around him, suffocating him until his lungs squeezed tight with pressure. He could feel the dizziness swallow him again, just as before.

But this time—it didn't last as long.

Something warm hit his face. Sunlight. Dry, summery heat caressed his skin, pushing back against the clinging ice that had gripped him for what felt like forever. The biting cold melted into balmy air like it had never existed, the disorienting unrealness fading as bright, golden warmth wrapped around him. The smell of green leaves mingled with something rich, mixing with the sweat prickling on his neck.

Wick staggered for balance as the world came back into sharp focus—and finally, his breath stilled. He blinked and blinked.

When he looked around, there was no snow.

Collapsing against the tree's base, gasping for air, Wick felt an overwhelming wave of relief crash through him. The dizzying nausea abated, leaving behind the solid, familiar sensation of warm dirt beneath his hands. He clutched at the grass, letting out a sob, or maybe it was laughter—it was impossible to tell now. Either way, he didn't care.

I'm back.

He was safe. Or was he?

***

Wick pushed himself onto his knees, glancing at the world before him.

Gone were the frost and ice-cracked trees. Gone was the heavy shroud of the sky on the verge of snow. Instead—*he was home. Or* what passed for home these days. The blistering midsummer heat hit full force, and just like that, he was back.

His breath hitched, but as Wick staggered to his feet, a familiar sight above the sea of trees calmed him—the red roof, sitting more than a hundred yards away, between the towering oaks and his family's old farmhouse just beyond. Gram's rose rock collection was sitting along the path leading to the porch.

He pressed closer to the house as his nerves pulsed with contradiction—relief and panic twining into a rhythm he couldn't escape. He had been gone for days. Hadn't he? His body could feel it. The exhaustion was pressed into every fiber of him, worn like a second skin.

And yet—something felt wrong.

As Wick drew closer, the sights and sounds of the house returned to him in full focus, alarming clarity settling over him now. The yard looked the same—a couple of chickens clucked lazily past the side hedges—and yet, somehow, the scene lacked urgency. There were no shouts, no agitation, no signs of anyone freaking out over his absence or sudden reappearance. Where was the panic he had feared?

I've been gone for two whole days, he screamed internally. *How can they be so calm?*

As he approached the house's porch steps, Wick spotted Nora standing on the porch with her hands on her hips, watching him quizzically.

"Where do you think you've been?" she asked, her voice full of amusement.

The question froze Wick in his tracks. "What?"

"You're dressed like it's a blizzard out here," Nora said, her eyebrow raised as though she didn't believe what she saw. "Where'd you get that coat? The attic?"

Wick stared at her. Was she serious? Didn't she see the state he was in? He sucked in a breath, trying to formulate a response, but faltered. Nora leaned against the railing and smirked, her eyes scanning him from his bedraggled boots to his collar.

"You look ridiculous. It's, like, ninety degrees. You know anything about that?"

"Where have I been?" Wick finally managed to stammer. "Where have I been? I've been gone for two days, Nora—two days!"

She stared at his outburst like he'd just professed to having woken up on Mars. "Dude, you've been gone for, what—fifteen minutes?"

Fifteen minutes! Wick felt nauseous, like someone had reached into his stomach and tied it in knots. "That's impossible—" His voice faltered.

Nora sighed dramatically, shaking her head. "Anytime you plan on wearing Halloween costumes in July, I deserve a heads up."

She turned and wandered toward the door, leaving Wick in a daze. *Fifteen minutes.* Everything felt off. Anger, confusion, and complete and utter loss washed over him.

Before he could press his mind to make sense of it, his eyes caught the figure ahead near the driveway—a man standing beside Gramps in a familiar broad-rimmed sheriff hat. Wick's pulse quickened.

What's the sheriff doing here? The picture started to shift, the tension in Gramps's features hardening as Wick stepped slightly closer. His stomach dropped—he could feel something brewing, far heavier than his brief disappearance.

"—Crystalis Vitalis—" The sheriff's words cut through Wick's mind like a knife.

***

Wick edged closer, his entire body operating on autopilot now. There was no room for thought, just muted dread coursing through him. He crouched behind the toolshed, catching snippets of the conversation between the sheriff and Gramps.

"Sorry to be the one to deliver bad news. They're forcing a decision—Quorum Court—condemnation," the sheriff said softly. "They think the mineral rights mean they can push you out. You know how sparse jobs are in the county."

"Mineral rights," Gramps spat. "It's all about the land, Tom." His face darkened with ire; his hands clenched into fists.

Wick's hands pressed over his mouth as the words registered. *Condemnation.* The land—Crystalis Vitalis—Vilnius. It was all connected. Everything.

"They don't care about the farm," Gramps continued. "It's the ground underneath they want."

"It's on the agenda a week from Monday," the sheriff added quietly. His words hung in the air, heavy as a storm cloud, ready to break. "You realize—if the Quorum Court approves and passes the emergency clause, which they probably will, you can live in the house, but the land is gone. Of course, they have to pay you for the land, but you no longer get to control or use it."

"Can we appeal and delay?"

"The only appeal you have is how much they pay, and that can take years to sort out, but the condemnation is immediate, no appeal."

This is all because of the crystal. The pieces are falling into place, aren't they? No way this is a coincidence. This—it's all my fault. Losing the crystal, letting all of this happen, and causing a timeline shift. Wick's thoughts raced; his heart pounded in his chest. *I need answers. I need to get to Billy. But first, I need Latesha's help!*

Chapter 8
A Call for Help

Wick needed to act, but first, he needed to think. *What can I do? Gramps? Billy? Is it time to open up to Gramps? Maybe Billy can shed some light. Latesha! Maybe Latesha can help!*

Wick went to the back porch and sat, eyeing the signal tree like he would keep an eye on an escaped convict. Wick pulled out his phone. *Finally! It works!*

He texted: *Latesha.*

Immediately, his phone rang. He answered quickly.

"Wick! Are you there? Thought you would call sooner."

"Yes, we're here. Just busy seeing Gram and Gramps and settling in."

"Is everything fine?"

"Well—"

"Wick. What is it?"

Wick took a deep breath. *How do I explain this? Should I tell her everything? About the crystal, Vilnius—no, not yet. I need to keep it simple. Focus on the condemnation.*

"Latesha, something's come up. It's about the land. The county is trying to force a decision—Quorum Court condemnation. They want the mineral rights. Gramps might lose the farm."

Latesha's voice grew urgent. "What do you mean? What happened?"

Wick explained everything he had overheard. The condemnation, the mineral rights, the looming Quorum Court decision. He could almost hear the gears turning in Latesha's mind.

"This is serious," she said. "We can't let them do this. We need to figure out a plan."

Should I tell her about the crystal? No. Not now. One step at a time.

"Yeah, it's a mess. I don't know what to do," Wick replied, his voice strained.

Latesha paused for a moment, then responded with determination. "Alright. I'll dig into everything I can about the Quorum Court and mineral rights. We need to gather as much information as possible. And remember that award I got for promoting clean streams around tribal lands? I've got 1.5 million followers. We need to mobilize; I can rally some serious support."

Wick's eyes widened. *This might work.* "Yes! The President's Environmental Youth Award. That's amazing, Latesha. We can use that to our advantage."

"Exactly. I'll organize protesters and get the local TV station to cover the story. The more pressure we put on the county, the better our chances."

"There's something else," Wick added hesitantly. "Our property has Native American heritage. Gramps told me it was once sacred land to the local tribe."

There was a brief pause at the other end. Then Latesha spoke, her voice charged with fresh energy. "That's huge, Wick! This gives us an even stronger case. We can leverage this to draw more attention and support. I'll highlight this in our campaign and ensure the local news covers it. That could be the key to stopping them."

"Wick!" his sister's voice called from behind him. He turned to see her standing at the door with a teasing grin.

"Hold on a second," he said, lowering the phone.

"Who are you talking to?" his sister asked, her eyebrows raised.

"Uh, Latesha," Wick admitted, trying to keep his voice casual.

His sister's grin widened. "Latesha, huh? Is she helping with the farm situation or—something else?"

Wick rolled his eyes. "Just helping with the farm."

"Sure, sure," she said, clearly not convinced. "If I didn't know any better, I'd say you two have a thing going on."

Wick felt his face flash hot. "It's not like that."

"Mm-hmm," she hummed, giving him a knowing look before returning inside.

Wick shook his head, a small smile tugging on his lips. Maybe something was there, but they had bigger problems to solve now.

He turned back to his phone. "Sorry about that. Let's do this. I'll update you on whatever I find out. Together, we can stop this."

Latesha's reply was swift and confident. "We've got this, Wick. We won't let them take your land. I'll let you know as soon as I put something together."

Wick put his phone away, feeling a renewed sense of determination. *I need to talk to Billy. Maybe he knows more than he's letting on.*

As he headed back inside, his thoughts raced. *Should I have told her about the crystal? About Vilnius? No. Not yet. I need more answers first.*

"Gramps, could I use your old truck to drive into town?"

"Sure, Wick. Help yourself. Just wait until morning. Never know when a deer will run out in front of you. Say, how was your hike?"

"Gramps. It was cool, really cool." *Frozen.* "Like taking a step back in time. Say, I bet you know a little about the local history. Have you ever heard of Riggsville?"

"Riggsville! Now, there's a name I haven't heard in a long time. Yes, it was a local community until after the Civil War, when folks up and moved to start Mountain View."

"So, there was no Mountain View at that time?"

"No Mountain View. So why do you ask?"

"Oh, I heard someone mention Riggsville and just wondered. So why did it move?"

"Stone County formed in 1873. They picked out a site in the center of the county for the county seat—Mountain View. I guess folks wanted to live in the new county seat. You can still see remnants of a road through Riggsville. I can show you sometime if you like."

"Thanks, Gramps. I guess I'm tired after a long day." *Two days.* "Say, do I have a place to crash?"

"Sure, Wick. Gram said you can choose between the futon in the living room, or the attic. The attic is drafty but gives you a full-size bed and some privacy. Why don't you try it, and if you don't like it, you can always take the futon?"

"Thanks, Gramps!"

Wick climbed the stairs to the attic. Besides cobwebs, he saw a maze of old wooden furniture draped in dusty sheets, hinting of forgotten times. Against one wall, a stack of vintage trunks and suitcases beckoned, each likely harboring relics of a bygone era. Shelves lined with mason jars, filled with mysterious preserved items, sparkled faintly in the dim light filtering through the small attic window.

An antique rocking chair creaked eerily in the corner as if it still held memories of countless hours spent there. Piles of yellowing newspapers and magazines lay scattered across the floor, their headlines and advertisements speaking of a different world. Boxes full of faded clothes, including hats, dresses, and suits, still reflected the elegance of their time.

Wick's eyes caught the glint of framed black-and-white photographs hung on the walls, capturing family gatherings, holidays, and moments of significance. A dusty bookshelf stood proudly, laden with classic literature, cookbooks, and children's stories, their pages yellowed with age. He noticed a bundle of handwritten letters tied with a ribbon, each a potential gateway to heartfelt stories of love, loss, and life.

In one corner, a collection of rusty hand tools, an old acoustic guitar, and a toy train set lay abandoned, whispering tales of their past use. A large cedar chest, covered in a fine layer of dust, promised treasures inside—perhaps handmade quilts, embroidered tablecloths, or crocheted blankets, carefully stored away.

Despite the allure of these hidden treasures, Wick was exhausted. The day's events swirled in his mind—Gramps's tense conversation with the sheriff, the looming threat of losing the farm, and his urgent call with Latesha. He still needed to understand so much, and many questions needed answers.

A sense of relief washed over him as he trudged to the small, cozy bed in the attic. Just the night before, he had been outdoors, freezing and keeping a fire going, haunted by the howls of wolves or coyotes in the distance. Now, in the warmth of the attic, with no risk of coyotes, he felt a profound gratitude for the simple comforts he had so often taken for granted.

Wick crashed into bed, his mind racing about what tomorrow might bring. He knew he had to talk to Billy, but that would have to wait until morning. For now, he needed rest to face whatever lay ahead.

Chapter 9
Back to Billy

Mountain View, the next morning

Wick snuck up the back stairwell, careful to avoid contact with anyone. Billy was asleep, his breakfast still on the tray beside the bed.

"Billy. Uncle Billy."

Wick coughed a few times to wake Billy gently.

"Wick!"

Wick put a finger to his lips to quiet Uncle Billy. "Shh. We don't want them to know I'm here. I need to talk to you."

"So glad you came back. But I can't think straight. Can I hold the crystal?"

"Uh, I don't have it with me, but I have questions about it."

Billy gave a snarly look. "I can't think straight. I need that crystal."

"I can't give it to you right now."

"I need my cat. Can you get Sailor?"

"Who?"

"Sailor. I need Sailor. Go get Sailor."

"Where?"

"My unit."

"I'm so confused."

"My unit, you know. In the home."

"Billy, I've never been to your *home*. Can't we go there? Besides, you were worried about the doctor and nurse watching. Wouldn't it be better to talk somewhere private?"

"Yes. Hand me those clothes."

***

Billy reached out to the cat and said, "Sailor, come here, girl," as she prowled the cramped studio unit at the assisted living home.

Sailor's fascinating blend of colors and textures revealed her many years. Her fur, a patchwork of different colors, was predominantly a mix of deep orange and pure white, with the occasional splash of black. Age had softened the vibrancy of her coat, giving it a slightly faded yet endearingly rustic appearance.

Her face was particularly striking, with one side mostly white and the other a rich orange, as if a whimsical artist had painted it. The cat's eyes were perhaps her most captivating feature—one was a piercing blue, while the other shone a warm amber, creating an almost hypnotic gaze.

Time had not been entirely kind to the cat. She moved with a slight limp, favoring her left hind leg, which appeared to have a minor defect. Despite this, she carried herself with quiet dignity, each step a testament to her resilience.

As she sat by the window, the sunlight streaming through highlighted the varied hues of her fur and the unique beauty of her mismatched eyes. Oddly, the bell on the Sailor's collar did not ring.

The cat walked past Billy and jumped into Wick's arms.

"She remembers you," Billy said, reaching for Sailor.

Remembers me? Wick thought, puzzled. *I've never seen this cat. But that's not why we're here.* He handed Sailor to Billy.

Billy seemed to calm down for the first time. "Now, Wick, you said you have questions?"

"Yes, I went through a time warp yesterday, almost froze to death, and barely made it back alive. What the heck is going on, and what is/was that crystal?"

Billy's voice rose. "Wick! This may come as a shock, but you and I have traveled that road many times together. Thankfully, it's all over now that we have the crystal back. As long as we keep that crystal, we win. Vilnius loses. He can't touch us anymore. Shoot, he can't do squat. I'll bet yesterday you thought I was crazy, didn't you? Don't answer that. Just listen. You shouldn't have gone anywhere, but it's okay as long as the crystal is safe."

Wick turned and stared out the window.

"Wick. Wick! Tell me it's safe. It is safe, isn't it?"

"Look, Billy, you didn't tell me any of this yesterday."

Wick told Billy everything that had happened, every detail. Billy sat stunned, covering his mouth with his hand. When Wick mentioned trading the crystal, Billy gasped, plopped his head into his hands, and shook it in despair.

After a long silence, Billy finally spoke. "Oh, my gosh. We didn't know. I didn't know. We always assumed it started some other way. We never thought our actions at the end of the road might start the whole thing. It's the missing piece. If only we had known."

"Can't we just go back and tell ourselves? Won't that work?"

"If only it were that easy. See, Wick, we learned a long time ago that reality is like a patchwork quilt made up of actions from both the present and the past. We just can't reset by changing one event early on. It could work, but it might cause disastrous consequences. No, my friend, we are better off repeating what we know we already did, hoping for some break along the way."

"Wait, what do you mean repeat? I've never done those things you mention."

"Well, for me, it's like looking back."

Wick shook his head. "But you know what to do, how to stop it, right?"

"I thought I did, but now I'm not so sure. The things you are telling me now, I would think I would know. It has all changed. We are on a new timeline. We're starting over."

"For me, it is just starting," Wick said. "You'd better fill me in, and this time, don't leave out any details."

"It's okay. You lost the crystal, but at least we have the knife. We do have the knife, don't we?"

"Oh, sure. And it should be even better now that Gramps sharpened it."

"Wick!" Billy put his head down in his hands again, moving from side to side. "Wick, Wick, Wick." Billy put his hand on his heart. "Oh, I can't take any more. The knife, too?"

"We still have the knife. It's just been sharpened and oiled."

"Look, the idea of using an artifact to jump back in time is to have something genuine from that date. It won't work if you change it, like sharpening the knife."

Billy described how the signal tree worked and how he first met Wick over seventy years ago. "You have to repeat those visits. It's our only chance."

"Okay. So, what do I need to do first? And explain again how I know what date I'm jumping back to."

"First, you need a crystal from the magic cave."

"Magic cave! Oh, come on! You have to be kidding. You're kidding, right? There's a magic cave?"

"Come on, Wick. You're the one who told me about the cave. I didn't believe it either. Keep up. Crystal from the magic cave, plus an item from the time/day you want to visit."

"Then why did I go back to 1855?"

"You had your Gramps's 1855 coin, right?"

"Yes."

"Well."

"Oh."

"First, you need to meet Kahoka, like you did for the first time."

"But we don't have a crystal—"

"You remember—oh, excuse me, you don't know about the crystal we hid in the trunk in the attic. Go to the attic in the old home. Lift the fake floor at the bottom of the trunk. Find the artifacts we hid, along with a crystal. Wick, if you lose that crystal!"

"I won't this time. I understand the importance now."

"There are two arrowheads. One will take you to your original visit to Kahoka. The other one will take you years later when Kahoka has a family. You want the first one."

"How will I know which one to take?"

"Sorry. Fifty years ago, I could have told you. One is gray. One is white. My memory is foggy. We should have labeled them. Fifty-fifty chance. Not great, but all we have for now."

"Okay, so say I get the right one. What then?"

"Take food, water, a knife, a fire starter, and a compass. You have a long trip ahead of you. Take the crystal and the arrowhead. Go to the signal tree. You know what to do next. After the time warp, mark a trail from the signal tree to Coon Creek. Using Coon Creek as your base reference, head due east several miles until you hit the next big creek. That should be Wallace Creek. If you can't find Wallace Creek, once you leave Coon Creek and top a mountain, just keep going over the mountain and then downhill. Follow Wallace Creek downstream several miles to the White River. You have to be exactly where Wallace Creek meets the White River, and you must make it there the same day you arrive, or he could be gone, and you might miss him. You once told me that's where you first met Kahoka.

"Now, Wick, most importantly, mark your trail along the way. Break limbs. Cut notches into trees. Set rocks on top of rocks. You are stuck if you can't find your way back to the signal tree. Use the creeks and mountain ridges as your landmarks. Time how long it takes you to get from the signal tree to the White River. If you have trouble, go due west about the same length of time to get back to Coon Creek, and from there, you can follow your blazed trail back to the signal tree. My guess is three to four hours each way. Prepare to spend the night just in case. Look, your life is more valuable to your family than the land is. We can live without the land. Don't try it if you're not up to it. It's okay just to let it go. There's no guarantee we can win anyway."

"What if I get the wrong arrowhead?"

"Try to cover and return as soon as possible to get the other arrowhead. Go meet Kahoka for the first time before he had a family."

"I was gone for two days, but when I returned, they thought I was only gone for a short while. What's up with that? Does it always do that?"

"Yes, and we never figured out why. It just does. Be careful. If you stay for twenty years, you may return an old man, like Rip Van Winkle."

"And what about injuries? Do they stay, or do they reset when I return?"

"Great question. I wish it were that easy. Injuries are injuries. If you get hurt there, you will be hurt the same when you get back. And if you die—"

"Die!"

"Yes, die. If you die, you're dead. Game over. Remember, you don't have to do this. I've been battling this for over seventy years. I'm tired. I don't have the energy to do much. Not like I did when you and I ran around together."

"But you tell me we were best friends. Does that mean your younger self helped me?"

"Oh sure, we went through a lot together. We're best friends. Or at least we were. Well, not at first, but later... Look, I'm tired. I need to rest. I'm not as young as I once was. Let me know later what you decide."

Too much for me, too! "Okay, Billy. I'm heading out. Do you want me to take you back to the hospital?"

"No, I think I'll stay here."

About that time, a nurse walked into the room. "Billy, Billy, Billy. You are here. Dear, you must inform the hospital when you want to check out. They were worried about you. I have to call and let them know you're okay." The nurse walked out, shaking her head and laughing.

"What about Dad? Is there any chance he's caught up in all of this?"

"Well, I don't trust Vilnius. If there was one reason to keep going, even more important than land, it would be your dad. There's no way to know, so keep your wits about you to see if we can learn anything about your dad and you don't fall victim to Vilnius."

"One last question. How old is Sailor? She looks ancient."

"Oh, almost as old as I am." Billy leaned back and closed his eyes.

Yeah, right. A cat that's almost eighty years old. Wick shook his head. "See you, Billy."

Chapter 10
Camp

Wick wasted no time in finding the crystal and two arrowheads in the hidden compartment at the bottom of the trunk. *Okay. Which one? Gray or white?*

Wick remembered Billy's instructions to carry food, water, a knife, a fire starter, and a compass. After packing the essentials—flint and knife—into an old backpack, he rummaged through the kitchen for snacks and filled an old canteen with water. A coat was added, just in case. Night brought silence and reflection as Wick settled in, replaying everything that had happened. He could walk away, or try to put things right. *Dad. The land. No way I'm walking away. Gray arrowhead it is. First light.*

***

Wick stood at the signal tree at dawn, backpack loaded, boots laced, crystal and gray arrowhead in hand. *Okay, gray, do me right.* He braced for dizziness and nausea, but stayed upright through the spinning transition this time. When the world settled, the house was gone, and the treescape had shifted—except the signal tree and large boulder still held their ground. *Okay. Blaze a trail to Coon Creek, just like Billy said. Then east to Wallace Creek.*

Wick moved briskly, snapping branches and stacking rocks. At least this way, I won't end up lost on the way back from Coon Creek. Now—east to Wallace Creek.

Before Wick traveled any distance, he saw a man sitting, hunched over, repeatedly striking two rocks together. He crept closer, making sure the man did not see him. After watching, he decided to ask if it was Kahoka. "Excuse me, sir, are you Kahoka? Excuse me, sir, can you hear me?"

The man spoke. "Hear you! A herd of buffalo makes less noise. Remember, Wick? Wolf hearing?"

Wick stepped back, both startled and confused. Wolf hearing? "Sure, Kahoka?"

"Yes, who else? Glad to see you, my old friend. The kids will be happy to see you. You brought their peppermints, didn't you?"

Peppermints? "Oh, sorry. Not this trip."

"Well, they will still be excited to see you. Let's go."

"Where?"

"To camp."

***

At a small encampment nestled in the back hills of the Ozarks, Wick noticed several campfires, some with hanging pots simmering for the midday meal. The air was filled with the aroma of cooking and the soft crackling of the fires. The terrain was hilly and rocky, with a small creek just beyond the camp. Tall bluffs loomed overhead, casting shadows over the teepees scattered around. The bluff area looked like it served as the central meeting site for the tribe, with seats gathered around, taking advantage of the natural windbreak and rain cover provided by the bluff outcropping. Deer and bear skins stretched to cure added to the rustic, historical feel of the place. Baskets and pottery were scattered around, reflecting the tribe's skill and artistry. Dogs and chickens roamed freely, adding a sense of life and activity to the camp. Several kids saw Wick and came running up screaming. The children wore clothing made of leather, adorned with colorful beadwork that caught the light of the campfires. Their moccasins were also made of leather and decorated with intricate beading patterns, highlighting the tribe's craftsmanship. "Show us your shot, Wick. We want to see it again!"

Wick quickly realized he had landed at the wrong time jump. *I should've picked the white arrowhead. I need to find a way out.*

Wick pulled Kahoka aside and spoke softly. "Kahoka. I can see you live here in a time of joy and peace, but I need your help. You called me *'old friend.'* Is that true?"

"Yes, of course."

"Look, I'm here by mistake. I'm making a mess of things. You may find this hard to believe, but I never met you before today, and I need to get back to the time when we first met, you know, on the White River. My dad's missing. They're taking our land. It's all a mess."

"Hold on, Wick. You mean you never met me before today?"

"No."

"You don't know how to shoot a bow."

"No, should I?"

Before Kahoka could answer, a voice interrupted from behind them.

"What? He can't shoot?"

Both men turned to see Waya, Kahoka's son, standing there with a look of disbelief and anger.

"Waya, calm down," Kahoka said gently.

"No, Father! This is nonsense. I should be the one to save the tribe, not him. I've trained all my life." Waya's voice was loud, filled with resentment.

"Waya," Kahoka tried to soothe, "it's not as simple as you think. We need to trust."

"Trust? How can I when this outsider doesn't even know how to use a bow? He's not worthy!" Waya's frustration boiled over, and he stormed off, disappearing into the woods.

Kahoka sighed and turned back to Wick. "It's okay," he said, his smile strained. "He'll come around. Let's continue."

"So, I need to learn—how to shoot?"

"Yes!" Pausing to watch Waya disappear into the woods, Kahoka's voice grew somber. "What we hold most dear depends on it."

"How do I get out of this? I feel terrible letting the kids down. I don't have their peppermints. I can't shoot a bow. I don't think I can do this."

"Wick. Take a breath. You can do this. I saw you do *'this.'* It was you. Have belief. Have confidence. You already did it in my book."

"I wish I could believe. I can't see it right now."

"Here, Wick. Do you see this arrowhead I was working on today?"

"Yes."

"Here, take it. When you get back to the farm, store it away. When this is all over, when there is no more risk, when you have the peppermints, and when you can shoot that bow, use this special arrowhead to return here, to this point in time. The kids will think it is still the same time, with only a brief pause in between. They won't know the difference. You will be a hero. Then we can all enjoy the squash, spinach, and squirrel feast we prepared. You will shoot that bow. You will hit the bullseye. We will laugh about how you got started. It will all be good. You will see."

"What else can you tell me?"

"I could tell you a lot, but you need to learn as you did initially. Go. It will be okay. Find the younger me by the river, as Billy told you. Use the arrowhead to come back when it is all done. We will feast, laugh, and have fun when you return to this point. Oh, and Wick, when we first meet, don't give up easily. Stick with it. If you give up at that point, it's all over."

"What do you mean?"

"Just go. You'll see. Just be yourself, but don't give up. Oh, and sorry."

Sorry. For what?

***

Back at the signal tree, Wick placed his hands against the bark and time warped back to the present, mastering how to avoid the nausea. He returned to his room in the attic, sat on the bed, and put his head in his hands. Tears welled up in his eyes, but he refused to cry. *I can't do this. Shoot a bow. I can't shoot anything.*

Wick thought about giving up. Billy had said: "It's okay just to let it go." *But Dad and the land for Gramps. I gotta go.*

He put Kahoka's new arrowhead in the hidden trunk compartment for future use, picked up the white arrowhead, and headed back to the signal tree.

Chapter 11
The Hawk

Wick finally felt he had the time warp down. He braced, tensing muscles like a fighter pilot preparing for G-forces. Shouldering his backpack, he touched the signal tree, white arrowhead and crystal in hand.

He immediately raised his arms, looking overhead to see clouds, lightning, and rain. He jumped as the thunder boomed. *Rain! I prepared for the snow. Oh boy.* Wick pulled out his coat and put it over his head. *Cancel? No, I can't do that. It might mess up the time.* Wick knew the way to Coon Creek. Downhill. He headed out, marking his trail to find his way back. *Get to the White River and find Kahoka.*

His trip to Coon Creek went quickly. *Doing good. Now, east to Wallace Creek.* Wick used the compass to continue east for about an hour until he reached a bluff. *I can't climb that! Billy didn't say anything about a bluff.* He sat, wondering if he should quit. *I've come this far. Kahoka said don't give up. I wish I could.*

He looked left, north, and right, south. *I'm going north.* He walked north until the bluff line eased. *I can go up that slope.* The ground continued to rise for a while. *Did I make it to the top? Hope so. Billy said go downhill to find Wallace Creek. Let's see. Downhill looks like southeast. I'll try that.*

Before he could go much further, the skies opened, releasing torrents that pounded the earth. He could barely see through sheets of rain. Just then, lightning struck a tree to his right. *Gotta keep going.* In the next few steps, Wick slipped on a rock, hurting his arm. Soaked and injured, he looked for any place he could find shelter. He walked further and found a small bluff outcropping, scooting back under the overhang to get a respite from the pounding rain.

The storm raged for hours and finally slowed down to a light sprinkle. Wick set out to find Wallace Creek, continuing his trek downhill, but soon encountered another bluff. *How many bluffs are out here?* He had to divert again to find a slope to go down. When he finally neared the bottom, he could hear a creek roaring in the distance, but daylight was running low. He thought about continuing into the dark but realized he could fall and sustain a serious injury or, worse, get lost altogether. He searched for shelter. Under a bluff, he found a prominent setback. He gathered wood on his way into the shelter, thankful for a few dry pieces under the bluff line to start his fire. *Make a fire and get dry.*

Wick rubbed his arms to break the chill. He used a packed candle to start a quick fire, squeezed the water out of his clothes, and laid them out to dry.

Wick considered the day's efforts, saddened he did not reach the White River in one day. *I can't believe I didn't make it there.* Billy had said a "few hours each way." *I wonder if he ever walked this.* Rain, lightning, and bluffs seemed to conspire to prevent him from reaching his destination. He wondered if he should keep going, but remembered Kahoka's advice to *"not give up."*

As the dark set in, Wick heard coyotes or wolves in the distance but was less concerned because they had not attacked the last time he had slept in the wild. The rain finally seemed to stop, and a hoot owl sounded from afar. Crickets chirped so loudly their sudden silence felt eerie; the kind of hush that made the dark feel watchful. Whippoorwills and bobwhites called out in the distance. The flickering flame and embers provided comfort, strategically placed between Wick and the open woods.

As dawn broke, Wick stood up, stretched, and rubbed his hip, thankful for dry clothes and no rain. He kicked dirt on the last embers and headed toward the creek. He could still hear the roaring water. As he neared the creek, the noise grew louder. He saw large limbs and debris being swept downstream. *No crossing that torrent. I hope this is Wallace Creek. It must go to the river.* Wick backed away from the briars, up slope, and followed the direction of the flowing water. *I hope the White River is close and I don't miss Kahoka.*

Wick reached down to untangle more briars from his jeans. Again, he backed away from the creek to avoid briars, keeping the creek within sight. He kept weaving to avoid downed trees, limbs, and rocks. As he continued downstream, he spotted an opening in the tree line ahead. *The river! The White River.* He rushed toward the river and slipped on wet leaves, taking a tumble. Sitting up, he checked his arms and head for injuries. Pulling himself up, he continued at a slower but steady pace. Finally, he reached the riverbank.

He looked out to see a vast river wider than two football fields. *Oh my gosh, that's enormous.* He sat pondering what to do. *Did I miss him? Do I sit here? How long?* He sat there for what seemed an eternity, just watching, waiting. *I've got to do something. Can't go downstream or cross where the creek meets the river.*

Wick started walking upstream along the riverbank. After a while, he saw a canoe upside down on the bank. He stopped and looked around. Seeing no one, he hollered. The canoe looked abandoned. He sat. *I'll wait here.*

After a few minutes, he saw a canoe on the other side of the river. He yelled, but the sound of the river drowned out his voice. *I'll bet that's him.* He shouted again, "Kahoka!" *I've got to get over there!* Wick flipped the canoe over and slid it into the water. *It floats.* He grabbed the paddle and hopped in, paddling into the current. Wick had to lean left to keep the current from capsizing the canoe. He paddled alternately on both sides to head across the current. Before he realized it, a giant tree came floating down the river. He tried to turn the canoe, but it was too late. A tree limb struck his canoe, causing it to capsize.

Wick went under. He could swim but had never tried it fully clothed in the middle of a roaring river. He managed to reach the surface, gasping for breath and yelling for help. The current pulled him back under. He fought his way back to the surface and heard someone yelling. He caught a glimpse of a man in a canoe approaching fast. Panicking, Wick grabbed the side of the canoe, capsizing it as well. Now, two people were struggling for their lives. Wick grabbed onto the person, pulling them both under. As they struggled to the surface, the man elbowed Wick, and then everything went black.

When Wick came to, he was staring at the sky. A fire blazed near him. He was on shore. He sat up but did not see anyone. Then he heard someone speaking behind him. "You! You caused me to lose my canoe and nearly killed us both! You are lucky to be alive. I should have let you drown."

"Kahoka!"

"What did you say?"

"Kahoka. You're Kahoka, aren't you?"

"Who is this Kahoka you speak of? I am not 'Kahoka.'"

"Oh, sorry. Who are you?"

"Well, the man who doesn't know how to use a canoe, doesn't know how to swim, panics in water, lost my canoe, and nearly killed us both—who are you?"

"Oh, sorry to lose your canoe. I am Finnwick. They call me Wick. And thank you for saving me."

Wick stood up and walked toward the man, extending his hand.

The man shoved Wick down the riverbank. He stopped short of the water and rolled over to look at the man.

"You are not my friend. I am called Tsiyi, and I have never lost a canoe. Never! Do you know how long it takes to build a canoe? In one day, you lost two canoes. You bring disgrace to us both. Do you know how to survive without a canoe? Can you catch fish? Can you stalk deer? Can you feed your tribe? I saved your life, so now I will go, but if you have no skills, where did you learn our language?"

"What language?"

"You speak with Cherokee tongue. Where did you learn it?"

Wick was taken aback. "Cherokee? I thought you were speaking English."

At that moment, a hawk glided in and landed between Tsiyi and Wick. Both men stopped talking and stared at the hawk. The hawk stared each man in the eye, then flew past Tsiyi and landed on a branch, staring at Tsiyi.

Tsiyi broke the silence. "This is a sign for me. The hawk is a sacred symbol for my people. I will follow this hawk. You stay here. I saved your life. Don't make me push you down again." Tsiyi walked to the tree where the hawk landed. The hawk flew a little further. and Tsiyi followed. As they went further, the hawk stopped. Tsiyi caught up with the hawk, but the hawk stayed only a moment then flew back to Wick. Tsiyi returned. Again, the hawk flew off and Tsiyi followed. This pattern repeated several times, and each time, the hawk stopped just within sight of Wick then returned to Wick.

After several tries, Tsiyi returned and said, "You follow the hawk." Wick did so, and the pattern was the same as when Tsiyi had followed the hawk, except now, the hawk kept returning to Tsiyi.

Finally, Tsiyi and Wick decided to follow the hawk together. This time, the hawk did not return to the riverbank but kept leading the two men away.

Tsiyi seemed reluctant to have Wick follow, but the hawk would not move away without both men. Wick wanted to find Kahoka but was mesmerized by the actions of the hawk and went along.

Neither man spoke until Wick broke the silence. "You are Cherokee. Have you ever seen a hawk act like this?"

"No," Tsiyi replied, shaking his head. "I have heard of spirit animals appearing but never leading men like this. They usually soar overhead or sit in a tree, but guide us like this? Never."

The two men continued to follow the hawk past Wallace Creek, over mountain ridges, and past several bluffs until reaching the top of a hill with moss-covered rocky outcrops flat with the ground—a plateau. At the edge of the bluff sat a gnarled cedar, its base disappearing into the rocky bluff, with no visible soil, and the tree's crown jutting up and out over the bluff's edge. The tree was no taller than the men, suggesting it could be young, but its thick, twisted, and tangled base and crown told a different story, suggesting it might be centuries old—the hawk perched in the cedar.

Wick suddenly realized. "I've been here before."

"What do you mean?"

"I've been here before. I saw a hawk, maybe this hawk, at this spot, in that tree, before. It seemed to speak to me, saving my life."

"Saving your life! What a coincidence."

"Yes, I think it is trying to tell us something. Something more. It brought us here for a reason."

The two men walked closer to the bluff's edge.

Tsiyi said, "I think I see something below." He lay down and peered over the drop. "Hey, there's a ledge under here, and it opens up!"

Wick hesitated, a chill tingling his skin. "Do you think it's safe?"

Tsiyi glanced back, eyes glinting with an energy that looked equal parts curiosity and caution. "One way to find out." He wriggled forward and lowered himself onto the narrow shelf.

Wick took a deep breath, heart pounding. *What if this is a trap?* He pushed the thought aside, slid onto his stomach, and inched forward, just enough to look down. A sixty-foot plunge loomed beyond the ledge where Tsiyi crouched. *I'd never have known this shelf was here if he hadn't gone first.* Tall trees stood just out of reach below. *If I slip, I'll have to jump and grab that tree.* A low growl echoed from the darkness beneath, sending shivers down his spine.

The hawk gave a piercing cry and took off, circling above them. Tsiyi turned to Wick, a grim look on his face. "Whatever's down there, we face it together."

Wick nodded, swallowing hard.

Tsiyi gathered a pine knot and some dried grass, wrapping the grass around the knot. He struck a flint against his knife, and sparks flew onto the grass, igniting a small flame. Soon, the makeshift torch flickered to life, casting eerie shadows on the bluff walls.

"This should help us see in there," Tsiyi said, holding the torch.

Together, they descended into the unknown, the darkness swallowing them whole, with only the torchlight flickering against the stone walls.

Chapter 12
The Cave

The opening was narrow. Tsiyi carried the torch in one hand, using the other to crawl. The passageway meandered. *I'm behind Tsiyi. Safe for now.* After several blind turns, the passageway opened into a large cavern. Crystals adorned the walls and ceiling, offering myriad reflections and shadows. Wick stood mesmerized until a stranger sight grabbed his focus. Across the room sat a little man in front of a small campfire. The man raised his hand to motion the men to join him. Tsiyi started toward the man. Wick slowly followed. They sat around the campfire. The air filled with anticipation as the fire's light danced across their faces.

The man cast a handful of material onto the fire. It blazed with red, blue, and green dancing colors. The man raised his hand, halting questions. "I am Kimi. I summoned you here."

Wick opened his mouth to speak, but Kimi lifted his hand, silencing him.

Kimi continued. "I come from the Cahokia. We were once a proud people, inhabitants of vast lands. Drought, disease, and warfare reduced my people to a remnant. We are no longer a nation. We have been scattered and reduced to obscurity.

"This place, this cave, has been sacred to the Cahokia for eons. My spirit has guarded and protected this cave, this land, guided by spirits more ancient than I for many years. My time is ending. I have chosen you as guardians, not only for this cave, but also for this land, your land, and your families.

"Tsiyi, your family was pushed out of Tennessee. You know what it feels like to lose your homeland. Even now, your parents and tribe search for a home on the river. They will find their home, but you will stay and make these hills your home. Sadly, your new homeland will soon come under attack, and you must work with Wick to defend it for the sake of your new tribe, your family, and Wick's family.

"Wick, your family was driven from your home by unseen forces, including your dad's disappearance. You experienced what it feels like to be lost and unable to return home. The assaults on your family and homeland are not finished. You must be strong and courageous, tapping into strengths and abilities you never knew you possessed.

"Tsiyi, I give you the name Kahoka, symbolizing my people's knowledge, honor, and strength. I bestow upon you my gift of wolf hearing," Kimi said, his voice layered with experience.

Wick and Tsiyi looked at each other, eyes wide with shared astonishment, their expressions mirrored in the cavern's eerie glow.

Wick jumped up. "Kahoka! So, you are Kahoka. I found Kahoka."

Kimi motioned for Wick to sit. Wick put his hands on the sides of his head, then sat.

"With wolf hearing," Kimi continued, "you perceive sounds others cannot—like whispering winds, a rabbit's cautious footsteps, or the distant howl of a wolf. Every rustle in the forest will speak to you, and your acute awareness will shield you from surprise or ambush."

Tsiyi stood, seeming to absorb the promise of heightened senses with every fiber of his being. Wick watched, intrigued and slightly envious, as Tsiyi turned, scanning the cave in renewed wonder.

"Do you hear that?" Tsiyi asked suddenly, his voice tinged with wonder.

"What?" Wick asked.

"That sound of water dripping," Tsiyi replied, a mixture of disbelief and excitement.

"I don't hear it."

Kimi motioned for Tsiyi to sit, his face serene, seeming to understand the profound gift he had passed on.

Tsiyi said, "Thank you. I accept the gift. I will make these hills my home and henceforth be known as Kahoka."

Kimi continued to talk. "Wick, to you, I give the name Tayen, symbolizing newness and an awakening of your heritage. You will learn about your heritage, and you must learn skills. Protect your family and work with Kahoka to preserve this land. To you, I give the gift of hawk vision. It will not enhance your sight but allow you to see through the eyes of the hawk. This power will take time to master, and its full potential can only be revealed through patience and practice."

Hawk vision? "Thank you."

Kimi continued, "You are brothers and must help one another."

Kahoka pressed his palm flat against his chest as he looked at Wick. Wick hesitated, then mirrored the gesture. The two of them locked eyes in the flickering firelight.

Kimi smiled. "You are brothers—through the blood that spans generations." Kimi looked at Tayen. "Kahoka is your ancestor."

Wick held up his hand to ask a question, only to see Kimi cast another handful of material on the fire, creating a fresh round of colorful flames. Kimi disappeared, leaving Wick and Kahoka stunned.

As the flames flickered, casting shadows along the cave walls, Wick and Kahoka faced each other. Wick's mind raced with confusion and awe. *What did all this mean?* He felt something deep within him shift, drawing him closer to a heritage he knew so little about. *How is this possible? Am I tied to this place, to these people, not just by words but by blood?*

Kahoka broke the silence. "I guess we have a lot to talk about."

Wick nodded slowly, his mind turning over ideas and questions. "Yeah, a lot to sort out."

Kahoka nodded slowly as they stood, eyes fixed on Wick. "We need a plan. I can see we're on the same side."

Wick heaved a deep sigh, his thoughts overflowing. "There's more. Kimi didn't tell the whole story." Wick explained he was from a different time and all that had befallen him. He explained how he went to Riggsville and Kahoka's camp and how Kahoka's son got angry.

Kahoka leaned back and sat on a rock, shaking his head. "A son!" he exclaimed.

Wick nodded and explained how his gramps thought the signal tree pointed to a sacred Indian site. Kahoka held up his hand and said, "Signal tree. Do you mean day star?"

Wick shook his head. "Day star? What's a day star?"

"You know, trail marker trees to navigate during the day, like stars at night."

Wick turned to look at Kahoka. "You navigate from stars?"

"Yes. I'll show you."

Outside in the diminishing light, the night seemed vast and limitless, stars stretching in their eternal dance.

Kahoka pointed. "The North Star is constant, always guiding the way. Two stars on the Big Dipper's outer rim point directly to the North Star." Kahoka continued to share celestial navigation tips. Kahoka faced the North Star and extended his arm right. "See, the river is that way. East."

Wick pulled out his compass, marveling, "Wow! It is," confirming what he already trusted.

"A compass. Where did you get a compass?"

"Don't you have one?"

"No. We trade only for what we need; a compass is a luxury."

"Well, you can have this. But you have to help me return to the signal tree, the day star."

Kahoka smiled. The two went back inside the cave.

Kahoka said, "Without a way to communicate, I don't see how we can help each other."

"Maybe there is a way," Wick explained, detailing how the coin and arrowheads worked with the signal tree.

Kahoka listened intently, nodding slowly as the concept formed in his mind.

Wick continued, "Perhaps an artifact, something hidden, could serve as a message if we need each other—something no one else would find or understand. Take something you make, something unique that won't disintegrate, like an arrowhead you just made that day, and hide it in that pocket on the cave wall. I will check each week. Once I get it and go to the signal tree, it should bring me back to the day you made the item. I will search for you at the signal tree, the cave, or the camp. If you don't see me that day, you'll know it didn't work, and you can try a different item. If I need to get a message to you, I will just come back and tell you."

***

In the morning, they decided to head to the signal tree. Wick thought he knew the general direction. As they walked, they came to a line that Wick had blazed. "Almost there. We can follow this line."

Reaching the signal tree, Kahoka turned and pointed back the way they'd come. "That's a day star—it points toward the cave." He listened for a moment, then looked toward the creek hollows. "I think I hear others—perhaps a neighboring tribe down the creek. I'll check that out. Any hawk vision yet?"

Wick shook his head, a frown creeping onto his lips. *No hawk vision yet.* His shoulders sagged, showing frustration.

They studied each other, their newfound destinies hanging in the air. The look they exchanged made it clear to Wick that their alliance, underscored by familial ties and overwhelming experiences, would be their greatest survival tool.

Wick nodded. "And I'll return home—for now."
"Till next time, Tayen," Kahoka said, his tone full of promise.
"Till next time," Wick echoed.

Chapter 13
The Van

As Kahoka disappeared into the woods, Wick took a pause. He lay beneath the archaic sentinel of the signal tree—the world around him still. The tree stood silent, an unwavering keeper of time's secrets—its branches twisting like outstretched hands bracing the sky.

Just a few days, he mused, and yet it had felt like a lifetime had stretched and compressed into tangled moments. The past had folded into the present, and it felt like however many days were too few to hold everything he'd experienced.

The resonance of Kimi's words clung to him. Kahoka, Tayen, and the gifts of wolf hearing and hawk vision weren't just names or stray abilities; they were anchors that tied him to something ancient yet unseen.

The encounter in the cavern swirled through his mind, echoing through the marrow of his bones, challenging his understanding of lineage and purpose. His life, once defined by the rhythmic clatter of city streets and wrestling mats, was now measured by the whispers of trees and the pull of things unseen.

Wick peered through the web of branches that caught the early morning light, watching lazy clouds drift by. In the city, time moved in a linear march forward—calendar pages flipping, classes starting and ending, and sports seasons marking the calendar like clockwork. Here, time had become a mosaic, each piece jagged yet fitting together in strange cohesion. He was losing his grasp on the flow of hours and days; time swirled around him in layers of past and present.

He commanded himself to focus and take inventory. By now, Latesha's internet campaign should be taking off, alerting her 1.5 million followers to the injustice. Protesters, TV coverage. Billy—he needed to update him. Shooting a bow—he couldn't think about that right now. Vilnius—no telling what he was up to now. His dad— had to be alive, but where? *And hawk vision—hawk vision!*

Wick closed his eyes and imagined what it must be like to see through the eyes of a hawk—soaring high—seeing for miles down to the slightest detail. *Nothing.*

Wick drifted off, exhausted from the whirlwind of events since arriving in Mountain View. He dreamed of strolling along Chicago's iconic Navy Pier, gazing at the clouds drifting over Lake Michigan, envisioning a perfect blend of city charm and nature's tranquility. His mind drifted to floating in the clouds. Looking down, he could see the top of the Sears Tower, the Navy Pier, and his apartment building. He saw jet boats performing synchronized stunts and the Thunderbirds performing thrilling aerial feats. Looking at his arm, he saw feathers catching the wind.

Wick startled awake. *The Chicago Air and Water Show! That was the Chicago Air and Water Show! It's this week, right now, in Chicago! Hawk vision!* That was hawk vision!

He tried closing his eyes to continue the vision, but nothing happened. He tried to fall asleep but was too wired to drift back off. *That was awesome! I've got to master this.*

Wick stood, resolved to consolidate fragmentary hopes into a tangible outcome to save his family's heritage. His journey wouldn't be without mistakes or missteps, but piece by piece, he would wrestle this mosaic into a coherent defense—a plan built on wit and welded by burgeoning friendships across time.

Before returning to the present, Wick looked around for a small stone. He lifted a larger rock and pounded the small rock until it broke in two. *From now on, I'm saving and labeling an object from each trip in case I need to return here and now.*

Wick took a long breath and touched the signal tree. He returned home instantly, trying to reorient his mind to the present time despite the three days he had just spent reaching the White River, nearly drowning, finding Kahoka, meeting Kimi, and learning about his appointment as a guardian and his gift of hawk vision.

Back at the house, Wick grabbed a handful of zip-lock sandwich bags, placed the broken piece of rock in the bag, and labeled it "Kimi–cave." He stowed it in the hidden trunk compartment.

Checking his phone, he saw an update from Latesha. "100 ppl ready 4 Quorum Crt mtg. Protest signs, 2 local TV stns, state paper. Hoping 4 national news. Standby."

Wick headed to town to see Billy. Pulling onto Main Street, he followed a van sporting a colorful logo—a set of hands holding crystals with flowing water. When the vehicle slowed, he drew close enough to read "Crystalis Vitalis." The van turned down an alley and stopped behind an old warehouse. Wick slowed long enough to see a man go inside.

Wonder if Billy knows about this?

***

Billy was slumped in his lazy chair with the TV blasting. Sailor Cat walked up and rubbed Wick's leg.

Billy woke and smiled. "You belong to her now. She just marked you."

Wick glanced down the hall and closed the door. "Billy. Lots happened since we spoke a few days ago."

"You mean yesterday?" Billy said with a puzzled look.

"Oh my gosh, yes, I mean, it's been three days for me, but yes, yesterday."

Wick told Billy about his adventures: meeting Kahoka at the camp, angering Waya, missing the White River on the first day, being saved by Kahoka, encountering a hawk, finding the crystal cave, meeting Kimi, experiencing hawk vision, and seeing a Crystalis Vitalis van parked behind the warehouse.

Billy shook his head. "As I suspected. It's all changed. It's not good that Waya overheard. I hope that does not mess things up. I'm glad you found Kahoka, found the cave, and saw Kimi. But I never heard you almost drowned. It makes me concerned we should stop."

"Oh, I'm not stopping now. And what's this business about shooting a bow? Is that even a thing?"

"It was in the past scenario. But now, I don't know. You should learn, but right now, we have other problems. Tell you what, it's getting dark. How about we park near that alley and see what's happening?"

Wick glanced out the window, the shadows lengthening across the street. "Alright," he muttered, steeling himself for what lay ahead. "Let's see what we're walking into."

There was no telling what danger might lurk in the darkness—what secrets would unveil when they dared to peel back the layers of deceit spinning out from the heart of Crystalis Vitalis.

Chapter 14
The Break In

Wick parked at Mountain View Square. Six small groups of musicians gathered near the square, playing folk tunes without amplification. The melodies of dulcimers and acoustic guitars, along with harmonized voices, filled the air. The scene's charm and the spectators gathered around each group, as well as cars and small crowds, made it easy for them to blend in. Casually walking past the front of the building, they saw a small sign in the window: "Crystalis Vitalis."

"You're right, Wick. They do have a building. But why would they need such a large building, and how could they afford it anyway? They aren't in business yet. At least not that I've heard."

Walking to the back alley, Wick noted, "That's where the man went. No lights on now."

Billy tried the door. "Let's go in."

"Are you crazy? That's breaking and entering!"

"It's only breaking if it's locked."

"It *is* locked!"

Billy pulled out his driver's license and slid it between the door and the jamb. "What if it's not locked?" The door swung open. Billy stepped inside.

Wick looked on in horror, motioning for Billy to back out, then whispered, "Billy! What's wrong with you? Come out of there."

Billy walked a little further, then turned. "Well, aren't you going to join me?"

Wick shook his head slowly and followed in disgust. "I don't like what we're doing here."

The bottom floor was mostly empty, with just some old shelves and tables.

Billy turned to Wick. "Where's your phone light? Let's see what's upstairs."

Billy headed upstairs with Wick close behind. The stairs led to a hallway with several doors. One room was empty. The second was a large conference room with plush leather chairs and an architectural model in the middle of the table. On the walls were several architectural drawings. Wick and Billy moved closer to study the drawings and models.

"He's planning a factory, a new hospital, and a high-rise building!" Wick said.

Adjacent to the conference room, they saw an office adorned with artwork, a large oak desk, and a filing cabinet. Billy opened the file drawer.

"Bitcoin. What's Bitcoin?" Billy said.

"Here, let me see that. Over 200 Bitcoin! Unbelievable! These statements go back to 2015."

"Is it worth anything?"

"Worth anything? Worth anything?" Wick said, his voice excited. "Billy, this is enough to buy an island or a small country. More than enough to build whatever you want."

At that moment, the lights came on. Billy and Wick turned to see Vilnius standing in the doorway.

"Find anything of interest, gentlemen?" Vilnius said.

"Mr. Whitmore," Wick stammered. "I'm sorry—"

Vilnius motioned for Wick to hand him the file. "It's quite all right, Wick. I'm glad you stopped by. I've been wanting to speak with you."

Just then, a broad-shouldered figure filled the doorway, muscles stretching the seams of his shirt as he surveyed the room. "Everything okay, Mr. V?"

"Oh yes, Mike. Everything is fine," Vilnius said, smiling.

Mike stepped back, and a young girl poked her head in. "I'm headed home, Daddy. Oh, hi, Mr. Jenkins."

Billy's face reddened as he looked toward the ceiling. "Hi, Abby," he said, struggling to find the words.

"Mike, could you drive Abby home?"

"Sure, Mr. V."

Mike and Abby left. Vilnius looked out and hollered, "Tank, you still here?"

"Sure thing, Mr. V," growled a deep, gravelly voice.

"Stick around. I may have a job for you," Vilnius said, staring at Wick. He motioned for Wick and Billy to move to the conference room. "Well, gentlemen."

Wick glanced at Billy, hoping he would know how to get out of this mess.

As they stepped into the conference room, the architectural model on the table looked even more elaborate than it had from Wick's phone light. The extensive drawings showed a new hospital, shopping mall, and high-rise apartment building. Near the exit stood a towering figure with shoulders broad enough to block the doorway and biceps that strained against his sleeves. His vigilant eyes scanned the room, appearing to ensure everything remained in order.

"Hey, Mr. V, do we need the police?"

"Not yet, Tank. How about you wait downstairs? I don't think these two mean me any harm."

Vilnius reclined and stretched his arms, a satisfied look on his face—seeming to find their predicament amusing.

"So, gentlemen, what have you discovered?"

"Nothing," Wick said. "We just got here."

"Wick. It's all right. You can tell me you saw the Bitcoin, the models, the planning. Tell me, but please don't tell anyone else. And what I want to know is, do you like it?"

"Like it?" Wick said, blinking at the question. "Honestly, no. Not if it means losing our farm. Not if it means destroying the land."

"Well, Wick. You're not helping that, are you? You seem to be making a mess of things."

"Well," Wick said. "What if we *do* tell?"

Vilnius reached over to move a computer mouse. After a few clicks, the wall monitor turned on to show eight camera displays in a grid. Vilnius clicked one, played it, and paused to show Billy sliding a card in the door. "Well, Wick. It would be tragic to see Billy live out his days behind bars. It would also be sad to see your college dreams shattered, not to mention the shame it would bring your family.

"Wick, I hold all the cards here. The money. The county's support. I'll get the land—one way or another. You can stop all that by giving me what I want. I don't need the whole three thousand acres. I just want the crystals. But if it takes three thousand acres to get the crystals, so be it. This can stop here and now if you tell me where they are. I'm more than willing to compensate your family. Join me now, and you can become a VP of a mega-company. Imagine, *Forbes '30 under 30'*! Think about it. Getting in on the ground floor of a multi-billion-dollar company. You'd be set for life."

"And what about my dad?"

"I have nothing to do with that. He is my friend. I'm putting all my resources into starting this company, but if you help me, it could free up my resources to help find your dad."

"And why are you doing all of this?"

"My daughter Abby. We will do anything to help our loved ones. Abby is all I have in the whole world. We lost her mom to cancer. I don't want to lose Abby, too. I think I can find a cure to end cancer. Think about it, Wick. We'd be heroes. Heck, I might even run for president; who knows? It will be worth billions."

"Can we go now?"

"Sure," Vilnius said, a ghost of a smile on his lips. "And Wick, remember—you get a free pass today. But if you cross me—if Big Mike and Tank catch even a whiff of subversion—all bets are off. I won't be so forgiving next time."

As Wick and Billy stepped back into the night, the chill in the air wrapped tightly around him, the tension hanging thick as the swirling wind. Wick grappled with the consequences of his choices—caught in a precarious dance between self-preservation and defiance. Standing against Vilnius was daunting, but Wick refused to bow to threats. He would find a way through this tangled web of deceit and danger. *What have I gotten myself into, and how will I get us out?*

Chapter 15
John

Wick and Billy returned to the assisted living unit. The recent encounter with Vilnius echoed in Wick's mind. The usually comforting surroundings of Billy's room now felt stifling, the night's revelations seeming to cling to the walls. He sat in a daze, his thoughts churning over towering henchmen, secret Bitcoin treasure troves, and architectural models that symbolized more than steel and concrete. The shock of facing a man with what seemed like infinite resources left him feeling simultaneously small and defiant. Sailor jumped into his lap, but the warm, furry presence barely registered. Wick absent-mindedly stroked the cat's fur.

Finally, Billy broke the silence with a sigh that seemed to rise from the floor. "Well, I guess it's over, right?"

Wick shook his head firmly. "Billy, if Dad were home and things were all right, I could walk away, but he's out there somewhere and he needs us. I can feel it. Vilnius is a snake in the grass. I don't trust him."

Billy frowned, the lines on his face deepening with worry. "He has so much more than we ever imagined—resources, money, and those henchmen, Big Mike and Tank. We're outmatched in every way."

"You're right," Wick admitted, his tone grim but his resolve sharpening like a blade. "He's got more resources than we thought. He must be time traveling—there's no other way he could manipulate investments perfectly, especially in something like Bitcoin, which didn't carry much value before 2010. Now, they're worth over $100,000 each. That gives him more than $20 million in leverage."

Billy's eyes widened as the realization hit. "Bitcoin—how could he have done it?"

"It has to be the crystal. The one I traded in Riggsville. It must have been passed down through the years and somehow ended up in Vilnius's hands. It's easy. If you knew what to invest in ten or twenty years ago, you could easily be a billionaire today."

Billy let out a heavy sigh, running a hand through his hair. The enormity of it all seemed to settle across his shoulders. "So, what are we going to do? We're no match for him physically, financially, or politically. Are we going to go back and invest like he did? We could outdo him there. Couldn't we be billionaires tomorrow if we wanted? With money, couldn't we hire muscle and donate to get political clout?"

Wick shook his head. "Gosh, Billy! Didn't you say, 'We learned a long time ago that reality is like a patchwork quilt?' And didn't you say, 'Changing one event early on could have disastrous consequences?' Would the farm still be the farm if the family had a billion dollars? I can't believe I'm saying this, but I like the farm and my life the way they are. I mean, look at Vilnius. He has money to do whatever he wants but still wants more. If that's what it's like to be mega-rich, no thanks."

Billy nodded and reached for Sailor Cat.

Wick leaned forward, a determined glint in his eyes. "Vilnius doesn't know about the public pressure we're about to leverage. Latesha's help will be crucial at the Quorum Court meeting. We'll come out in full force. Protesters. TV stations. Maybe even national coverage. Public image is everything to a politician. The Quorum Court will be forced to back down. Vilnius will be history. End of story."

Billy nodded slowly, doubt casting a shadow over the shimmer of hope. "Okay, we can try that, but I feel there's more to it than a court meeting."

"Maybe," Wick mused, the thrum of possibility threading through his voice, "but let him underestimate us. It works in our favor. He thinks we're weak and defeated, but we're just getting started."

Billy's eyes sparked briefly with hope, the idea taking root. "You think we have a chance?"

"We have to believe," Wick said firmly, his words a quiet rallying cry. "Vilnius has heavy hitters and deep pockets, but he doesn't have the public on his side. We use that to our advantage and hit him where it hurts the most—in the public eye. Without the support of the Quorum Court, no condemnation. He has nothing."

The room grew silent again. Despite the enormity of their task and the unspoken fears simmering beneath the surface, a tenacity sparked between them. Wick knew they couldn't back down—not when so much was at stake.

Billy broke the silence again. "What will you do when Vilnius finds out you crossed him and those heavy hitters come after you?"

"Well. I am a top wrestler at my school. It's no match for that strength, but I know a move or two that might catch them off guard. And I ran cross-country. So, mostly, I'll just run. I guess you might be challenged in that department. Say, could the younger you run very fast?"

"Wick. You don't know how good you kids have it, getting a car at the age of seventeen. Why, back in my day, we walked or ran everywhere. There was no cross-country because everything was cross-country."

"I thought you rode horses—"

Billy raised his hand. "Let me stop you there. We had one horse, and my dad used it to plow the field and pull the wagon to church on Sundays. Yes, I learned to ride, but I walked most of the time. It was several miles to school and uphill both ways."

"Now, wait a minute. 'Uphill both ways?'"

"Well, you walk it, then tell me if it ain't uphill both ways."

"Pass. I walked to the White River and back. You're right. With the creeks and hills, it would be uphill both ways. Sorry. Go on."

"Back to if I could run fast. Yes, I was a good runner, but we didn't have track or cross-country at school. The school was too small, and other schools were too far away for sports. Working on the farm was sports enough."

"The other day, you told me we were—excuse me—are best friends. You said your younger self helped me. But you were tired and needed to rest. Is that still something I/we need to do? Do I still need to go back and meet your younger self?"

"Wick, think about it. If you don't go back and meet me as a young person, how would I ever know about the crystal, the cave, or Vilnius? Sure, you could skip that, but every action or inaction has an impact. Say you didn't go back and meet my younger self. As soon as you decide, you might visit me and find I don't know anything. Of course, that could happen anyway at my age. Everything could change. Would it be for the better? Who knows? But that would be a huge change, and I don't think we can take that risk."

"So, I need to go back and meet your younger self? How would I even do that?"

"See that valet tray on my dresser? The one with my wallet and keys? Look in the corner and pick up the dime."

"Wow! This dime has a hole in it. What happened?"

"My brother—"

"Wait! You have a brother?" Wick interrupted.

"Had a brother. My brother gave me his single-shot .22 rifle before he left for the war. It cost a whole whopping five dollars. I bet a rifle like this would cost about $300 new today. I shot that dime at twenty-five paces. Open sights. I could plink a squirrel right between the eyes out of the tallest tree."

"Well, what happened to your brother? What's his name?"

Billy stopped talking and stared across the room. He pressed his fist to his mouth, bouncing it gently, searching for words. "John—John—" He fell silent again. Then he opened his hand and rubbed his eyes. After a long pause, he shook his head. "I can't do this right now. You caught me off guard. I'd be glad to tell you about John—just not now."

"Okay," Wick said, sorry for bringing it up. He had never dealt with a situation in which a grown man became emotional.

Wick stood up, wondering if he should go, stay, be quiet, or keep talking. After another awkward pause, Wick asked, "So, the dime. You mentioned the dime. Is that how I go back to meet you for the first time?"

Billy let out a slow breath, shoulders easing as the conversation shifted. "Yeah. That should get you to the right day—but you'll have to find out where I am when you land. Start at the old Russ Grocery store near Chalybeate Springs. It went out 'round 1931, but what's left is still standing. Watch out for rattlers—don't go walking in the building. The boys and I played there some afternoons after school. If we're not at Russ's or the Kahoka Post Office nearby, try the Pritchard Sawmill in Pleasant Grove. I need to rest now."

"Okay, Billy. I'll let you know how it goes." *Though, if I'm right, you'll already know the outcome by the time I get back.* Wick nearly laughed at the thought. "Just one more thing. It's not winter there, is it?"

"Oh no. It's warm."

"Good."

Chapter 16
WW2

Back at the house, Wick saw Gramps sitting around the campfire.

Gramps called out, "How do you like the old blue Ford truck, Wick?" His voice carried a mix of pride and nostalgia.

"Gramps, it's awesome. I have always wanted a new car, but I like it better than a new one. What year is it, anyway?"

"It's a '74 model. Got it when your mom was born. That might be why I'm so partial to it. You don't miss all the electric gadgets like power windows and air conditioning?"

"Naw. I will look around for something like that when I go to college. It will be cool."

"Well, Wick. I'm glad you feel that way because it's yours."

Wick shook his head in shock. "You're kidding?" He hugged Gramps. "I love you, Gramps." Wick felt warmth spread through him, surprising himself with the strength of his emotions.

Wick continued, "Uncle Billy mentioned his brother, John, but got all choked up and couldn't finish telling me about him. Did you know him?"

Gramps cracked a big smile like he was about to laugh, then slumped his head into his right hand and rubbed his face and head as if deep in thought.

Oh no! Not again. First Billy and now Gramps!

After a moment, Gramps straightened and offered Wick a sheepish grin, as though brushing away the heaviness. "Wick, you're talking about my dad, John."

"Your dad?" Wick's surprise mingled with embarrassment. "Sorry—I didn't know."

Gramps adjusted in his seat, drawing Wick closer to the legacy he suddenly felt tethered to. "That's okay, son. How were you going to know without talking like this? My dad, John, died in World War II, commonly referred to as WW2."

"Sorry, I didn't know. Can you tell me his story?"

"Can I?" Gramps said with a burst of energy. "Of course I can. War broke out on September 1, 1939, when Nazi Germany invaded Poland. I was born in the spring of 1940. The US entered World War II on December 7, 1941, following Japan's surprise attack on Pearl Harbor. When I was two, my dad, John, and two of his buddies enlisted. Two out of three soldiers at the time were drafted, but my grandpa, Elijah, said John and his buddies volunteered for service to keep America free."

Gramps's voice caught. He shifted in his chair.

"I lived here then with my grandpa, Elijah; my grandma, Myrtle; my mom, Sarah; and Dad's younger brother, Billy. Yes—my uncle, your great-great-uncle Billy. He was fourteen when John died in the war."

Wick scrambled to process the connections—his family tree taking tangible shape before him. "What happened to John?"

"Well, it was tragic. During the largest amphibious invasion in history, where Allied forces stormed the beaches of Normandy, France, on June 6, 1944, many of John's platoon drowned before they ever got to shore. John lost his helmet in the rough waters. If he'd been wearing a helmet, he might have survived."

"That's sad. But the ones that drowned! Why—how could they drown?"

"Well, they carried about ninety pounds of gear—weapons, ammunition, clothing, food, and water."

"Yeah, okay, but I still don't understand how they drowned."

"Many amphibious vehicles never made it to the beach. They stopped in six feet of water due to rough waters and enemy fire. Some soldiers were too proud to wear a life preserver, while others wore them around their waist. When they hit the water, the heavy gear pulled their head under, and they drowned. If they had worn the preserver on their neck and shoulders and strapped their helmets on, that might have helped. John beat the odds, fighting for two years. D-Day was where it ended for him. He was shot on Normandy's Omaha Beach, June 6, 1944. I was almost three at the time."

Wick leaned back, struck by the depth of history he'd never known. "Wow, Gramps! I guess I still have a lot to learn. Did he receive any medals?"

"Oh sure, the European Campaign Medal. The WW2 Victory Medal. But the Purple Heart honors those wounded or killed in action, symbolizing sacrifice and bravery. It's my favorite. Even got a signed regret letter from Franklin D. Roosevelt. John's name is on the memorial in front of the courthouse downtown."

Wick sensed the pride in Gramps's voice. Wick asked quietly. "Did a lot of people die?"

Gramps hung his head and stared at the ground. "It was the deadliest military conflict in history. Almost three hundred thousand US soldiers and over fifty million worldwide, not counting those who died from disease and famine."

"Ouch! That's insane."

"Have you heard the saying 'all gave some, some gave all?'"

"No."

"Well, ponder that, and next time we talk, let me know what you think it means."

"Okay. Thanks, Gramps. I'll think about it," Wick said, the depth of their talk still sinking in.

***

Back in his room, Wick's phone bathed him in blue light as he delved into history. *John—Billy's brother, Gramps's dad, my great-grandpa. Wow!* Wick typed "all gave some; some gave all" into the search bar, the phrase resonating like an unspoken anthem. The song "Some Gave All" by Billy Ray Cyrus came up, a poignant accompaniment to his reflections. Wick listened to it several times and then nodded his head. I get it now.

Wick filled his pack for his next trip. *Tomorrow morning, 1947.* The thought of meeting a younger Billy and seeing history play out before his eyes both thrilled and unnerved him. *What will Billy be like at seventeen?* Would he share the wisdom Wick had come to rely on—or would seventeen-year-old Billy be entirely different, colored by the past Wick had only just begun to unravel?

As he packed, Wick's mind buzzed with questions, each one a thread pulling him further into the tapestry of time. *What if I get caught up in something I can't control?* The stakes seemed to rise with each layer of history he pieced together. He double-checked his gear—ensuring everything was ready for a trip where the mundane might tip into the extraordinary.

In a fleeting moment, he recalled his brief encounter with hawk vision, a potential yet untapped, always hovering at the edge of his consciousness. Could it guide him in finding his dad? His father's disappearance remained a shadow he could not shake, a mystery entwined with the land and its secrets. How deep did Vilnius's grasp reach into this tangled web?

Wick paused by the window, the night whispering through the trees, carrying fragments of a world he was about to plunge into. His heartbeat quickened—not from fear, but from the thrill of stepping into another moment filled with unknown possibilities, where answers and dangers coexisted just a breath away. As he turned from the window, a quiet resolve settled in. Tomorrow was more than a journey through time; it was a journey toward truth— one step closer to uncovering secrets that stretched from his blood to the land he stood on.

He couldn't help but wonder: could this journey bring him closer to his father, to an understanding of Vilnius's reach, or might it unleash something unforeseen, changing everything again?

With one final glance at his packed bag, Wick knew—there'd be no turning back once tomorrow dawned. The past awaited, brimming with potential—both for confrontation and discovery.

Chapter 17
Russ Grocery

Wick ran his fingertips over the circumference of Billy's dime, stopping abruptly at the jagged hole. The once-smooth center now bore a rough edge, a palpable reminder of the .22 caliber bullet's force. A tiny shard caught against the pad of his thumb, anchoring him to a pivotal moment across time. The dime, combined with the crystal, tethered him across decades as he touched the signal tree. The world blurred and shifted instantly, settling into the summer of 1947. The air smelled different here—fresher, unburdened by the complexities of the modern world.

Taking a deep breath, Wick glanced around, adjusting to the mid-twentieth-century sights and sounds. Gramps's farm burst into life before him.

Wick stood in awe of the lively 1947 farm. In stark contrast to its modern counterpart, the 1947 version of the farm was bustling with activity. The barn stood proud, a sentinel amidst verdant fields, where cows and a solitary horse grazed leisurely. Nearby, a chicken coop teemed with clucking hens and curious guinea fowl. Dogs barked merrily, chasing after a playful six-year-old boy: Boyd, Wick realized, his future grandfather.

The expansive garden sprawled next to the house, every row meticulously tended, bursting with life and color. Wick marveled at the covered back porch, where a chain and pulley descended into the well, an example of utility and simplicity.

Wick exhaled, blending gratitude with nerves as he knocked. The open door let the breeze flow through the wooden screen door, mingling the scents of fresh-baked bread and the earthy aroma of well-tended soil.

A woman with an inviting smile answered. "Billy's off somewhere."

Wick thanked her, his head spinning from the lively contrast to his era's quiet homestead. "Can you give me directions to the old Russ Grocery?"

She pointed down the road. "Just follow that and turn the corner."

The dirt road stretched before him, winding its way to the old Russ Grocery store, where Billy mentioned starting. Wick approached cautiously, spotting the faded remnants of what once had been a bustling hub.

As Wick neared, he recalled Billy's warning about the rattlesnakes lurking in the ruin and hesitated to venture too close. The distinct sound of a rattler's warning confirmed his decision; its dry rattle unsettling in the otherwise quiet surroundings. Wick shivered—not from the chill but from the eerie familiarity of stepping onto history's stage.

With Russ Grocery yielding no sign of Billy, Wick turned toward his next lead: the Kahoka Post Office. A group of boys loitered around, their voices carrying easily on the breeze. Wick approached, asking if they'd seen Billy. A few exchanged glances before one replied, nodding toward the sawmill in Pleasant Grove with a casual shrug.

The sawmill's rhythmic hum echoed through the trees. Wooden planks stretched toward the sky in formation, long shadows casting patterns beneath the mid-morning sun. Wick spotted a boy matching Billy's description, barefoot and carefree, caught up in jovial camaraderie.

Gathering his resolve, Wick moved closer, only to witness younger Billy's antics firsthand. Billy displayed a flair for dramatics, his laughter infectious, even as he engaged in harmless jostling—a playful shove here, mischief-laden taunt there. When Wick approached, Billy's expression shifted between intrigue and mockery.

"You lost, stranger? Where'd you get those fancy shoes? What's the matter? Too good to go barefoot?" Billy quipped, his voice light but eyes assessing.

"No," Wick replied confidently, locking eyes with him. Billy approached, stepping in closer, causing Wick to stumble backward over another boy who crouched behind him. Laughter erupted as Wick regained his balance, determination burning brighter.

Billy and the boys began to head off, casting Wick a mistrustful glance as he followed.

"You stay here, fancy shoes," Billy quipped.

Desperate, Wick needed something, anything, to capture Billy's attention. "What's the matter, Billy? Afraid to wrestle?"

Billy's eyebrows arched, a grin spreading over his face. Turning to his friends, his laughter was boastful. "This city boy thinks he can take me on—let's show him how it's done!"

The match fired up instantly—a clash of skill and grit, as Wick found Billy a formidable opponent. Each tactical maneuver yielded new insights into strengths, both hidden and overt. Wick discovered a wrestling hold unknown to him, showing Billy's rural expertise despite Wick's years of formal training.

Their tussle ended in a breathless draw; camaraderie forged amidst competition. Billy gestured toward the vibrant life overhead, challenging Wick to follow him into the sawmill's rafters. Hesitation gripped Wick, but the allure of curiosity and challenge nudged him forward. Surrounded by rough-hewn beams and machinery's rhythmic whir below, Wick felt his pulse quicken—a dance between thrill and danger on the knife's edge.

The boards trembled beneath them, but Billy's assured steps lit a path, guiding Wick to safer beams.

Life here seemed stark and unyielding, much like the wood being milled. Every splinter and creak spoke of toil and perseverance. Yet, there was a certain beauty in this rawness. Each plank was evidence of the hard work and craftsmanship that built this place, a legacy Wick could appreciate, even if he hadn't milled the wood himself. He felt a kinship with the place—a quiet pact between man and machine, both striving and enduring.

From their perch, Wick attempted to share his unbelievable story, history's whispers threading through the air.

Billy smirked, disbelief coating his words like sap. "Who do you think you are—John Carter from 'A Princess of Mars'?"

"Never read it," Wick replied, genuinely curious.

"You got to read Edgar Rice Burroughs. John Carter transported from Earth to Mars—you're claiming to do the same thing, just through time."

Wick's eyes widened as the realization hit him. "I am, Billy. I need you to trust me," he said, his voice firm with conviction.

Billy's skepticism didn't waver. He crossed his arms, leaning back slightly, a challenging glint in his eye. "Trust? I need proof—a show of faith."

Wick hesitated, pressure building inside of him. His mind raced, knowing what he had to do. "Alright," he said slowly, "I'll try something I've never done. I'll bring you with me—to the past."

Billy's eyebrows shot up in surprise, but he nodded, curiosity gleaming in his eyes.

They traveled to the signal tree, hearts pounding as they touched its gnarled bark, holding Gramp's 1855 silver dollar. The world dissolved and reformed, snow chilling their breath. A crisp winter air enveloped them, and they saw their exhalations turn into puffs against the chill.

Billy staggered, dizziness washing over him like a sudden wave, and he almost fell. Wick grabbed his arm, steadying him.

"First time's rough," Wick said, a knowing smile on his face. "I nearly lost my lunch the first time it happened to me."

But in the marvel of time slipping away, levity emerged. Embracing newfound wonder, Billy scooped up a handful of snow and playfully launched a snowball at Wick. Wick grinned, retaliating as laughter punctuated their snow-draped surroundings. Their laughter echoed through the cold air, adding warmth to the snowy scene.

They quickly sculpted a snowman with twig arms and features, representing their impromptu adventure. Stepping back to admire their creation, they burst into laughter again, the simple joy of the moment overwhelming them.

Shivering in their summer attire, they glanced at each other, a shared understanding dawning. "Okay, okay!" Billy chattered. "I'm convinced—let's go back, quick!"

Within moments, they reappeared under 1947's unrelenting sun, Billy's newfound belief sparking another demand—one Wick hesitated to entertain.

"You've got to go back and stop my brother from enlisting, Wick," Billy implored. "If anyone can do it, you can."

Wick thought of the ripples their actions could unleash, the enormity of his mission juxtaposed against Billy's plea. *Could I live with the consequences of altering the past so directly?* he wondered, the burden of his mission colliding with Billy's plea.

"I can't do that, Billy. I'm just here to save my family and the land," Wick replied. The enormity of an entire family's fate swirled within him.

"Oh, I see. Save your family but not mine?" Billy's voice wavered a blend of challenge and hope, plunging Wick deeper into a sea of choices.

"Billy, I'd love to help, but I don't know." Wick hesitated, wrestling with ethics, uncertainty, and the desire to make a difference.

"Well, you need my help, and I'm not helping unless you help me."

Wick turned to gaze at the signal tree—a tangible reminder of lives affected far beyond his depth of wisdom. A resolve crystallized within him, an urge to act against the specter of regret simmering beneath his skin. *Every step I take in the past creates ripples. Could this possibility steer things toward balance?*

"Okay, Billy. We're in this together. I'll try, but what if he says no? What then? Are we good?"

Billy's eyes twinkled with a mix of challenge and amusement. "If John says 'no,' I'm good. Just ask him why, and don't ask my nickname."

Wick paused, considering the hurdles ahead. "But what if John asks for proof? You did."

Billy nodded, acknowledging the need for a secret only they would know. "You're right. You could tell him about the time I almost fell off the cliff. Mom always warned us to stay away from the cliffs, but John took me up there one day. He said to be careful. I was walking along the bluff when a rock shifted under my weight. I lost my balance and nearly fell. John barely caught me and pulled me to safety. We tried to push the rock off the cliff, but it was too heavy to move. It's strange that it was so nearly balanced that it shifts when you step on it. John called it the 'seesaw' rock."

"Are you sure that's secret enough he will know you sent me?" Wick asked, his voice tinged with skepticism.

"Oh yeah," Billy assured, confidence in his tone. "We never told anyone. Wouldn't want to worry Mom and didn't want to get in trouble anyway."

"Okay. I will use that if I need to," Wick agreed, mentally filing away this personal history as a potential key to winning John's trust.

They returned to Billy's house. Electric lights with bare bulbs and pull chains cast warm glows throughout the room, creating a cozy contrast to the vivid summer light outside. A wood stove in the kitchen emitted an inviting warmth despite the season, its presence an authentic nod to earlier days. The walls were adorned with patterned wallpaper, typical of the time, enveloping the room with gentle nostalgia.

Billy retrieved a letter from his brother, John—a tangible time marker, written the day before John shipped out to go overseas for World War II. He also displayed a photo of John and Sarah, taken on the same day, standing on the bluffs overlooking the large boulders above the creek. Wick marveled as he met Elijah and Myrtle Jenkins, his great-great-grandparents. Their hospitality was warm and reminiscent of his grandparents, evoking a comforting familiarity.

He felt an overwhelming urge to reveal the truth but knew he must keep it hidden. The purpose of his mission deepened, a silent bond between past and present tugging at his conscience. John and Sarah's photo grew heavier in his hand, joined by the letter tucked aside—not just a marker but a silent promise of intent.

With the letter secured, Wick steeled himself, stepping once more into the uncertain void of time. Would this be his family's salvation—or their undoing? Together, Wick and Billy carved the unknown, step by courageous step. With a new friendship cemented and a new path begun, they faced the challenges ahead with newfound resolve.

Chapter 18
John

Wick steadied his breath, holding the sealed letter to his chest as he stood at the signal tree. Everything about this day felt surreal. Clutching Billy's crystal, he braced for the familiar lurch of time travel. The world blurred, colors and sounds swirling until, with a gentle thud, he landed in 1942—on the day before John deployed for Europe.

The moment Wick opened his eyes, he sensed the farm was in a different state than in 1947. The paint gleamed and the roof looked fresher—less worn by the elements. The same barn and outbuildings stood, but their timbers shone, reminding Wick that five years of wear during wartime had not yet taken their toll. The place exuded the same warmth as before—cows in the field, chickens pecking the ground—yet the shadow of war hung just out of sight.

He soon learned that John and his wife, Sarah, had walked to the bluffs, making the most of the warm spring day. Wick followed a meandering path lined with budding wildflowers, their colors a cheerful backdrop for the bittersweet mission, drawing him onward.

At the bluff's edge, he spotted John and Sarah quietly leaning against one another, staring into the vastness of the valley below as the creek babbled in the distance. They were so calm, so untroubled in each other's presence, it made Wick's heart ache knowing what lay ahead.

"Excuse me," Wick said softly, not wanting to disrupt the moment. "John?"

John turned, and though he initially appeared surprised, a strange recognition surfaced in his eyes. "Well, now," he said, a hint of a grin tugging at his mouth. "I was wondering whether you'd appear today."

Sarah's gaze shifted curiously between John and Wick, but she only smiled politely. "Mind taking our picture?" John asked, handing Wick a camera. "We want something to remember this day by."

Wick obliged, snapping the photograph—an image he knew all too well and had carried in his pocket: John and Sarah side by side, the bluff's rocky landscape behind them—a circle in time completed.

Once the shutter clicked and the moment was captured, John turned to Sarah. "Would you mind giving me a minute with—my friend here?" Sarah offered Wick a nod and headed back along the trail, seemingly content to let them speak privately.

"I'm from the future," Wick said, his voice trembling more than he intended. "Billy sent me to warn you that if you go, you may not—" He paused, tears threatening to break. "May not come home."

To Wick's surprise, John offered a gentle smile. "Kimi told me about you," he said. "Said you'd show up and, in time, take over as guardian. I might've teased you if we had more time, but I'm glad to meet you."

The words warmed and unbalanced Wick equally; John knew of his role, possibly even better than Wick did. Still, Wick pressed on. "You have a choice, John—Billy fears you won't return."

"Does America win?" John asked. His calm acceptance brought a lump to Wick's throat.

"Yes," Wick answered solemnly. "But it's costly. We keep war away from Arkansas, from our land, but many men like you—"

"That's why I'm going," John said, gaze firm as though all was decided. "To keep that darkness from coming here, from touching those I love. My family, your family. Even you, whether you realize it or not." He reached out and clasped Wick's shoulder. "You're my great-grandson, after all."

The significance of those words made Wick's knees feel weak. He stared at John's earnest expression and quickly folded into a rough embrace. In that moment, he understood how deep love could stretch across time.

Pulling away, Wick remembered the caution he desperately needed to impart. "John, if you invade by sea, promise me something. Wear your life preserver around your neck and shoulders, not your waist, and always latch your helmet. Tell your men, too. It might save—" He swallowed.

John nodded. "I promise. Every precaution helps. And you— have you already started learning the bow?"

Wick blinked, startled. "The bow? How do you—?"

"I've heard the story from Kahoka. About the tribes and the tournament. About how you're meant to step in. We wouldn't even be here if Kahoka's tribe hadn't won the bow shoot, and we owe that all to you." John's eyes glimmered with fond amusement as Wick stammered, unsure how to respond. "You'll need to practice, Wick. It's important—for all our sakes."

Before Wick could ask more questions, they were interrupted by a gentle voice calling from down the trail. Sarah returned, holding a bouquet of purple and white flowers.

"Where'd you get those white fringe-like flowers?" Wick asked.

"Oh, you've never seen a grancy graybeard?" She pointed to a tree near the bluff's edge.

Wick turned to see a delicate cascade of fluffy, white, fringe-like flowers that filled the air with a sweet fragrance, creating an ethereal and enchanting display. "Wow! I've never seen one."

"It's Mom's favorite. She planted it with her father when she was a kid. We're heading back to the house for dinner. We'd love for you to join us."

Wick didn't have the heart to refuse. He followed John and Sarah down from the bluffs, weaving between stands of cedar and pine trees. As they rounded the final bend, they saw a neighbor with a large wicker basket step out from behind the broad trunk of an oak.

The neighbor hoisted the basket, revealing a wriggling litter of tiny kittens. John paused, eyes gleaming as he rummaged amidst the fuzzy mewls. Finally, he gently lifted a kitten with fur strikingly similar to Billy's cat, Sailor—one side white and the other a rich orange—one eye blue, the other amber.

John stepped aside with Wick, lowering his voice. "Billy's been torn up about my leaving. Take this kitten to him," he whispered, stroking the kitten's tiny head. "Something to ease his heartbreak." He pulled a small bell from his pocket, prying the metal ball free. Producing a small crystal fragment, he placed it inside, sealing it shut around the kitten's fragile collar.

"This might help him live a good, long life," John murmured, half-joking, half-believing in the powers that ran through their family's secret power.

Wick's mind spun. Could this be the cat he'd seen with Billy in 2026?

They arrived at the farmhouse with a cheerful throng—Elijah and Myrtle, John's parents, John's younger brother Billy at twelve, and Boyd, just a toddler of two. Inside, dinner was a hearty spread—fried chicken, mashed potatoes, gravy, beans, cornbread, and fresh greens from the garden.

"This is the best fried chicken I have ever eaten," Wick said. "Where'd you get it?"

"Out back," Elijah said, pointing toward the chicken coop, chopping one hand on his arm.

The conversation was warm, the family brimming with laughter, each moment infused with love. Wick was on the verge of tears, reminded of how little they knew that John would likely never sit at that table again.

At times, twelve-year-old Billy stared at Wick sideways, curiosity dancing across his face, but Wick remained quiet, wary of interfering. Boyd climbed up and sat in Wick's lap. Elijah and Myrtle chatted about how the farm's workload had doubled with more men leaving to fight. Sarah passed the plates. John's eyes shone with pride as he looked around the table, soaking in precious minutes.

After supper, John nudged Wick outside, letting the murmur of conversation remain behind them. Evening shadows stretched across the yard as cicadas chirped in a slow, rising chorus. John lowered his voice: "Wick, I have something else to ask. If I don't make it back—" He let the sentence hang. "In the spring, pick a bouquet of purple dwarf bearded iris flowers—Sarah's favorite. They grow along the creek bottom. Add some grancy graybeard and dogwood flowers if you can." He pressed a sealed note into Wick's hand. "Deliver them to her with this."

Wick's throat tightened. "I promise," he said, voice hushed from the enormity of it all.

While they stood beneath the early stars, Wick suddenly realized he needed the restroom. Trying to keep his composure, he asked John quietly. John smirked and led Wick toward a small outhouse behind the chicken coop, its door adorned with a crested moon cutout. Wick's eyes bulged at the rudimentary design—two wooden panels open for ventilation and not a shred of toilet paper anywhere—just a tattered catalog. Wick made do as best he could, mortified by the unfamiliar routine.

When he emerged, John ducked inside. Moments later, John opened the door a crack and beckoned Wick over. "That sack of lime in the corner is what you sprinkle down the hole," John explained through a conspiratorial grin. "Nothing fancy like plumbing in these parts. So, it's always an adventure using the facilities."

They both laughed, Wick's face burning red from embarrassment. "I guess that's something they forgot to mention in history class."

As night enveloped the sky, John guided Wick upstairs to the attic. The lumber smelled of new roof beams, raw and unblemished by time. John showed Wick a trunk with a false bottom. "I built this to store important odds and ends," he proudly explained. "One day, you might find it useful."

Wick ran his hand over the clean edges, thinking of the trunk he used in 2026, now old and creaky. The sense of time folding onto itself overwhelmed him. He realized how many small threads held lineage together, bridging hearts long separated by the tides of history.

"Remember, Wick," John said softly, "every choice you make could alter someone else's life. You're a trustee of this knowledge now, so use it carefully."

Tears threatened to surface, but Wick forced a small smile. "I'll do my best."

"Good," John answered. They clasped hands with solemn understanding.

John led Wick back downstairs, where the family—lounging on the porch with little Boyd cuddled on Myrtle's lap—continued their pleasant chatter. Wick excused himself with a heavy heart. "Thank you all for having me," he said, trembling ever so slightly. "I won't forget your kindness."

"You come on back now, anytime you like. Ya hear?" Myrtle said.

Wick felt the signal tree beckoning. Once more, he clutched the crystal, the farm dissolving around him as the tapestry of time re-stitched itself. Moments later, he landed face-to-face with a seventeen-year-old Billy in 1947's summer heat. Billy's gaze narrowed when Wick gently extended the tiny kitten.

"John wanted you to have this," Wick said softly. "He thought you might need a friend."

Billy's eyes widened, surprise sparkling when the kitten mewed.

Wick ran his thumb over the newly fashioned collar with the silent bell. "Take care of him, Shooter," Wick teased, grinning at John's nickname for Billy. Billy laughed, the tension in his shoulders easing.

Wick recounted, in broad strokes, how John was resolute in his duty to protect family and country. "He loves you, Billy. He doesn't want you to hurt. But he has to fight to keep all of us safe."

Billy nodded, hugging the kitten protectively. "Shooter, huh?" He let out a grin. "Thanks, Wick. Thank you for going to see him."

Wick exhaled, feeling the swirl of possibilities that still lay ahead. "I need to get back," Wick said, thinking of his modern time—of Latesha organizing protests and the land condemnation threatening his family. "Time might stand still in 2026, but I'd better check to be sure everything's okay."

Billy understood, resting a hand on Wick's shoulder, the new kitten purring in his arms. "Good luck."

Wick turned to the signal tree that'd become both gate and guide. Hardly a step away, he paused, glancing over his shoulder at

Billy. The boy cradled the kitten, already forging a bond that might carry across unimaginable years.

"Until next time, Shooter," Wick said, mustering a grin with a chin lift. The sun beat down, and the wind ruffled the leaves overhead.

Time beckoned, possibilities vast. Wick pressed his hand to the bark, the crystal in his grip, his resolve steady. *If I can keep them safe, I'll do anything.* With that final thought, he touched the tree and disappeared, leaving behind the promise of a future and the love of a family stretched across centuries.

Chapter 19
Secrets in the Past

Wick stumbled forward, feeling the familiar lurch of the signal tree's temporal shift fade behind him. The abrupt change from summer 1947 to midday 2026 left him disoriented. He steadied himself, pressing his hand to the trunk to recall where—and when—he stood. His heart still raced from parting ways with Billy, that tiny kitten mewling in the teenage version of his great-great uncle's arms.

Wick's mind roiled with the knowledge he'd gleaned. John had chosen to fight. Billy had hoped beyond hope John would change his mind. *That would be something, if John made it.*

Uncertain what time, if any, had passed in 2026, Wick glanced around. The house and yard remained unchanged since he had left for 1947. Birds chirped along the fence, and a distant car rumbled down the gravel road. *No panic. Good.* He drew a deep breath, relieved to see no immediate crisis in the modern yard.

Wick walked behind the house and found Gramps tending a small campfire pit near the porch. It was one of Gramps's daily activities, his way of keeping memories alive, and keeping mosquitoes away, Wick supposed.

"Hey, Gramps," Wick said, voice subdued as he approached.

Gramps looked up, a crooked smile forming. "Thought you'd gone exploring again." He pointed to an empty chair. "Sit a spell?"

Wick obliged, lowering himself gingerly onto the old wooden seat. Sparks from the campfire danced on the breeze, and for a moment, he relished the simple warmth. "Gramps," he ventured, needing to confirm what he'd just learned from John. "So, John, your dad—he died on D-Day, correct? June 6, 1944?"

Gramps gave him a curious glance. "No, that's not quite right." The older man's expression grew solemn as he stirred the ashes with a charred stick. "He was injured on that day—received his first Purple Heart—but he pulled through. Didn't come home, though. Went back into action soon after."

Wick's heart jolted. "He went back?"

Gramps nodded. "Fought hard. On August 10, 1944, he was shot while attacking a machine gun stronghold and died of his wounds. He saved much of his company that day—and earned a second Purple Heart. The Army recognized courage even if it cost him dearly." Gramps's voice cracked, but he continued. "We don't see enough of that kind of selflessness anymore."

Wick inhaled slowly, remembering John's promise to strap on his helmet and wear his preserver correctly if an amphibious assault happened. His small warning seemed to make a difference—John survived Omaha Beach. But in the end, the war claimed him. Wick swallowed, fighting the urge to explain. He had to keep silent about his travels, about how John knew he wouldn't return. That knowledge settled in Wick's chest, but he found some solace in knowing John's sacrifice, along with that of millions of other US soldiers, had helped preserve America's freedoms—for his family, for their land.

"Thanks, Gramps," Wick said quietly, forcing a small smile to chase away the sadness in his voice. "That's such a sacrifice. Hearing his story—living here. I feel like I know him a little bit now."

"And what about that saying? Have you given it some thought?" Gramps asked, his voice steady.

"All gave some; some gave all? Yes. I think so. John, for instance, gave his life—he gave all. Others supported the war effort and lost loved ones, so they all gave some. But I imagine some of those who gave some felt like they gave their all. How many fathers, mothers, and brothers would gladly trade places with loved ones they lost if they could? It's heavy. I get that."

Gramps patted him on the shoulder, a rare smile touching his lips. "True. So true. You *do* get it. You've gone a lot further than I thought you could."

Wick nodded. *You got that right.*

Wick changed the topic and updated Gramps on the protest Latesha was organizing.

"Protest?" Gramps repeated, taking off his cap to wipe his forehead.

"Yeah, a public demonstration against the condemnation. Latesha's roped in local activists and reporters—you name it. She's determined to show we won't sit back and take this."

Gramps held his cap, his gaze shifting to the old farmland. A mix of responsibility and uncertainty lined his face. "I see. Well, it might help. I'm not big on stirring the pot, but if it saves our farm, so be it."

Wick nodded, relieved Gramps wasn't outright opposed to Latesha's tactics. "She's got a big social media following. Between that, the tribal significance, and media coverage, we might force them to reconsider condemnation."

Gramps sighed. "Or make 'em rush it through." He glanced at Wick's worried expression. "But if you trust her, then I trust you."

***

Wick headed to visit Billy in town. He found Billy in his room at the assisted living facility. Sailor Cat dozed on a sunny windowsill.

"Hey, Billy. Wanted to update you," Wick said quietly, closing the door behind him.

Seeing Wick, Billy perked up. "Finnwick! What'd you find out from younger me?"

Wick leaned in, sharing his encounter with younger Billy in 1947. He explained how he'd been asked to warn John, but John refused to stand down, accepting his fate to keep the war away from his family. Reaching to pet Sailor, Wick added, "John even gave me this kitten to pass on—one with mismatched eyes. So she is that old?"

Billy laughed softly, looking at the ancient feline. "So, you figured it out." He shook his head in amusement. "Sailor defies logic, though I guess time travel does too."

Their laughter filled the small room, a moment of levity in the swirling uncertainties. Wick updated Billy on the upcoming Quorum Court battle. Billy nodded, eyes shining with hope and caution.

"I may have figured Sailor out, but I still need help with the knife and bow."

"The knife was our way back to a critical time, at least in the original timeline. But it's been sharpened, so we must find a different way to link back. Besides, we can't be sure we need to go there now. We'll wait to see. But in the original timeline, you returned and worked as a blacksmith apprentice."

"A blacksmith apprentice! Awesome."

"Yes. As for the bow. Kahoka was injured, and you had to step in to win the competition."

"What competition?"

"The land. The whole shebang."

"The land? What do you mean? Kahoka lived there, and it passed down through the family over the years."

"In Kahoka's time, tribes were being pressured out. The land was perfect for their needs, with abundant deer, bears, squirrels, and fish. Creeks, bluffs, rocks, and ridges made it difficult for wagons, so settlers moved on to easier terrain. Two tribes lived there, but the limited hollows couldn't sustain them, so one had to leave."

"You're telling me they had to leave?"

"They had to move to the reservation in Oklahoma."

"How awful! I read about that in history, but it sits differently when it's your family."

"Sad but true. Each tribe chose its most proficient bow shooter for a cornstalk shoot."

"Wait—cornstalk shoot?"

"Cornstalk shoot. A bundle of corn stalks, about three feet wide, set up at a hundred yards. The one with the most hits wins. Kahoka was the best in his tribe, but he got hurt. In the original timeline, you stepped in and won the tournament."

"Wait. You keep saying 'original timeline'. Does that mean I may not have to shoot the bow?"

"Wick. Do you want to bet your family's land on a 'maybe'? You'd better learn to be an expert shooter. And not with a modern compound or crossbow; we're talking about a bow fashioned from wood like hickory, Osage orange, or walnut—not a fancy laminated recurve bow. Wooden arrows with real feathers—no aluminum."

"Billy—it's too much! Dad's missing. The county's taking the land. V's henchmen are lurking who knows where. Now, you're telling me I need a hundred-year-old bow with vintage arrows and learn to become an expert." It was more of a question than a statement. "It's just *way* too much!"

"Wick, slow down. Take a breath. I didn't say today. Take it one step at a time. Remember, you can go back and spend a day, a week, or even a month learning to shoot. But there's a sequence to doing this—one step at a time. You will know when it's time to go back for the bow shoot. Just save that for last and ensure you know how to shoot that bow before then."

"Okay." *But I may be an old man before that happens.*

"Stay safe, Wick. Vilnius is cunning. Like you say, Big Mike and Tank could be lurking anywhere."

"I will."

Chapter 20

The Kiss

Back at the house, Wick's phone buzzed with an incoming call from Latesha. "I'm almost to Mountain View," she announced, excitement blending with urgency. "Things are heating up. I have about twenty supporters following me by caravan—there are more at the courthouse square. Mind if I crash at your place?"

Wick felt a jolt of nerves. "Sure, let me ask my mom." He found her flipping through the day's mail and explained the situation.

"That's fine, honey," Mom said, no hesitation in her tone. "Your friend can share Nora's room. Nora can take the trundle bed. Nora might roll her eyes, but she can deal with it." She grinned. "One more girl in the house won't kill us."

Wick paused, reflecting on how Latesha's heritage differed vastly from his family's. "Mom, do you think Gramps will be cool with—?"

She raised a brow and looked up. "Wick, your gramps would never judge. Over the years, he's had enough bias thrown at him to know better. He'll welcome Latesha in the same way as anyone. Quit worrying."

She hesitated for a moment, then took a deep breath. "You know, Wick, there's something I never told you. When I was eight,

I traveled with your gramps and gram out of state. We stopped at a restaurant and they turned us away. I felt so diminished and ashamed. No one should ever be made to feel that way, and your gramps would never do that to anyone. He knows what it's like to be judged unfairly."

Exhaling, Wick thanked her, relief flooding through him.

Wick returned to the kitchen, his footsteps echoing in the quiet room. He ran a hand through his hair, which had become slightly damp with sweat. His eyes darted around, unable to settle on anything for more than a second. He tapped his fingers on the countertop, a rhythmic yet erratic beat, and occasionally glanced at the clock, anticipating something. The soft creak of the floorboards followed him as he paced, adding to the tense atmosphere.

Nora walked in and shot him a knowing look. "What's up with you?" she teased under her breath. "You look like you're expecting your date to show up." Then, in a quieter tone, she raised an eyebrow. "Bet you're excited Latesha's coming, huh?"

Wick felt heat spread to his cheeks. "Nora, it's not like that," he sputtered.

"Uh-huh," she said, smirking, letting him squirm. Nora glanced down the hallway. "Anyway, she's staying in my room, right? Just great," she added with a small, irritated sigh. "I enjoy having my bathroom; her hair routine could tie it up!"

Wick gave her an apologetic grin. "Thanks, sis. Sorry for the inconvenience. But it'll be worth it, I promise. She's helping us big time."

Nora rolled her eyes and dropped her voice. "I get it—good cause and all. But you owe me. Big."

Wick nodded. "Deal."

Twenty minutes later, Latesha's sporty compact car rumbled up the driveway, protest signs rattling in the backseat. She flashed a bright smile, her vibrant hair shimmering.

"Hug?" she asked teasingly, stepping out of the car.

Wick offered a quick squeeze, a playful spark in his eyes. "Thanks for doing all this," he said, gesturing at the signs. "It means a lot."

"No problem—let's show them we mean business. Love the trees," she said with a smile. "Brings back memories of our days in Grant Park, right?"

Wick smiled and took her to meet Gram and Gramps.

***

The following day, Wick found the courthouse yard teeming with supporters holding signs: Save Our Heritage; Stop the Condemnation; Crystalis Vitalis is a Corporate Giant—hands off! Protesters marched around the courthouse and along the sidewalk from the courthouse to the annex building. Latesha, wearing a T-shirt emblazoned with an environmental slogan, gave a statement to a local radio reporter. A camera crew from a regional TV station hovered nearby, capturing every angle.

"This land," Latesha explained passionately, "has deep indigenous roots, which this condemnation threatens to erase. The family's Cherokee ancestry isn't just a line on paper—it's a living heritage."

Wick felt an unexpected surge of pride watching her speak. Latesha had not only mobilized the media, but her calm yet passionate perspective lent dignity to their cause. Her leadership was evident in every detail, from the organized protesters to her articulate statements.

Wick stood in front of the candy store, near the giant wooden rocker, across from the courthouse. The sight of protesters was in stark contrast to welcoming Ozark culture. Wick started feeling optimistic until he caught sight of Vilnius standing across the block, looking his way. Wick's heart quickened. He turned right to avoid his glare and saw Tank. Wick turned left and saw Big Mike. He shifted his weight from one foot to the other and looked around nervously, hoping for a way out. He felt cornered as Vilnius headed his way.

Vilnius leaned against the storefront next to Wick, looking at the protesters. "Hello, Wick."

Wick cleared his throat, wiped his palms on his pants, and forced a smile. He swallowed and stared at the protesters, considering his options. His eyes darted around, searching for an escape. "Hello."

"Nice demo, Wick. Does this mean you're turning down the VP job? You know I'm going to win in the end."

"You haven't won yet."

"Okay, Wick, but remember what I said if you turned me down." Vilnius turned to walk away and glanced at Tank and Big Mike, giving a subtle head gesture toward Wick.

The message was clear—Wick was on borrowed time.

Gramps arrived moments later, wearing pressed work slacks and a nicer-than-usual collared shirt. He caught Wick's eye, and Wick hurried over, thankful to leave Tank and Big Mike behind.

"You doing okay?" Gramps asked.

"Sure. You?"

Gramps shrugged. "Never thought I'd see the day cameras and signs lined the square. But I suppose we do what we must."

Gramps turned and nodded toward a granite memorial near the courthouse lawn. The structure stood solemnly, seeming to watch over the crowd. At the top, an eagle sculpture perched, wings outstretched in a silent salute. The inscription read, "In Loving Remembrance of Our Stone County Sons who paid the supreme price of their lives in the First World War, the Second World War, the Korean War, and the Vietnam War, and who now await reunion with us in eternity as we, their friends and loved ones who gather here, keep their memory alive in our minds and hearts."

Wick followed Gramps, heart tightening as he saw John's name etched among many. A swirl of emotions churned—gratitude, awe, and a lingering ache. Gramps's eyes grew misty. He reached out with a trembling hand, fingers grazing John's name. His throat tightened. Wick swore he saw him try to speak—but no words came.

Wick swallowed, imagining the cost carried forward in each chiseled name. "He'd probably be proud of how we're fighting for the land he left behind—how we're standing free."

Gramps offered him a faint, sad smile. "I'd like to believe so."

He gestured toward the courthouse, where local sandstone blocks rose in rough-hewn rows. "See that stone, boy? Notice how it looks—like it's braced itself for a thousand storms." He laid his palm on a stone. "Native rock from the Ozarks, red and brown pigments swirling. Every ridge and crack are part of Stone County's story."

Wick leaned in, drawn by the specks of color glimmering in the morning light. "Looks alive somehow."

Gramps nodded. "It's been weathered, chipped, hammered into shape—yet here it stands since 1922. Reminds me a little of us right now."

At that moment, a hush fell on the small gathering. Wick sensed a presence behind him, the soft rustle of delicate fabric. He turned to find Abby, Vilnius's daughter, approaching in a pastel, southern-belle-style dress that brought a vibrant pop of color to the courthouse lawn. Without a word, she leaned in and kissed Wick's cheek, leaving a deep red imprint.

Before Wick could speak, a nearby newspaper reporter snapped a photo, capturing Wick's stunned expression—Abby's lips still close to his cheek. *Did Latesha see?* he wondered with sudden panic.

Wick stiffened, heart hammering. As fast as she arrived, Abby stepped away. Her dress ruffled about her ankles, ribbons fluttering in the gentle breeze. Across the street, Vilnius stood with arms folded, lips curved in a subtle smirk. His pulse thundered. *I've been set up.* Gramps just gaped in wonder as he formed a slight smile that expressed wonder.

Wick wiped the back of his hand over the spot, cheeks heating. The swirl of events—the protest, Vilnius, Abby, a suspicious photograph—threatened to overwhelm him. Gramps appeared speechless, shaking his head slowly.

But Wick had no time to sort this out now.

Chapter 21
Judgment's Edge

Inside the county annex building, the Quorum Court rolled into session. The room filled, and many of the protesters had to stand outside. The county judge—the county's chief executive official, not a trial judge—tapped a gavel to draw attention. The judge finally got down to business after an hour of other agenda items. "Under new business, we have an ordinance to condemn property for commercial development."

The county attorney stood next, reciting the dreaded plan. "This action would transfer control of the Jenkins family's three thousand-plus acres to the county—except for the family home and a five-acre parcel. The county could then transfer or sell part or all of the remaining acreage to Crystalis Vitalis for commercial development. A future appraisal would determine the final compensation to the family, using fair market value."

Murmurs rustled among the protesters who'd managed to crowd inside despite the no-cell-phones, no-TV-cameras rule.

Gramps walked to the podium, his shoulders squared, and introduced himself. He spoke in a resolute voice. "My family has owned this land since right after 1800. It was one of the earliest deeds recorded after Stone County was formed in 1873, but our connection goes back even further. My Cherokee ancestors used that land well before paper deeds came along. We have always preserved this land, honoring the legacy of those who came before us. This land isn't just soil and trees; it's a sanctuary for wildlife and the guardian of our clear, pristine streams. My father, grandfather, and countless family ties are woven into every acre. This condemnation tears our heritage from us."

The judge—the county's chief executive—leaned in. "We're not unsympathetic, Mr. Jenkins. However, the county believes the mineral resources could invigorate growth for jobs, taxes, and prosperity. Unless the law says otherwise, we have the right to ensure the property's best use for the public good, and we promise to compensate you and your family fairly."

Gramps set his jaw. "Look. Land heritage in Arkansas, where property has passed down from Native American ancestors to their modern-day descendants, is rare. Is the court just going to disregard that?"

The judge looked over at the attorney. "Bruce. No one mentioned Native American heritage to me."

The attorney cleared his throat. "Judge, we searched public records back to 1900 and didn't find a deed. If ownership dates back to Native American heritage, we were not aware of that. If Mr. Jenkins can provide a title or deed establishing ownership from that period, that could change things based on legal precedent in case law."

Gramps slapped the podium in excitement. "If you need a deed, we'll show you one."

Wick looked over at Vilnius, hoping to see an acceptance of defeat on his face, but instead, he saw Vilnius point to Tank to exit the room. *I wonder what that was about.*

The room grew loud. The judge tapped his gavel. "Mr. Jenkins. We are tabling this action until a special session next week to give you time to get the deed to Bruce and for him to provide a legal opinion on the specific facts."

"Tabled, not canceled?" Latesha whispered to Wick. "That's a postponement, but at least it stops them for now."

Members of the Quorum Court murmured assent. Tension in the room slackened. Cautious celebration flowed among the protesters. Applause broke out, and the judge gently rapped the gavel for order. "We'll reconvene in one week unless the Jenkins show proof sooner."

Outside the annex building, Wick and Gramps paused for Latesha to speak with the radio and TV stations. As they stood there, a fire truck came wailing by.

After media interviews, Latesha pumped her fist with excitement. "We did it, Wick—no immediate condemnation!"

Gramps exhaled in relief. "All I have to do is get a copy of the deed from the county clerk. It should be easy enough. I could've done it before, but I never thought we'd need to prove ownership."

"You have it at home?" Wick asked as they walked the five blocks from the annex to the square.

"Surely somewhere, but it would be easier to get it from the county clerk," Gramps said.

Wick and Latesha exchanged a triumphant look, trailing behind. She gently patted Wick's shoulder. "Your land, your heritage—safe for now."

Wick tried to smile, but lingering worry gnawed at him. *Did Latesha see that kiss?* He felt like he was on shaky ground—for the land; for his friendship.

Then he spotted a commotion near the courthouse. Thick smoke poured from the side entrance. Firefighters scrambled, hoses spraying.

"Oh my gosh," Latesha gasped, pressing a hand to her mouth. Protesters around them stood in stunned silence.

Gramps pulled one of his firefighter friends aside. "Frank, what happened? Anything damaged?"

"Mr. Jenkins, it's the strangest thing. A fireproof records vault. Can you believe it? Someone left the file drawer open, and the fluorescent ballast above it overheated and caught fire. Thankfully, nothing burned except some old records dating back to before 1900. The building's fine."

Frank hurried off to help. Wick's stomach twisted. If earlier records were destroyed, the deed might be gone. Latesha gripped his arm, her gaze still tinged with unease—and, Wick suspected, questions about Abby's bizarre moment.

Wick's knees threatened to give way with realization. If those records were destroyed, producing the deed wouldn't be so simple. He glanced at the building, heart pounding, as Latesha tightened her grip. *Was this an accident, or sabotage?*

Latesha stared. "Wick—"

He couldn't pull his eyes from the swirling smoke. Gramps's voice wavered. "Without the deed, we're lost."

Wick inhaled shakily. *I won't let them destroy our land.* But as smoke rose into the sky, his mind flicked to the image of Abby's kiss, the reporter snapping pictures, and Latesha's unsettled expression. He could do nothing except stand by while everything he cared about teetered on the edge of ruin.

He blinked, feeling guilty. "I—I'm sorry," he mumbled, wondering if she heard.

Latesha locked eyes with him, a silent question burning there. He had no words.

He shivered, fearing more than the property deed might go up in flames.

Chapter 22
Where the Snow Falls

Wick stood on the courthouse lawn, the afternoon sun pressing on his shoulders. The laughter and chants of the earlier protest faded into a hum, replaced by a knot in his stomach. He couldn't stop replaying the day's events—Abby's kiss, the photo, the fire, Latesha's wary expression. Everything was jumbled in his mind. He glanced at Gramps, who paced near the courtyard's rock fence, waiting for word on the fire damage.

Latesha hovered nearby, arms folded, her gaze shifting toward Wick, then away. He felt her distance like a cold breeze. *I have to fix this.* Fear nagged that his friendship with her might vanish along with the records.

They waited two hours for updates. One of Latesha's followers—a lanky man clutching a half-written sign—tugged on her sleeve and said, "Saw someone bolt through the alley across from the courthouse; too dark to see a face, but they ran quick." Latesha traded a glance at Wick. He suspected Big Mike or Tank, but he couldn't prove it.

Moments later, the fire chief walked out, helmet in hand. He nodded at Gramps. "Found evidence an accelerant was used. The ballast fixture was an attempt to cover up. Fireproof vault or not, if the drawer's left open and soaked with something flammable—" He shook his head, sighing. "All the old docs from before 1900—gone. No sign of a Jenkins deed or anything similar."

Gramps's face went ashy. "I see."

"Sorry." The chief tapped his helmet and stepped away.

Wick set a hand on Gramps's shoulder, but he noticed Latesha backing off. Her face carried a strain he'd never seen. Everything Wick valued—his family land and his hope for Latesha—seemed to evaporate.

***

The next morning, Gramps phoned the county clerk, voice subdued. Wick listened from across the living room. The clerk explained that no digital backups existed for the older records—the county had started digitizing from 1900 forward, with the pre-1900 files scheduled for next year. No luck. They suggested Gramps locate another copy if it existed.

Gramps hung up, shoulders slumping. "We might have it in the family files." He eyed Wick, expression weary. "Help me search?"

They rummaged through trunks and weathered boxes, among birth certificates, old marriage licenses, and random receipts for feed and seed. For hours, they overturned dusty corners. Nothing. Gramps let out a trembling exhale, murmuring that the family always relied on "good faith" inheritance. "Never needed probate. Didn't do any official changes."

Wick squeezed his arm. "We'll keep looking," he offered, but Gramps only nodded, eyes distant with worry.

***

Around noon, Gram carried in the local newspaper with an apologetic frown. "Wick, you might want to see this."

Wick's heart plummeted. On the front page was a photo of Abby leaning in to kiss him on the cheek, capturing his stunned look. Next to that, an image showed smoke billowing from the courthouse roof. The headline read: "Things Heat up on Courthouse Square."

Latesha peered over his shoulder, her jaw clenching. "All that protesting, everything for the land, and *this* is the front page?" Her voice cracked. She tossed the paper onto the table. "Guess they prefer a scandal over real issues."

Wick felt her anger radiate like a furnace. He opened his mouth to apologize, but no words came. She stormed from the room, leaving him in silence.

***

That afternoon, the search for the deed resumed. Dust motes danced in the attic's dim light as Wick and Gramps shuffled through old ledgers and letters. Latesha floated in and out, rarely meeting Wick's eyes. Each time, he felt a twist in his gut—a sense he was losing her. *I don't even know Abby. Why can't I say that?* But Latesha barely gave him a chance to speak.

By evening, the family had found nothing. Gramps set aside a final box with shaky hands. "Must've had it once. Or maybe your great-great-grandfather never kept a copy. Or we lost it over the years." His voice trailed off. "I don't know."

Wick set down a handful of letters, exhaling quietly. The absence of proof and the absence of trust threatened to unravel everything. He stole a sidelong glance at Latesha, who hovered by the attic steps, arms crossed. She offered no comfort, the corners of her mouth tight.

Then Gram called them for supper. Latesha left first, descending in swift strides that didn't invite conversation. Wick's heart pounded—someone else might shrug off Abby's random kiss, but Latesha was different, and he respected her enough not to trivialize it.

****

After dinner, the moon rose over the pines. Wick found Latesha in the backyard, tossing her duffel bag into the trunk of her car. She caught sight of him and folded her arms.

He approached slowly, words tangled in his throat. "You're leaving?"

She gave a curt nod. Her gaze flickered with hurt. "Figured the county's burning, the deed's gone, the news exploited your—kissing debacle. Nothing left for me to do." She swallowed. "I'm sorry." Her tone implied the opposite.

He reached out a hand. "Wait—Abby blindsided me. I don't know her at all. Vilnius set me up. Please believe me."

Latesha met his eyes, then looked away, voice shaking. "It sure looked friendly."

Latesha got into her car and started the engine.

Guilt rushed Wick. He stepped in front of the car and put his palm on the hood. "Wait! One last thing before you go, please. I won't try to stop you if you still want to leave after that. Promise."

She hesitated, then turned off the engine. "Ten minutes."

Wick nodded, dashing inside to grab two coats, boots, and mitts. He returned, balancing them awkwardly. Latesha frowned. "What's all that?"

"Trust me. Let's walk to the s-curved tree," Wick said, pointing toward the signal tree.

"Fine," she muttered.

***

They walked to the signal tree, its branches weaving in the twilight. Wick held out his hand. Latesha stared at him, tension evident on her face. "Wick—this better not be some nonsense."

He held her hand as he reached to place his other hand against the bark. "I need you to hold on to me." He inhaled. "Deep breath."

She opened her mouth to protest, but their world spun in a swirl of color and knocked Latesha off balance. She gasped, nearly collapsing, as Wick caught her in his arms. He glimpsed into her wide, astonished eyes for a few moments, and then they stood in a stark white landscape—snow stretching for miles beneath a leaden sky. She quickly put on the coat, boots, and mittens Wick had brought. He noticed goosebumps prickling Latesha's neck. She clutched his arm, unsteady, her breath catching.

He could see her struggling, but finally, she spoke in quivering syllables. "Wha—how?"

Wick guided her toward a leaning tree by an elephant-sized rock. He gathered twigs and moss, striking a flint until a small fire crackled, warming the icy air. He sat next to her, letting the prolonged silence fill with possibilities. Then, softly, he spoke.

"I've wanted to tell you. I just couldn't without risking more chaos."

She swallowed, face colored with shock. "We—we traveled?"

He nodded. "Through time, yeah. I know it's insane."

Her eyes bore into his, a finger jabbing the air between them. "You explain everything."

He inhaled slowly. "Short version: There's a crystal—my Uncle Billy gave it to me. A special one. Mix that with a historical artifact, like an 1855 coin or arrowhead, and the signal tree is a time portal. I ended up in 1855 by accident and nearly froze to death. Then I went again, found Billy when he was younger, discovered the cave with an ancient guardian named Kimi, met my co-guardian and ancestor, Kahoka, who's from the past, and I nearly drowned in the White River." Wick paused, glancing at her expression. She looked stunned but not dismissive.

He pressed on. "Vilnius corners me every chance he gets. I think he has something to do with Dad's disappearance. Dad vanished months ago. Vilnius wants our land for crystals—I suspect it's about their temporal properties. Yesterday, after the protest, he threatened me a second time. Then Abby—well, that stunt on my cheek. I think he set it up to sabotage my personal life. And honestly, it's working, because you nearly drove away."

Latesha's mouth opened and closed. "You ported through time, uncovered an entire web of new conflicts, and you suspect Vilnius is behind your father's disappearance?"

Wick nodded. "Vilnius is cunning. I think he used the time portal to play the Bitcoin market. He's trying to push us into signing over the land." He exhaled. "I'm not sure if Dad's alive. But I suspect Vilnius is connected."

As they sat on the ground, she pulled her knees to her chest and hugged them tightly. Her face was a mask of tension, every muscle rigid with unease. "And you never told me because...?"

He ran a hand over his snow-covered hair. "Because if time travel changes the timeline, it can cause bigger problems. I have to be careful. Uncle Billy said meddling can break the continuity. I already meddled. I lost the crystal Billy gave me and messed with 1855. The last thing I needed was more complications—like telling everyone."

She studied the fire's flickering glow, lips parting in a shaky smile. "That's—a lot."

A hush fell, broken only by the fire popping. Then she leaned closer, pressing her head on his shoulder. He blinked in surprise. Her voice tremored softly. "I'm sorry for storming off. I was so mad about that photo—like you didn't care. And then I was worried everything we worked for would vanish."

Wick felt gratitude inside him. "I'm sorry, too, for keeping you in the dark. You're the only person aside from Billy who knows. I trust you."

She listened silently for a moment, then eased her arms around him in a lingering hug. Snow continued drifting, dusting hair and coat. She tilted her chin and planted a gentle kiss against his cheek, lips curving in a careful smile.

Relief nearly overwhelmed him. "Stay," he whispered. "I need your help. Another pair of eyes and ears."

She swiped at a floating snowflake, nodding. "I can stay a week or two. That's all I can promise."

Wick breathed a laugh. "Two weeks is plenty. Time stands still at home when I'm gone. I could spend months away and only a few minutes pass at home."

She blinked. "Are you kidding?"

He grinned. "Here, I'll show you. Let's walk here, and you'll see when we return."

She glanced around the white emptiness. "All right. I still have many questions. Let's walk."

He helped her to her feet, smothering the fire. They wound through the snowy hills, steps crunching softly, hearts unburdening with each shared word. At last, they returned to the leaning tree near the big rock, hands entwined. He set a gloved palm against the trunk, the crystal in his pocket, and the same swirl of dizzying color enveloped them.

***

Moments later, they were back in 2026, the evening sky unchanged. Latesha inhaled sharply. "Time—didn't move?"

Wick shook his head, a grin blooming. "Welcome to my reality."

She gazed at him with new warmth in her eyes. "Guess we're in this together now."

Wick exhaled, tension lifting from his shoulders. Tomorrow, the condemnation fight would rage on, the deed lost; but Latesha was by his side for tonight, and a budding alliance—maybe more—sparked anew in the quiet Ozarks.

Chapter 23
Threads of Disappearance

Wick rolled out of bed, tension rippling through his shoulders. Yesterday's chaos lingered: Abby's confounding kiss, the courthouse fire, and the damning front-page photo. Another hurdle came: meeting with an attorney to salvage what remained of their land claim. He forced himself to his feet, hoping the morning would yield answers or a new plan.

***

Wick and his gramps reached town mid-morning, parking near the square. Sunlight gleamed on the adjacent storefronts. One sign read "Randall & Associates," and the other "Crystalis Vitalis." Wick frowned at the side-by-side entrances, which shared the same brick strip. He scanned for Vilnius's black SUV, but there was no sign. *Maybe we'll avoid him.*

A small desk and a short corridor greeted them in the law office lobby. A lone receptionist politely adjusted paperwork, and Gramps clutched a thin folder of notes as they waited.

Gramps patted his pocket, lips tightening. "My reading glasses—left them in the truck. Wick, fetch them, please? I don't want to embarrass myself by squinting at these property tax receipts."

Wick nodded and slipped back out, heart hammering as he jostled the door. Outside, the air felt uncomfortably still. *Don't run into Vilnius. Don't run into Vilnius.* He circled the truck, spotting the glasses on the seat, and hurried back.

When he reached the office door, a hand pressed against the glass, stopping him. Vilnius stood there, his gaze assessing, his voice low.

"Wick," he said softly, glancing at the glasses in Wick's hand. "Quite a tragedy, that courthouse fire. It amazes me how fragile old records can be. Have you located your copy of the deed?"

Wick fought to suppress a glare, refusing to let Vilnius see his anger. His knuckles whitened as he tried to yank the door open, but Vilnius's firm grip kept it shut. "You're gambling here, building a pot you might not be able to cover. Are you sure you want to keep raising the stakes? Sometimes folding early is wise." Vilnius's tone carried a subtle menace.

Pulse thudding, Wick forced himself to be calm. "We won't give up." He jerked the door open with sudden force, stepping inside. He could feel Vilnius's stare drilling into his back.

***

Returning to the lobby, Wick passed the glasses to Gramps. Just then, a trim, middle-aged man with gray flecks in his hair stepped forward, hand extended.

"Mr. Jenkins, I'm Randall. Ready?" His gaze paused on Wick. "And you must be Finnwick?"

Wick offered a tense smile. "Yes, sir."

"Follow me," Randall said, motioning them into a small corner office. A sturdy wooden desk, shelves of law books, and a scattering of papers gave the space a cramped but studious feel. Sun filtered in through a single window high on the wall.

He gestured at two chairs facing the desk. "Please, have a seat. How can I help?" Randall leaned forward, pen in hand. "Let's hear everything."

Gramps cleared his throat. "We've had the property dating back to our Native American heritage around 1800. We've never faced trouble like this. The county wants to condemn our three thousand acres of timber and farmland. The county clerk had a deed from 1873 destroyed in that courthouse fire. We never did probate. We just passed it down from generation to generation."

Randall tapped a pen on his notepad. "So, no probate, no modern chain of title. That means you lack a paper trail bridging each generation to you. The county could argue the land was never lawfully transferred. They'll say you must prove your inheritance was legitimate, which is tricky minus the deed." He pursed his lips. "You mentioned your Cherokee roots—some claims can be validated if the land was recognized in certain treaties, though that's rarely straightforward. The government might argue they have the authority to decide land ownership following Native American occupation, complicating things further."

Wick leaned forward, voice tight. "We also thought about adverse possession. We've lived there exclusively—except maybe hunters or neighbors crossing through here and there. Nothing official."

Randall grimaced sympathetically. "Exclusivity is everything. If outsiders roamed at will, it would undercut that. Also, forging a claim to all three thousand acres, presumably pristine in spots, can be difficult. A judge might limit you to the homestead portion if you can't prove you maintained the entire boundary."

He continued, "Without an accurate survey, defining the exact boundaries of your claim is another challenge. If there were any easements or rights-of-way granted over the years, it could further weaken your case. Plus, the lack of formal probate proceedings might complicate the legal standing of your ownership. You might need affidavits from longtime residents or historical records to support your claim. There is a good chance you could lose, especially with the destroyed deed and potential competing claims from neighboring land users."

Gramps's voice shook. "But we've lived there forever. We have receipts for property taxes and some old letters referring to farm improvements. That should count, right?"

Randall sighed. "Taxes help. Yet, for adverse possession claims, you need exclusive, continuous possession. If hunters or neighbors roamed your woods without explicit permission, exclusive possession is harder to prove. Also, three thousand acres is a lot to monitor. The county might argue the family never enforced boundaries."

Wick glanced at Gramps, seeing the worried look on his face. *If we can't prove exclusive use, we lose a massive chunk of land?*

Gramps exhaled slowly. "So, we're facing an uphill battle?"

Randall nodded regretfully. "Look, I'm amazed you got public sympathy on the part of the county to reconsider the action if you can produce proof of ownership dating back to 1873. That's as close to a win as you can hope for here. But if you can't produce a deed, and they move forward to condemn, they could pass the emergency clause and submit to the circuit court within days."

Gramps shook his head. "So, is there any hope past that point?"

Randall sat back, leaned his head, pursed his lips, and sighed as he tapped his fingers on his desk. "I have to be honest with you," he began, choosing his words carefully. "Reversing a condemnation is quite rare. Courts tend to defer to the government's determination of public use and necessity, making it challenging for property owners to overturn such decisions. Once it is condemned, proving ownership is strictly for compensation—it won't get your land back."

Wick and Gramps exchanged glances, their eyes locking in a silent plea for saving grace that didn't materialize.

Randall continued. "See what you can find—historical records, letters, diaries, older tax stubs—in case we have to rebuild your title chain from scratch. But without that title, you could lose your land within days."

Gramps folded his hands. "Yes. We'll do our best. Thank you."

"Of course." Randall stood, guiding them back out to the lobby.

Gramps rubbed his temples. "I never wanted it to come to this."

Wick saw a resolve in Gramps's tired eyes—like a battered oak refusing to fall.

***

They stepped into the lobby when Wick's phone vibrated. Mom's name blinked on the screen. He answered, bracing. "Mom?"

"Wick—is Nora with you?" she blurted, voice trembling. "We can't find her anywhere! She didn't say anything. Latesha left to meet her friends, but Nora wasn't with her. We can't find her."

Wick's heart lurched, nearly dropping the phone. "Gone? Hang on—we'll be right there." He ended the call, turning to Gramps with dread in his eyes. "Nora's missing."

Gramps stiffened. "Let's hurry home."

They rushed onto the sidewalk. Wick spotted Vilnius leaning by a planter, Big Mike behind him—no sign of Tank. A red wave of fury slammed through Wick. *My sister's gone—he's behind it.* Boiling anger overcame caution.

Charging forward, Wick seized Vilnius by his lapels and shoved his back against the brick front. "What did you do with Nora?" he snarled, shaking him. "Tell me where she is!"

Big Mike shifted, ready to pounce, but Vilnius smiled and waved him off, eyes glittering.

"Wick! First, your father disappears, and now your sister. Tragic indeed. If I ever finalize my business plan, I could free up resources to help your family. Pity we're all stuck, *hmm*?"

Wick hissed, but Gramps grabbed his arm, pulling him off Vilnius. Wick's breath heaved, tears of rage stinging his eyes as Gramps pulled him away.

"Easy, son," Gramps pleaded. "We need to go."

They bolted toward the truck. Wick's thoughts raged: Dad was missing, and now Nora—no deed, no sure path to saving the land. *Everything is unraveling.*

As they drove, Gramps said, "Don't worry, Wick. She's probably just gone for a walk. She will be okay. This reminds me of when I went missing when I was three and fell into a well. Or rather, was thrown into a well."

"What old well? You never told us that story. Besides, the well at the house looks too small for a kid to fit in."

"Oh, not one of those fancy drill rig wells. This one was dug by hand. It is about four feet wide and forty feet deep—big enough for a grown man to fall in. Back in my day, kids roamed the farm. Grandpa was always plowing, cutting down trees, or working other jobs. The dogs probably watched me more than anyone. One day, I was standing in our garden when some stranger came running along, scooped me up, and threw me into the well. I would have drowned, but another stranger came along, jumped into the well, and pulled me out. Saved my life."

"Gramps! If it's so dangerous, why haven't you filled it in, covered it, or warned us?"

"Oh, it's not a danger now. It filled in over the years: limbs, dirt, leaves. We'll check, but Nora couldn't fall into the old well. Just trust she's okay."

They screeched around winding curves, tires gripping the pavement as the car hit steep inclines and plunged sharp descents, engine howling with the strain.

Mom phoned—still no word about Nora.

Wick's thoughts blurred in panic. A single question thundered in his mind. *Where is Nora?*

Chapter 24
Racing the Shadows

Gramps's truck sped along the winding Ozark highway, flanked by dense woods with rocky outcrops blurring past each curve. A sunbeam flashed across the windshield, highlighting Gramps's white-knuckled grip as he floored the gas, as if hoping to outrun their anguish.

"Wick, call Tom," Gramps said, voice tight. "He needs to hear this firsthand."

Wick nodded. He fumbled for his phone, thumb trembling as he selected the sheriff's number. There was a faint ring, and then the gruff voice answered.

"Sheriff."

Wick's throat felt parched. "Tom, it's Wick—Nora's missing. We're rushing back to the farm. Can you—?"

Sheriff Tom cut him off gently, "I'll send Sterling—he's nearest. He'll be there in five. I'm right behind him."

Gramps cleared his throat. "Thank you, Tom."

The call disconnected, leaving an anxious hush in the cab.

***

They screeched into the driveway, dust swirling around the fenders. Wick slammed the truck door and sprinted toward the porch. His mom, eyes rimmed red, stood there, phone clutched in a sweating grip. He needed only a second to see panic etched on her face.

Not even a minute later, Deputy Sterling pulled in, lights strobing. He hopped out of his cruiser, footsteps crunching in the gravel as he hurried up the stairs.

"Ma'am," Sterling said firmly, "when did you last see your daughter?"

Mom swallowed hard. "About an hour ago—she stepped out the back door with a granola bar and water bottle—said she needed air." She faltered, voice cracking. "And she's not answering her phone."

Sterling wrote notes on a small pad, each scribble filling the tense silence. Moments later, another set of lights bled through the yard; Sheriff Tom stepped out.

He set a hand on Mom's arm. "We'll do what we can, I promise. Usually, teenagers wander off to cool down. No need to panic yet."

Wick's lips tightened. *Nora doesn't just wander off.* Latesha's car squeaked to a stop nearby, and she dashed to Wick.

"Any news?" she asked breathlessly.

Wick shook his head, teeth clenched. "Nothing."

Deputy Sterling and Sheriff Tom fanned out, scanning the yard. Gramps led them around the side, viewing the yard and oaks beyond. At the edge of the canopy, they froze. Nora's water bottle lay on its side, half empty. A half-eaten granola bar sat on leaves. And, heartbreakingly, her phone glinted in the dirt.

Tom's expression darkened. "Everybody, back away. We don't want any evidence destroyed." He raised his voice, calling to no one in particular. "What was she wearing?"

Mom stepped forward, voice trembling. "A gray hoodie, jeans, and blue-white sneakers."

Tom nodded, stepping aside to speak quietly into his radio. Wick and Gramps edged closer.

"Send out an Amber Alert," Tom told dispatch. "And call the K9 volunteer team." He paused, then added, "Sterling, see if you can locate any ring cams on the road; see if you can find out who's come or gone."

Sterling jogged away, voices crackling through on his radio. Wick twisted his hands, knuckles popping. *Where could she be?*

Remembering Gramps's story, Wick said abruptly, "What about that old well you mentioned?"

Tom, Gramps, and Wick trudged deep into the overgrown property. Thorns snagged Wick's jeans as Gramps pointed out a depression in the forest floor, half-filled with rotted limbs and moss. They peered in, pushed the leaves aside, and found only damp soil and an abandoned fox den. No hazard remained. Wick exhaled, relief jagging into frustration. *So not that.*

***

Hours ticked as the rural K9 team arrived, a swirl of wagging hounds. Mom gathered one of Nora's jackets for the hounds to scent. The dogs whined and sniffed, then bolted toward the signal tree. Tails wagging, they circled the tree's base, fixated for a moment before dropping their noses. Their wranglers frowned, pulling them off. They kept expanding their search in arcs, each loop returning to the signal tree.

Two hours later, the K9 lead approached Tom, shaking his head. "They're stumped. The trail stops at this tree. We're sorry."

Tom pinned his hat against his thigh and nodded. "Thank you. We can't force outcomes." He turned to the family with a quiet apology. "If the dogs can't find a track, a large-scale search won't help either. Something's off here. My best guess is a four-wheeler or some vehicle, but no tracks. We'll keep at it."

That pronouncement felt like a punch to Wick's gut. *Nora vanished into thin air. They took her. They took her back in time. I just know it.*

The lawmen departed, leaving the family and Latesha gathered in the kitchen. The fridge's hum sounded loud in the hush.

***

Latesha pulled Wick aside, voice low, eyes fierce. "You have to tell them about the signal tree, time travel, all of it. They deserve to know."

Wick's breath caught. He glanced at Gramps, then at Gram seated on the sofa, and finally at Mom, pacing with an empty cup. "What if they freak?"

Her gaze cut to him. "Too late for half measures. We're losing everything. Let them help you."

Nodding, Wick walked to Gramps, beckoning him outside so they wouldn't alarm Mom. They settled near the fire pit, night air carrying the scent of pine and the faint aroma of smoldered ashes. Wick took a moment to collect his thoughts, then unloaded the entire story: the signal tree's warp, the crystal, Kimi and Kahoka, his near-drowning experiences, how Dad might be trapped in time, and his suspicion that Vilnius manipulated events, possibly abducting family members.

Gramps listened without interruption, eyes dark, face etched in wonder. Only when Wick paused, voice cracking, did Gramps speak. "I knew—something was odd. You've changed. You did all that?"

Wick nodded.

Gramps continued. "My dad, John, told me wild tales when I was tiny. I always wrote them off as fairy stories. Now I see he meant them. You have my trust."

Wick exhaled shakily. "So do we—tell Mom?"

Gramps patted his hand. "We should. I'll explain. She might accept it better coming from me."

They moved inside, gathering the family in the living room. Gramps relayed the same story, layering in the old legends about John's role as guardian of the land—how that duty had passed to Wick. At first, Mom's face registered disbelief, and her initial disapproval of Wick risking himself was evident. But the dread of losing Nora overcame any cynicism. Eventually, she whispered, "If this is true, save Nora. Save Dad."

Wick's chest burned with empathy and fear. "I promise."

Mom found a shred of composure. "But you're still a kid. How can you—?"

Gramps spoke gently. "He may be young, but you don't know the half of what he's survived." He met Wick's eyes. "I have faith."

Gramps left the room and returned with a shotgun. Mom protested, thinking it was for Wick. Gramps cracked a smile. "It's not for Wick. It's for any of Vilnius's men if they think they can take anyone else." Mom smiled, a small sense of relief breaking through her worry.

Her voice wavered, tears brimming. "Alright. I don't like it but do what you must. Just—come back."

Wick nodded, turning the conversation to the final piece: time paused during his trips. He said he could jump now—tonight—and return moments later in their view. "I need to leave immediately to stop the clock and save what time we have left before the Quorum Court condemns the land."

"How does that help?" Mom asked.

"It saves present time but gives me unlimited time to travel back in time to solve this problem. Just as long as I don't come back looking like Rip Van Winkle," he joked, trying to lighten the mood. "We don't need another Gramps around here." A nervous laugh rippled through the room, tension easing for a moment.

Latesha drew in a breath. "Then I'll go with—"

But Mom stepped forward, voice hoarse. "I can't allow that. Your mother wouldn't forgive me."

A hush fell, and everyone was gripped by worry. Wick felt compelled to protest on Latesha's behalf—but the thought of risking her safety pounded guilt through him. After a tension-laden silence, Wick nodded and left the room to pack. Latesha followed.

Wick spoke softly to Latesha. "Look, let me scope it out. I will come back and update you. I may need your help."

***

That night, shadows sprawled across the yard. Wick stepped outside, the signal tree's silhouette looming. Donning a pack, he held the crystal and a battered artifact. A swirl of conflicting emotions tightened his throat: excitement, terror, guilt. He had to find her if Nora was stuck somewhere in time.

He cast a glance at the house. A light glowed in Mom's bedroom, comforting—yet tinged with sorrow. Then he turned to the ancient tree. *Here we go again.* He braced for the swirling color and the all-too-familiar head-spinning feeling.

Heart pounding, Wick pressed a palm to the bark. The world began to tilt, darkness rippling into bright fractals. One final thought seared his mind: *Hold on, Nora—I'm coming.*

Chapter 25
Whispers in the Past

Wick ported to 1947. He had left under a silent moon, but the sudden blaze of daylight jarred him. He squinted to adjust to the bright sunlight. As his eyes focused, he saw Billy enter the back porch door with Sailor Cat. He needed time to think before explaining everything that had transpired since handing John's gift of Sailor Cat to Billy: Nora missing, the land threatened, V's henchmen.

Wick slipped into the woods and headed to the cave. Perhaps he could find Kimi there. Or maybe Kahoka hid an artifact like an arrowhead in the pocket on the cave wall.

As he neared the top of the bluff, he noticed the same flat rocks, dried moss, and the old cedar at the bluff's edge. He eased over the bluff's edge onto the ledge below. Peering over the edge, he saw the perilous rocks and heard the stream babble in the distance.

Wick remembered the torch Kahoka had made. *This flashlight is a lot easier than a torch.* Getting on all fours, he crawled through the passage into the cave.

He was once again mesmerized by the expansive crystals surrounding the cave. The flashlight beam broke into a thousand fractals. "Hello," he called. "Kimi? Hello." Wick heard echoes. He searched the pocket in the cave wall, hoping Kahoka had sent him a message over time. Exploring the cave, he found several openings that could lead to other passageways. One passageway was too high to reach without a short climb—a second wound out of sight—a third seemed to angle deeper. *Not trying that today.* He leaned back on the cave wall, trying to focus on hawk vision. *How could I see Chicago but see nothing here?* He exited the cave and shimmied back to the top of the bluff.

Wick sat at the bluff's edge, looking past the cedar tree. He laced his fingers behind his head, leaned back, and stared at the sky. Nothing. He grabbed the edge of the rock bluff until his knuckles turned white. Still nothing. Trying harder, he squeezed his eyes shut and gritted his teeth. Frustrated, he opened his eyes, clenched his hands, and pounded the rock before planting his forehead in his palms, shaking his head in defeat. He leaned back, blinking rapidly, taking deep breaths. He rubbed his eyes and dropped his head back in his palms, feeling deflated.

Where are you, Nora? It's all my fault.

Wick couldn't face Billy yet. He couldn't face anyone. He knew Kahoka wouldn't be there in 1947, but he had to check Kahoka's camp.

Wick could still imagine the vibrant scene at camp—deer hides, campfires, baskets, pottery. No visible traces remained. Trees had overgrown the central meeting site beneath the large rock outcropping. Wick did not know why he went there, or what he was searching for, but he searched anyway. He found arrowhead chips. *I wish Kahoka were here.*

Staring out toward the creek, he absentmindedly drummed the base of his fist against the tree like he was testing a ripe melon for the perfect, hollow sound. He stopped, wincing as a sharp pain radiated through his hand. He opened his fist, staring at the reddened skin. *How long have I been doing this?*

He was lost—not physically but strategically. Searching for someone lost in time was like trying to catch a whisper in a storm. Finding someone's location without a lead was challenging, but the prospect of finding a specific location across the time spectrum was mind-boggling. He had checked the cave and the campsite. *I guess I can check around town.*

Wick followed Coon Creek as it wound toward Highway 5 and started walking toward town. A truck pulled over.

"Hey there, young fella. Headed to town if you want a lift," he said, pointing to the passenger seat.

Wick thanked the man and hopped in. He liked the open windows, except when they met another vehicle, which kicked up dust. Wick was amazed the driver did not seem to notice or care. He was also amazed people in 1947 would offer a ride to a stranger.

As Wick settled into the seat, he fidgeted, looking for a seat belt. The driver raised an eyebrow. "What are you doing there, son?"

"Uh, looking for the seat belt," Wick replied, feeling sheepish.

The driver chuckled. "Seat belt? Do you mean like a regular ol' pants belt?"

"No, I mean a strap to hold you in the car if it wrecks."

"Ain't never heard such a thing in cars, son. Hold on tight, and you'll be fine."

No seatbelt. Mom would croak.

Wick realized how strange his request must have sounded, given the truck rarely reached speeds of 30 mph.

As they approached the town square, the driver flipped on his turn signal, pulled over, and rolled to a stop. "Headed toward Turkey Creek. I'll let you out here, son."

Wick thanked the man and noticed how the square differed from modern times. Most men wore fedoras—stylish, soft, wide-brimmed hats with a creased crown and a pinched front, reminiscent of Humphrey Bogart's classic style in Casablanca. The courthouse looked timeless, unchanged, except that the "Our Sons of Stone County" memorial had not yet been constructed. In place of the Mexican restaurant, a motor company thrived. He headed in that direction.

Walking into the motor company, he marveled at seeing antique cars in pristine new condition. *1947 Ford F-1 for only $1,199? Gramps would love this.* Stepping outside, he saw a Greyhound bus pulling to a stop. A few people filed off, and others boarded. *Wow! I guess people took a bus before Uber and Lyft.*

Wick's stomach growled, a reminder he needed to find food soon. He glanced around the bustling square, searching for a place to eat. His eyes landed on Buster's Café, just across the street. As he walked over, he clutched the vintage currency Gramps procured. *Two $20, four $5s, and fourteen $1s. Hope this goes further than it looks.*

Approaching Buster's Café, Wick noticed the beer signs adorning the building. *Beer? I thought this was a dry county.* Spittoons were placed in public areas with signs reading, "No Spitting on the Sidewalk." *Chewing tobacco. Ugh.*

Inside, he found a seat where he could view the street from the window. A waitress approached with a friendly smile. "What can I get you?"

"I'll have the blue plate special and a Coke, please."

As she noted his order, Wick couldn't help but mention, "I noticed the beer signs outside."

The waitress chuckled. "Oh, those? They're leftovers from before. The county went dry two years ago. No beer served here anymore."

Wick nodded, taking in the history. "Interesting. I guess some things linger longer than we realize."

"Exactly," she said with a wink. "Enjoy your meal!" Wick was surprised smoking inside the restaurant was common—an ashtray at every table.

He settled into his seat, glanced out the window and his heart nearly stopped. Big Mike was strolling along the sidewalk, his hulking figure unmistakable. Wick's mind raced. *He shouldn't be here—did Vilnius send him?*

Before he could process the shock, Big Mike and Tank sauntered into the café, scanning the room before choosing a booth dangerously close to Wick's. Wick grabbed the menu and held it up, trying to shield his face. Just my luck, he thought. The waitress brought his ticket—sixty cents. Wick's hands shook as he reached for a dollar bill.

He strained to hear Big Mike and Tank's conversation but could only catch snippets. "Billy—Boyd—"

Wick's heart pounded. *Billy? Boyd? I have to warn Billy at the family farm!* He knew he had to act fast but couldn't risk being seen.

He observed the men. They seemed engrossed in their conversation. With a deep breath, Wick slipped out of his seat and headed toward the back of the café. He pushed through the kitchen doors, the clatter of dishes masking his escape. Without looking back, he found the rear exit and slipped out unseen.

Once outside, Wick walked briskly, determined to reach the family farm before it was too late.

He must warn Billy. He turned a corner and felt a heavy hand clamp onto his shoulder.

Chapter 26
Shots in the Dark

He spun around, heart racing, to face Big Mike, a scowl on the man's face. "Sneaking off so soon?" Big Mike asked, guiding Wick into a quiet alley.

As Wick tried to move away, Big Mike pinned him against a brick wall, his voice gruff. "We've got business, kid. Hate for you to wind up lost like your dad and sister." Wick's pulse throbbed. *He's working for Vilnius—gotta stay calm.*

Big Mike steered him deeper into the alley, Tank trailing behind with a menacing grin. Wick's mind raced. *I have to warn Billy. No time, no backup. Keep it together.* Big Mike leaned in, his tattoo-covered arms flexing as he blocked Wick's path. "You know why we're here?"

Wick swallowed hard, willing himself not to crumble. *If I stall, maybe I can slip out.* "Guessing you're not here for a friendly visit," he managed, voice cracking slightly.

Big Mike smirked. "Remember what Vilnius said? '*If you cross me—if Big Mike and Tank catch even a whiff of subversion—all bets are off.*'" He leaned closer, lowering his voice. "So where is it, kid? You gonna take us there? Save us both some trouble. Where do we find the crystals?"

A sudden noise drew their attention. A shop worker stepped out to throw away some trash. Big Mike and Tank glanced toward the distraction. Wick seized that moment to twist free. He sprinted, nearly stumbling on broken crates. *Run—faster!* he told himself, ignoring shouts behind him.

He ran across the main street, weaving through the startled townsfolk, through a backyard, over a picket fence, and kept going. His breath raked his throat as he glanced behind him—no sign of Big Mike. *I can't get caught. Billy needs me.* Wick needed to reach the farm first, but couldn't risk getting caught.

He saw a church and ducked inside, leaning over, panting. Startled when a hand gently touched his shoulder, Wick spun around and came face-to-face with an older gentleman dressed in trousers and a dark-colored button-up shirt with a white clerical collar. "Son, are you okay?"

Shaking his head, Wick leaned over again, gasping for breath. He pointed toward the door.

"That's okay, son. Take a moment to catch your breath. Have a seat and take a sip of water."

After a few minutes, the man continued, "Son, you pointed toward the door. Now, what's ailing you?"

"Men—" Wick shook his head after his breathless reply and tried again. "Some men are after me."

"Men! Do you need the sheriff?"

Wick shook his head. "No, sir—it's complicated. Bad men are after me. I need to get to my family. Until then, I'm outnumbered."

"When you say outnumbered, have you counted God?"

Wick looked up to see if the priest was serious.

The priest asked again. "Have you counted God among your numbers?"

Wick shook his head. "That sounds good, but what do you mean?"

"Well, in Second Kings 6, when the Syrians surrounded Elisha, he told his servant, *'Those that are with us are more than those that are with them.'* Then, he asked God to open his servant's eyes. They had chariots of fire protecting them. It's a great story. You should read it sometime."

"I'll do that. But for now, I could really use a ride."

The priest smiled and nodded.

***

As dusk settled, Wick caught up with Billy at the farm.

Billy had a perplexed look on his face. "Wick, you just left, and now you're back?"

Wick nodded and updated Billy on everything—Nora missing, the land threatened, and the encounter with V's henchmen.

"I've got to tell Dad," Billy said. They went to Elijah, sitting in his wicker rocker on the porch.

Billy and Wick sat with Elijah and explained that some men were after Wick.

"Well, the dogs will tell us if they come 'round." Elijah leaned over and patted his double-barrel shotgun leaning against the wall. "And if they do, we'll greet 'em proper." He checked his pocket watch, stood, and motioned to go in. "Time for the Jack Benny Show."

Gathering in the living room, Elijah switched on the radio. Jack Benny played a few notes on his violin, humorously off-key, followed by a comedic monologue. The show's announcer, Don Wilson, introduced the cast and the evening's entertainment, including Mary Livingstone (Jack's real-life wife, who often played the role of his long-suffering wife) and guest star Humphrey Bogart. Wick couldn't believe his ears when the Lucky Strike commercials touted the health benefits of smoking—weight loss, improved digestion, and avoiding obesity—with a doctor's endorsement, no less.

Are they serious? Smoking—healthy?

Wick felt the comfort of a joyous family gathering, a rarity in his recent day-to-day life. There was Boyd (his gramps as a six-year-old boy). Then, John's wife, Sarah, and Billy with his parents, Elijah and Myrtle.

As the show ended with "Hooray for Hollywood," Elijah switched off the radio and announced he was turning in for the evening. Wick lifted the family Bible and read Second Kings 6, which the pastor had quoted. He pondered verse 22: *'Thou shalt not smite.'*

Hmph. Big Mike needs that tattoo.

***

As the family settled in, Wick kept watch from the front window. He drifted in and out. He checked to ensure the dogs weren't alarmed each time he awoke. He would stare intently toward the driveway before drifting again. The open, screened windows made it easy to hear noises outside—frogs, crickets, cicadas, bobwhite, whippoorwill, and the occasional hoot owl gave a nightly serenade. After a while, he stood to go to the restroom. *Oh, shoot, no indoor plumbing. Outhouse. Really? And in the dark. Ugh.*

As he stepped onto the porch, the dogs rose but soon returned to their sleeping positions. The coyotes started howling in the bottoms as he stepped off the porch. The crescent moon provided a faint glow. Wick could see his shadow in the moonlight. The dogs paid no attention, and for Wick, the coyotes seemed more like a distant friend saying hello than a threat.

The frogs and cicadas suddenly went silent. The dogs were now on their feet, frozen, hair bristling, listening. He glanced down the driveway and saw headlights go off. Rushing to the porch, Wick went inside and stared out the window, wondering if he should awaken Elijah. After a few minutes, the guineas sounded with a raucous blend of squawks and trills. The dogs jumped up again, this time barking and growling at the dark. One dog stayed out front, and one ran toward the chicken coop.

Elijah appeared in the living room, holding his H&R shotgun. He stepped out the screen door onto the porch and shot two rounds in the air. He swiftly opened the gun, the barrels hinging downward with practiced ease, deftly inserting fresh shells before snapping it shut with a decisive click.

Wick was bewildered. Did Elijah see someone? Did he shoot at anything? Why didn't anyone else get out of bed? As Elijah stepped in, Wick asked, "Did you shoot anything?"

"Naw, but whoever or whatever it was knows we mean business. If it's a critter, it won't stop till it hits Coon Crick, and if it's a person, they'll think twice 'fore coming 'round here ag'in."

Elijah nonchalantly headed back to bed. The guineas settled down, and the dogs returned to their post on the porch.

Wick sat frozen. *No way I'm sleeping.* He peered wild-eyed into the darkness, wondering if Big Mike prowled just beyond the moonlight. What if the intruder didn't scare so easily?

Chapter 27
Shadows at Daybreak

Wick awoke to sizzling bacon and sausage aromas so powerful he momentarily imagined he was in 2026, strolling through a brunch buffet. Opening his eyes, he found himself in 1947, gazing at a wooden ceiling instead of a modern apartment. The roosters crowed, and not a single car horn blared outside. Without city noise or fluorescent hum, the silence unsettled him, like a reminder of the ticking clock he'd abandoned in his own time.

At barely six in the morning, Wick stood, bleary-eyed, in the living room where he had dozed off. He glanced through the window screen, half-expecting to see Big Mike or Tank lurking behind every tree. Elijah's gunshots from the middle of the night still played in his mind, but the farm seemed tranquil, maybe too quiet.

In the kitchen, a scene from an old magazine greeted him: Elijah, Billy, and the others gathered around a table loaded with eggs, buttermilk biscuits, and gravy. He'd never eaten anything like those biscuits and suddenly realized his nose and stomach agreed wholeheartedly on breakfast. *This sure beats Hardee's.*

"Join us, son," Elijah said, pulling out a chair. Wick eased himself onto the seat. They offered a blessing over the food and then passed the plates and bowls. Wick tried to savor it but worries gnawed at him. *How can they look so untroubled? Did they forget last night's disruptions?*

After breakfast, Billy took him outside for chores. Each step reminded Wick of how foreign this world felt and how he kept one foot in 2026, desperate for leads on Nora, anxious about Vilnius, and guilt-ridden over the farmland condemnation fight. They needed extra hands ever since John, Elijah's son, perished in the war. Milk had to be churned, and eggs collected.

"Let's start with milking," Billy said with a grin, leading him to the barn. Wick eyed the cow warily, remembering the automated milking machines from a school trip to a dairy farm. Billy's hands moved smoothly. Wick's attempts produced no milk, or angled jets missed the bucket entirely. The cow's udder felt alien. He'd never live it down if his wrestling buddies could see him now. Billy snickered, then mischievously squirted a stream at Wick's face. Wick sputtered, half irritated, half charmed by the farm boy's teasing.

Next, Billy pointed him toward a chicken coop. Wick squared his shoulders, basket in hand, and confronted rows of hens glaring from the shadows. *Don't peck me,* he repeated, inching his way under a giant hen and retrieving one egg at a time. By the time he emerged with a half-filled basket, his pulse finally slowed.

Under the blazing sun, it was off to the garden. *Hoeing weeds? Who needs a gym when you've got all this?* Rows of vegetables looked more vibrant than any supermarket produce: tomatoes glowing red, peppers dangling proudly, bean vines spiraling around stakes. Billy showed Wick how to spot perfect tomatoes. Wick tried to appear knowledgeable, but Billy and Boyd were faster, plucking vegetables with experienced precision. Though Wick's mind drifted to modern grocery stores, everything felt so comforting and straightforward. *What would Nora say if she saw me knee-deep in pole beans?*

He noticed the dogs skittering around, barking at the slightest movement. Tension skated beneath the surface—Wick imagined Tank or Big Mike stepping from behind a tree. Once or twice, Billy turned in confusion at Wick's nervous glances, but Wick forced a grin. *I must be ready. They could be out there watching.*

When it came time to muck the stable, the stench hit him so hard his breakfast hit the back of his throat, but Billy endured it without complaint, moving a pitchfork with practiced efficiency. Wick felt a new respect for the family's grit. He thought of how they did this daily, hands shaking as he heaved manure. *I'm panting like a dog, and we just started.*

As Wick crossed the hog pen, Billy shouted, "Look out for Brutus!" Wick leaped onto the gate, narrowly escaping a collision with a 250-pound hog. *That would be tragic, getting run over by the holiday ham.*

When Billy mentioned the well, Wick expected a modern water pump—some chrome contraption humming with precision. He didn't expect the relic hanging on the back porch, its spindly pulley swinging from the ceiling like a remnant from frontier days. Instead, Billy demonstrated a torpedo-shaped well bucket attached to a chain lowered by hand. Wick hauled chain after chain of water. He quickly learned the pulley's true purpose: mocking him with each creak of begrudging compliance.

The first few runs were a novelty, but at bucket number six, his arms quivered. Billy pointed to a 55-gallon drum. "We'll need it full," Billy said, as though announcing the weather forecast. Wick whimpered inwardly, cursing the day he'd volunteered. His thoughts longed for the effortless luxury of home, where water sprang forth at the mere twist of a faucet—no pulleys, no quivering arms, just blissful modernity.

"You ever plan on a pump?" Wick asked, rubbing sore shoulders.

Elijah overheard. "Not unless we find a way to pay for it. A hundred bucks might as well be a thousand. We manage with what we have."

Wick nodded, suddenly humbled by how easily he had taken modern conveniences for granted. Meanwhile, 2026 stood frozen, Nora still gone—everything undone.

Feeling the summer heat, Wick wiped the sweat from his brow and realized Boyd wasn't with them. "Where's Boyd? He was picking tomatoes," he asked Billy, tension prickling his neck. "You check the house; I'll look around out back."

He headed behind the barn, scanning the tall grass. Dogs barked, and a child's scream ripped the air. Wick sprinted, heart pounding, and saw Tank storming down the slope with Boyd slung under one arm. "Billy!" Wick shouted, voice echoing. "Get your dad—Boyd's been taken."

As Wick charged after Tank, the dogs bounded ahead, barking furiously. In the distance loomed a wide, old dug well—its gaping mouth framed by a rock wall, like a relic from a time when safety regulations were just a suggestion. Tank roared as the hounds bit at him. With a snarl, he hefted Boyd up and dropped him into the open well. The child vanished from sight. Wick arrived just as Tank disappeared into the woods, the sound of snapping branches marking his retreat.

Wick peered over the rock edge. Boyd splashed into the water forty feet below, emerging with a sputter before sinking again. "Gramps! Hold on!" Wick yelled, the irony of the nickname lost in the moment. His eyes darted to a rope tied to a tree, a battered bucket dangling at its end. Without hesitation, he lowered the rope and slid down, his palms searing as the rough fibers tore at his skin.

The icy water closed over his ankles as he landed. Wick lunged forward, grabbing Boyd's shirt and yanking his head above the surface. "You're not drowning today," he muttered, his voice tight with adrenaline. "Are you okay?" he shouted, his breath coming in gasps.

Boyd coughed and gasped for air. Wick propped Boyd on the bucket, a makeshift perch in the darkness. "Are you okay, Gramps— I mean, Boyd?"

Boyd nodded.

"Can you hold this rope while I climb out?"

The boy sobbed, "Don't leave me!"

"I have to climb out to pull you to safety, okay?" Wick said.

Boyd hesitated, then shook his head.

Wick's stomach twisted. *I have no choice.* "Listen, you're brave. You'll be a protector one day, just like I am right now," Wick murmured, his voice low but steady. "Hold that rope, and don't let go—I'll do the rest."

Boyd nodded, eyes wide.

Wick scaled the rope, bracing his feet against the wall, each move stealing what little strength he had left. Elijah and Billy arrived and quickly helped Wick over the side.

Elijah yelled into the well, "Boyd! Boyd! Are you okay?"

Boyd sobbed, "Yes."

The three quickly hauled Boyd free, breathing relief. Billy glared at the tree line, shotgun in hand, scanning for Tank.

Boyd's feet hit the ground, shuddering on impact. Elijah wrapped his arms around the boy. Elijah turned toward the house, his footsteps urgent and steady, the boy cradled like a fragile ember.

Wick followed behind, adrenaline still coursing through him. Guilt gnawed at him. *If I had used hawk vision, I might have seen Tank coming. This is on me.* He pictured Nora—kidnapped, lost— and now Boyd nearly kidnapped and drowned. He had to do more than wait for another crisis.

Elijah kept watch on the porch, shotgun at his side. Boyd was safe for the moment. As Wick recovered, he turned to Billy, voice unsteady. "I'm going to find Kahoka. I need to understand how he mastered wolf hearing. This has to stop."

Billy's eyes widened with concern. "You sure you want to leave? Tank could be out there."

"Yes. But I have no choice." Wick set his jaw, gaze drifting toward the signal tree. Maybe time with Kahoka would help him hone his abilities, maybe end the chase. Or perhaps everything would crumble if he failed.

Wick wanted to check on Boyd one more time before he left. He reached into his pack, where he kept the peppermints for the kids at Kahoka's camp. "Hey, Boyd. Have a mint. Are you feeling better?"

Boyd smiled, nodded, popped the mint into his mouth, then stood up and hugged Wick. "Thank you for jumping in the well to save me."

"You're welcome, buddy. I'm sorry that happened to you." Wick hugged Boyd again, stepped onto the porch, and headed out, mind-churning, still shaken by how close his Gramps had come to disaster.

Billy waved, "Be careful and come back soon."

Wick offered a tight nod, gazing at the signal tree. "I will, Shooter." *This has to end—before someone else gets hurt. I have to make this right.*

Chapter 28
Crossroads of Trust

Before touching the signal tree, Wick bowed and closed his eyes. *God, please protect Gramps, Billy, Sarah, Elijah, and Myrtle. Help me find Nora. We need a break. I don't have any leads.*

Looking around, Wick considered his next steps. *Okay, back to 2026 to get the arrowhead, visit Kahoka, and learn how to use hawk vision.*

As Wick weathered the shift, he paused to let his eyes adjust to the night and was startled to hear Latesha.

"Wick, you're back!"

"Latesha! Is everything okay?"

"Yes, but don't freak out."

"Uh oh, what's going on?"

"It's Abby—"

"Abby! Oh no, what's she done now?"

"Wick, it's nothing bad. Now don't blow up—she's here."

"Here! I didn't invite her..." Wick blurted, his voice tight with panic. He raised his hands, trying to ward off blame. *Latesha can't think I planned this. Not after everything.*

Latesha lowered her gaze and shook her head, extending her hand to stop him. "Wick, hold on. I know you didn't invite her. She's not here for drama—she's here to help."

"Help? And you trust her? You saw what she did. It's got to be a trap, an ambush!" Wick scanned the shadows, eyes straining against the dark. Every snap and rustle made his gut tighten, half-expecting Tank or Big Mike to lunge out. *Is this it? Is this another trap—or is this the help I prayed for? Besides, how could she help anyway?*

"Wick, slow down. You can at least hear what she has to say."

"Okay, but you have to be my chaperone."

Latesha motioned for Wick to follow. The campfire burned low, its embers casting faint glows against the dark silhouettes of the forest. The crisp scent of pine intermingled with smoke. A whippoorwill called in the distance, its solitary notes heavy against the hushed backdrop of night insects. Abby was waiting by the fire.

Abby's hands twisted in her lap as she stared into the flames. Her lips pressed together, but her shoulders gave her away—a mix of tension and vulnerability. When she noticed Wick, she quickly stared back at the fire.

The fire crackled to life as Wick heaved a log. Spitting sparks climbed into the night sky, and a plume of smoke mingled with the cool evening air. His gaze fixed on Abby through the shifting flames. Popping wood broke the uneasy silence.

"Wick," Abby hesitated, her voice tremulous as though the words scraped against her resolve. "I'm sorry." Her grip tightened on her hands. "I don't like what Vilnius has done."

"You mean your father, don't you?"

Abby shook her head and looked up, her brow furrowing. "Don't call him that. He's not my father."

Wick and Latesha exchanged looks.

Abby continued, her voice softer now but unwavering. "My dad died in a naval accident when I was three. Vilnius married my mom. She died from breast cancer when I was twelve. Vilnius is my stepdad. I don't have any other family. I thought it was a joke when he told me to kiss you on the square. I didn't know it would cause you trouble."

Wick shook his head. "So why are you here?"

"I don't know everything Vilnius is planning, but I caught wind of something—your sister's name came up. After that, I couldn't just sit by and do nothing. Tell me how I can help."

Wick stood. "That's great. Where is she?"

"Well—I don't know where they took her."

Wick rolled his shoulders, each motion like a volcano on the brink of an eruption. His grimace twisted as if his restraint had a breaking point. Latesha reached up, clasping his arm with both hands—a firm but gentle touch that anchored him. Her fingers lingered as she tugged, a quiet insistence pulling him toward the chair beside her. Wick let out a sharp breath, his tension simmering, but he sank into the seat anyway.

Latesha placed another log on the fire, the flames igniting the dry bark. The warmth stretched out, a fragile balm against the cold tension. Her tone and how she looked at Abby suggested she was trying to calm things down. "Abby, what can you help us with?"

"I overheard something, but I'm unsure what it meant."

Latesha nodded, seeming to encourage Abby. "Okay, what did you hear? Maybe it will help."

"Well, I heard Tank and Mike talking. They said they stole items from a hidden compartment in the attic trunk. They took the items and used them to *'travel back and make copies.'* I don't know how, but they said this would allow them to *'follow Wick'* to special places so they could *'mess him up bad.'"*

Wick put his hands on the sides of his head and stood up. Grabbing Latesha's arm, he muttered, "We'll be right back, Abby," and pulled Latesha away from the firelight.

The forest's darkness encased them as they moved beyond the fire's glow. Overhead, the wind stirred the branches, their creaks and rustles making Wick's nerves fray further. He glanced up sharply, half-convinced Tank might be out there, lurking in the shadows, listening to every word.

"That's it, Latesha."

"What's it?"

"That's it. That's how they found me in 1947."

"Wick! You can't be serious! You don't mean—"

"Yes, they were there." Wick gave Latesha a quick rundown: spotting Tank and Mike in the café, slipping away unseen, the priest's unexpected help, the chaos at the farm, and Boyd—Gramps—nearly drowning in the well.

Latesha's brow furrowed. "That sounds horrible." She stepped closer, wrapping her arms around Wick in a fleeting hug, brief but steady, like she was trying to lend him her strength. The embrace was just long enough to stifle the jagged edges of his panic. She hesitated, her voice softening as she pulled back. "But what does she mean by 'copies'?"

"Copies," Wick said, his frustration sharp. He paced a few steps, clenching and unclenching his fists. "They probably used the items to travel, grab a new artifact from that time, and then return the originals. That means they can follow me anywhere. No time zone is safe. This is terrible news. They don't need to know when I'm going—they can try each one until they cross paths with me. That explains how they were in town the same day I was in 1947." His mind latched onto the spiraling possibilities. *What if they sabotage something vital in 1855 or 1947? What if they've already done it?*

He raked a hand through his hair, the pressure tightening in his chest. "I have to move fast. I need to find a new place to hide the artifacts and master hawk vision before they cause any more disruptions. Otherwise, we'll be dealing with one mess after another."

"So why would they return the originals?" Latesha asked, her voice steady but tinged with concern.

"Maybe to catch me in the past. Maybe to harm the family in the past, like they tried to get Boyd—Gramps." Wick exhaled sharply, gazing toward the firelight. As much as he wanted to run from everything piling up, there was no time to stall.

Latesha nodded. "Do you think she knows about the signal tree?"

"Maybe not. Or she could be leading us on. Let's finish talking with her."

"Abby, thanks for the info. Maybe that can help. Please call us if you hear anything about Nora. We have to find her—soon. And by the way, sorry to hear about your dad and mom, and also sorry you have cancer."

Abby looked up in surprise. "Cancer? I don't have cancer. Who told you I have cancer?"

"Vilnius."

Abby shook her head. "I should have known. I don't have cancer."

Wick was stymied. "That's why Vilnius said he wanted to find a cure for cancer—to help his daughter. I mean—I saw you in the hospital walking with an IV."

"Oh, treatment for my inflammatory bowel disease—every two months."

Wick nodded. "Ah. Well, please let Latesha know if you hear anything else, and thank you for offering your help."

Wick and Latesha watched as Abby got in her car.

"One last question, Abby," Latesha said. "Do you know anything about Wick's dad?"

Abby shook her head. "Sorry."

Latesha waved as Abby drove away.

Latesha looked at Wick. "So, what do you think? She wants to help, right?"

"Maybe, but I keep getting blindsided. Still, I did pray for help. Maybe this is the answer. But I have to keep going—I need to find Nora. I'm headed to see Kahoka. I hope he can help me develop hawk vision. But first, I have to hug Gramps. Nearly losing him in that old well still feels surreal."

As Wick headed toward the house, Latesha grabbed Wick's arm and spun him around. "Wick! I'm going with you."

Wick hesitated, his gaze dropping to the ground as his thoughts churned. *Could I really bring her? What if she got hurt—or worse?* His stomach twisted, guilt and responsibility churning. "Latesha, you heard my mom. She won't approve."

"Wick, look at it from my perspective." Her voice was steady, but an urgency was behind it—a need to be understood. "Your dad's missing. Your sister's missing. What's next—you? If you disappear without a trace, how will I know where to start helping you, your dad, or your sister? And besides, I want to see Kahoka's village. You're headed there, so take me along. You can bring me back right after."

"Well, are you going to ask my mom?"

"No. I don't want to make her mad, but I'm going."

Wick let out a deep breath. He rubbed the back of his neck, torn between concern and admiration for her resolve. "Okay, but she may think you've been kidnapped if we don't tell her."

"I can leave her a note. Anyway, if what you say is right, that time stands nearly still here when we travel back in time, I might be back before she knows I'm gone, right?"

Wick nodded as they headed to the house.

Inside, Wick found Gramps standing in the kitchen and wrapped him in a bear hug.

"Easy, Wick. What's this about?"

Wick stepped back, grinning, shaking his finger at Gramps. "You knew, didn't you? You knew it was me who pulled you from the well."

Gramps nodded, grinning and looking flushed. "I thought it was you, but I didn't want to mess with your path, just in case."

Wick lunged and gave Gramps another big hug, not letting go.

Gramps patted Wick on the back. "That's okay, son. I'm okay. Now find your sister. I want a group hug from you, Latesha, and Nora soon."

"Gramps, can you help us out? I don't want to upset Mom, but I need Latesha to go with me to see Kahoka. It should be safe. We can leave Mom a note."

"That's okay, Wick—no need for a note. I'll tell your mom I sent her with you to help scope things out. Just hurry back, or your mom will worry me to death." Gramps winked, a smile creeping onto his face. "I may have to come join you too."

"Really? Okay." Wick turned to Latesha. "There are briars and snakes out there. Wear jeans and boots, and pack snacks and water."

Latesha smirked, her arms crossing. "Briars and snakes, huh? Sounds like you're trying to scare me off."

Wick raised an eyebrow. "Just making sure you're prepared. Jeans and boots are for our protection, not scare tactics." He reached the top of the fridge, pulling down a large bag of peppermint candies. "And these—we'll need these for the kids."

"And my hair kit."

"Hair kit? You don't need a hair kit? Really?"

Latesha opened her hair kit, revealing compact mirrors, brushes, ribbons, hair bands, hair clippies, and other assorted items. "You have stuff to do, and so do I. You take care of the guys, and I'll take care of the girls."

Wick shook his head and handed Latesha an extra flashlight.

As they gathered supplies, the practicality of her resourcefulness struck him. She wouldn't just survive in the 1800s—she'd thrive. Her knack for connecting with people and quick thinking under pressure could make all the difference.

Wick and his gramps exchanged smiles as Wick and Latesha headed out.

Both were equipped with backpacks, the straps snug across their shoulders, each bag stuffed with essentials. Wick adjusted his pack and glanced at Latesha, who shifted the flashlight, tightening her grip. The dark outside wrapped around them like a cocoon, the cool night air brushing against their skin as they approached the signal tree. The forest was alive with the distant calls of night birds and the soft rustling of unseen critters. Wick reached out to Latesha. She clasped his hand without hesitation, their fingers lacing together.

"Ready?" he murmured.

She nodded, her eyes steady despite a hint of unease. Together, they pressed their palms against the rough bark of the signal tree. The moonlight filtered through the branches, illuminating their determined faces as the forest seemed to hold its breath around them.

Chapter 29
Braids and Branches

After porting, Wick caught Latesha before she could stumble, sweeping her into a graceful dip. Their eyes locked, the moment hanging. "It gets easier," he murmured.

Latesha groaned, one hand on her stomach and the other shading her eyes. "I don't know—still woozy. Teleporting feels like being wrung out and left to dry. I should've grabbed my sunglasses. Is it far to Kahoka's camp?"

"Less than a mile—maybe thirty minutes to an hour."

"Oh, I usually walk that in twelve minutes. Is your mile longer than mine?"

"Don't judge until you hike it."

Wick paused, turning to the signal tree. "Before we go, look at this tree. It's your anchor point. If anything happens—any trouble—run back here and touch it. It'll take you straight back." His tone softened. "Promise me you won't hesitate if it comes to that."

Latesha frowned, shading her eyes as she studied the tree's gnarled branches. "Got it—signal tree on the hill. But you're not planning on leaving me, right?"

Wick shook his head, a wry smile tugging at the corners of his lips. "Not unless you bolt first."

He stopped, his expression turning serious as he held out his pinkie. "No joking, I need you to promise. No hesitation if trouble hits. You leave me and run." His little finger stayed extended, unwavering in its insistence.

Latesha sighed, rolling her eyes but linking her pinkie with his. "Fine. Pinkie promise." Her lips curved despite herself, and a glimmer of amusement broke through the tension. "Now I'm officially bound by sacred oath."

Turning downhill, Wick warned, "Prepare for rocks, creeks, and hills."

Latesha smiled. "Still not running me off. Let's go!"

Wick led the way, brushing through a tangle of undergrowth. He barely noticed the branches whipping back as he passed—until he heard a low yelp from behind. Glancing over his shoulder, he stifled a grin. Latesha was mid-duck, her hands up like she was warding off an invisible assailant.

"Do you have a personal vendetta with the trees, or just me?" she muttered, batting away another offending branch.

Wick shrugged, smirking as he turned back to the path. "They're testing your reflexes. Hiking's not just about walking—survival of the quickest."

Latesha huffed, dodging another swiping branch. "Great. An obstacle course with sarcasm included."

His grin widened. "Consider it part of the charm."

As Wick let another branch go, he heard another yelp. "You know what? I'm taking point." She sidestepped around him, tossing a glare over her shoulder. "Let's see how you like getting slapped."

Wick chuckled, falling behind her. "Be my guest."

It only took a few paces before Latesha halted abruptly, arms flailing as she walked face-first through a delicate web. She froze, letting out an unsteady breath. "Wick," she said, her voice dangerously calm, "tell me that wasn't a spider."

"Well," he drawled, crossing his arms, "technically, it was its home."

"*Ugh!*" She danced in place, furiously swiping at her face and hair. "Why does nature hate me?"

Wick bit back a laugh. "Want me to lead again?"

She shot him a look before stepping aside to let him pass. "Fine. You win. You can lead—but I'm keeping my distance."

As Wick moved ahead, her muttering under her breath followed him—something about branches, spiders, and how she might never trust him on a hike again.

As they neared Kahoka's camp, Latesha quickened her pace to catch up with Wick. "So, does this camp come with modern conveniences? Say—a restroom?"

Wick glanced over his shoulder, eyebrows raised. "A covered pit. Moss or leaves for paper. Fancy enough?"

Latesha's jaw dropped slightly before she let out a laugh. "You warned me about rocks and snakes but somehow left *that* part out?"

He smirked. "Figured it was implied."

"Well," she said, a touch of exasperation in her voice, "I need to—uh—step away for a minute. Could you maybe walk ahead? Give me, you know, some distance?"

Wick chuckled, shaking his head as he continued down the path. "Sure thing. Let me know if you need directions to the moss."

Her groan followed him, mixed with muttered words about rustic living and why anyone thought leaves were a solution.

Arriving at camp, Kahoka walked up to Latesha, introduced himself, and asked jokingly, "So, did you find the moss?"

Latesha blinked, momentarily stunned. "Wait—how did you—?"

Wick leaned casually against a nearby tree, a lopsided grin tugging at his face. "Oh yeah, Latesha, our friend Kahoka here has the special gift of wolf hearing. He can hear a conversation at a quarter mile."

Kahoka gave a modest shrug, clearly enjoying her reaction. "Some call it a gift. Others—an inconvenience."

Latesha turned to Wick, grinning but narrowing her eyes. "Another fact you forgot to mention, huh?"

Wick raised his hands in mock defense. "Hey, I like to leave some surprises for later. Keeps things interesting."

Kahoka chuckled. "Don't worry, Latesha. You're not the first to underestimate just how much I overhear. And for the record—good choice with the moss."

Latesha groaned, covering her face with one hand while pointing a mock accusatory finger at Wick with the other. "This is your fault."

Wick laughed, shaking his head. "Consider it part of the learning curve."

Before Latesha had time to adjust to the camp's bustle, a group of kids sprinted toward her and Wick, their faces lit with excitement. "Did you bring the peppermints?" one boy asked, practically bouncing on his toes.

Latesha blinked in surprise, then looked to Wick for an answer. He reached into his backpack and pulled out a small pouch. "You think I'd come empty-handed?" he teased, tossing the pouch to Latesha.

As she opened it, the kids crowded closer, eager hands reaching out. Her smile grew impossibly wide as she knelt, handing out the treats. "Here you go! No pushing, okay?" Her laughter rang out as the children thanked her with gleeful grins and scurried away to savor their treasures. Kahoka smiled and reached for a handful.

Wick watched her, a hint of a smirk tugging at his lips. She looked at ease, like she'd been doing this for years.

Before he could comment, a few older girls—perhaps a year or two younger than Latesha—approached, their eyes bright with curiosity. One of them pointed to Latesha's hair, her tone admiring. "Your hair—it's so beautiful. How do you do it?"

Latesha straightened, her cheeks glowing. "Oh, thank you! I love yours, too. It's so beautifully braided." She reached out, hesitating, before one of the girls nodded her permission. "I've never seen such intricate patterns before."

The girls exchanged delighted glances. "Come," one said, tugging Latesha's hand gently. "We'll show you how. You can teach us your styles, too."

Latesha glanced back at Wick, torn between staying by his side and following the girls.

Wick waved her off with an amused grin. "Go on. We'll catch up with you at the squash, spinach, and squirrel feast."

Latesha paused mid-step, her smile faltering just slightly. "Squirrel?" she asked, her voice tinged with uncertainty.

Wick chuckled, clearly enjoying her hesitation. "Freshly roasted. It's a camp favorite."

Her lips twitched as if deciding between a grimace and a grin, but in the end, her excitement won out. Beaming again, she grabbed her hair kit and allowed the girls to tug her toward one of the teepees. The prospect of bonding over braids and hairstyles seemed to outweigh her apprehension about the evening's menu.

As she walked away, Kahoka chuckled. "She's fitting in well."

Wick shrugged, a subtle smile pulling at the corner of his mouth. "Yeah. She's got a way about her."

"Nice move, remembering the peppermints. You redeemed yourself." Kahoka gestured for him to follow. "Come on. We've got things to discuss while she's busy."

Wick exhaled in relief. This was the reason he'd come back. "Sure."

Wick looked back once more. Latesha was already deep into an animated discussion about hair braiding. She glanced up, caught his eye, and waved, seemingly telling him, "I'm fine—go on." He waved back, a small surge of fondness for her pluck and willingness to jump into the unknown.

With a nod, Wick followed Kahoka, leaving Latesha to her hairstyling exchange as the camp settled into its lively rhythm.

Chapter 30
Focus

Kahoka led Wick along a winding path past the camp's edge, the hum of voices fading behind them. The terrain changed, with dense trees giving way to a clearing bathed in dappled sunlight. They emerged onto a vast open stretch of flat rock in the middle of the creek. The creek trickled softly along one side of the expanse, its gentle stream carving patterns into the edges of the flat stone. Scattered across the flat rock were circular indentations, smooth and shallow, carved by high waters that had swirled and ebbed over countless eons.

Kahoka gestured to the spot with a sweeping arm. "This is it," he said, his voice carrying a note of satisfaction. "It's quiet. Good for thinking—talking."

Wick nodded, his gaze sweeping across the tranquil scene. He stepped onto the rock, feeling warmth from the sun-soaked surface. The faint scent of water and moss filled the air, blending with the gentle murmur of the creek. "I can see why you like it," he said. "Feels—untouched."

"It is," Kahoka replied, standing at the edge where the stream meandered. "Places like this remind you why it's worth it."

Wick crossed his arms loosely, his stance more pensive than guarded. Letting silence settle between them for a moment, he took in the scene—tranquil, yes, but with an undercurrent of purpose. The stillness was broken only by birds' distant chirps and the water's soft babble. Finally, he exhaled, his focus shifting. "We need to talk," he prompted, finally turning to Kahoka. "A lot has happened since we last visited."

Wick unfolded his arms, his tone measured but laced with urgency. "My dad's been gone for months—missing. It's a loss, but we've come to terms with it, at least for now." He paced a few steps along the sun-warmed rock, the creek's gentle murmur, an unsettling contrast to his words. "The deed to the land—missing too. Boyd—someone tried to take him. But Nora—" He stopped, his voice hitching. "She's gone. Vilnius's henchmen took her—just recently."

He stopped, his eyes locking on Kahoka. "I need your help," he said, desperation in his gaze. "I don't know what they'll do to her." His hand briefly raked through his hair before falling to his side. "Vilnius—he's been making threats like he owns the world, sending his people after my family, and it's all coming apart."

Kahoka's expression darkened, his usual calm giving way to quiet intensity. "How can I help?"

In that moment, Wick felt the years stretching between them, an unspoken gap. Time had barely brushed past him—he was still the same seventeen-year-old who'd befriended Kahoka. But Kahoka had aged years in what felt like days for Wick. No longer the teen who once teased him, Kahoka had grown into a figure Wick could hardly recognize—a husband, a father, a leader. *We started as equals, but he's miles ahead of me now.* A sense of admiration stirred within Wick, woven into Kahoka's every word and measured step. *If Kahoka can grow into this, maybe I can, too.*

Wick exhaled, pushing the emotion aside and sharpening his focus. "You've mastered something I haven't," he said. "Kimi gave you wolf hearing, and you got the hang of it in one day. Kimi gave me hawk vision, but I've only seen it once, and now it feels like a dream. I've tried, but I keep coming up empty. I need to learn it to find Nora. I need to see what I'm missing, literally."

Kahoka stepped closer, the creek's faint mist brushing his skin. "Sit. Close your eyes. Hear those bird chirps?"

Wick protested. "Wait, I asked about vision, not hearing."

"Wick. Trust me. Sit. Close your eyes. Hear those birds?"

Wick lowered himself to the flat rock, muttering a reluctant, "Yes."

"Focus on the birds—just the birds."

"Okay. Now what?"

"Good. Now focus on the kids at camp."

Wick turned his head. "I—don't hear any kids," he said, his expression tightening in confusion.

"Sorry—forgot I have wolf hearing. How about the breeze through the treetops? Focus on the breeze. Hear it moving the leaves?"

Wick nodded. "Okay."

"Now, just the water in the stream. Notice how the others fade each time you focus on a new item?"

"Yes."

"Ever notice how you can focus on one person talking in a noisy crowd?"

"Yes."

"Hearing is all about focus. Hawk vision must be the same. Think about it as three vision modes: near, far, and hawk vision. You unlocked it once before. How did you do it?"

"I don't know. I lay below the signal tree, staring at the clouds. I drifted off. It felt like I could see everything—where we used to live, clear as day."

"Okay. Try that now. See the clouds? Focus on the clouds. Concentrate on the sky."

Wick focused on the clouds and sky. The world seemed to slow as his senses narrowed. Suddenly, he was soaring, his perspective sweeping high above the creek, hills, and trees. Wick startled, breaking his concentration. The vivid imagery dissolved, pulling him back to the rock. He looked at Kahoka with a coy smile.

Kahoka smiled and nodded, seemingly knowing Wick had had a breakthrough.

Wick hopped to his feet, a grin spreading across his face. Without a word, he extended his hand to Kahoka, clasping it firmly. Their hands locked in a solid bro shake before Wick pulled him into a quick, back-slapping hug. His excitement blazed. *Latesha has to know about this!*

"Thanks, Kahoka. I needed that," Wick said, his voice lighter now, a spark of determination returning to his eyes.

Chapter 31
Aquafall

Wick practically jogged toward the camp's central circle, eager to share his breakthrough with hawk vision. However, the moment he saw her, the excitement in her eyes immediately drew his attention.

"Wick!" she exclaimed, rushing over. "Look!" She ran her fingers through the neat twists and plaits of her hair, her face glowing with pride. "Isn't it beautiful? The girls taught me how to do it. It took some time, but I finally mastered their braiding technique."

Wick realized his news of hawk vision would have to wait. There was genuine joy in her expression, and he wanted to reflect on that. "It looks amazing," he said softly. "They're pros, and you're a quick study."

Before he could continue, she seized his hand and pulled him to a nearby bluff. Clear water streamed from a crevice in the rock, sparkling under the afternoon sun. She crouched and cupped her hands, letting the cool flow pass over her palms. "Taste it," she insisted. "It's fresh spring water—like nature's own faucet." She drank a small mouthful, grinning from ear to ear. "It's better than

Acqua Panna—pure luxury without the markup! If we could bottle this, we'd make a killing," she joked.

Wick leaned in, taking a cautious sip. It tasted remarkably pure, with a faint mineral tang that gave it a crisp edge. Latesha laughed with triumph. "And you claimed they didn't have running water."

He chuckled. "I stand corrected."

Her eyes shifted to him. "You wanted to tell me something?"

Wick's excitement burst forward. "Kahoka helped me with hawk vision—I finally nailed it!"

Latesha beamed, throwing both arms around him. "That's incredible!" She pulled back and studied his face intently. "So can you see—like, everything?"

His grin widened. "Not everything, but it's a start." A shadow passed across his face, unspoken thoughts on his mind. *I've got to use it to find Nora.*

They wandered back to camp, the promise of a feast beckoning. Smoke rose softly from cooking fires, and the rich aroma of roasted squirrel floated through the camp. Wick observed Latesha's first bite—her expressions ranging from curiosity to cautious delight. Much to his surprise, she sampled a second spoonful of stew with squirrel chunks, followed by a third.

"You're gonna eat the entire pot if you keep going," Wick teased.

She laughed, cheeks flushed. "I didn't expect to like it—guess I'm braver than you thought." Her grin widened as she wagged the spoon at him.

After dinner, the sun slipped lower in the sky, and villagers gathered around the communal fire. Voices rose in gentle chatter and subdued laughter as children crouched near the fire, poking sticks into glowing embers. Each poke sent a cascade of sparks swirling into the air, their faces lighting up with delight at the fiery dance. Wick and Latesha found themselves relaxing on woven mats. A faint breeze carried the sweet, lingering scent of peppermints and other treats from the earlier part of the day.

Eventually, Kahoka showed Latesha a small family teepee made ready for her. "You can sleep here," Kahoka offered. "Wick and I can camp by the main fire."

Dusk settled soon after, and a thousand stars glittered overhead. Resting near the warm coals, Wick's thoughts turned to his hawk vision. The day's events looped through his mind—he'd succeeded, but could he refine his control?

An image flared behind his closed eyelids. He soared across modern-day Mountain View, seeing busy streets under broad daylight. Shocked, he shot upright and nudged Kahoka awake. "It's night here," Wick whispered, voice trembling with excitement, "but what I saw was daytime."

Kahoka's face registered surprise, but then an idea lit his gaze. "Focus on the day we first met, when the hawk guided us to Kimi's cave. Sharpen that memory and see it through a hawk's eyes."

Wick obliged, mind focusing. A new vision emerged—the White River. He saw glimpses of him slipping into swirling currents and younger Kahoka hauling him onto the bank. Breaking the link felt like being tugged out of a dream.

Kahoka inhaled as if measuring the enormity of what Wick had just witnessed. "My wolf hearing only works in the moment, but your hawk vision cuts across time and distance." He exhaled slowly. "No wonder Kimi said, *'Your power will take patience and practice for its full potential to appear.'* Perhaps you're fulfilling that."

Morning brought goodbyes sealed with lingering hugs and promises to return. Latesha handed out hairbands and ribbons to her new friends while Wick exchanged warm handshakes with the elders he'd come to respect. Just before they were set to leave, Kahoka pulled Wick aside, his expression serious.

"What about your archery?" Kahoka asked. "Have you practiced?"

Wick shook his head, frustration flaring like a stoked ember. "No. Once I find Nora, I will work on that, but first, I have to bring her home."

Kahoka's gaze didn't waver, the force of his words unmistakable. "Understood. But don't wait too long. Step back to that day unprepared, and it all falls apart. We could lose everything."

Wick nodded. "Yes, you warned me before." His thoughts churned. *What day? Everything?*

As they moved away from camp, Wick glanced at Latesha, her quiet smile lingering as she waved goodbye to the girls. "Hey," he called to her, "didn't you forget your hair case?"

Latesha shook her head, the smile widening. "Nope. I left it with the girls as a gift."

Wick raised an eyebrow, impressed. "That's generous of you. They'll love having it."

"They already do," she replied, brushing a braid from her face. "Besides, leaving a part of myself here with them feels right."

As they continued down the trail, Wick's gaze caught on something hanging across Latesha's shoulder—a bandolier bag, ornate and intricate. His steps slowed as the craftsmanship drew him in. "Where'd you get that?" he asked, nodding toward the bag.

Latesha glanced at the bandolier and adjusted the strap. "The girls gave it to me—from Kahoka's wife. It's like his family signature."

Wick's brow furrowed as he traced the exquisite details with his eyes. "This must have taken—what—a hundred hours to make?"

"At least," Latesha agreed, her voice soft and amazed. "I can't believe they gave me something so special."

Wick shook his head, marveling at the gesture. "You must've connected."

Latesha smiled, brushing the fabric lightly. "I hope so. I'd hate to leave without saying goodbye properly."

Leaving camp, Wick and Latesha trekked toward an old bluff where Wick remembered meeting John. He hadn't been back since, but the memory of it had stuck with him—a secluded sanctuary etched into the land. Purple wildflowers dotted the creek bottom, lush and alive, and a row of white grancy graybeards glimmered on the hilltop under the early sunlight. When they reached the edge of the bluff, they paused to take in the sweeping view of the treetops, stretching endlessly under the morning light. The secluded setting felt like it existed outside time, untouched and serene. The creek wound below, glittering in the sun like a silver ribbon. They sat near the bluff's edge, letting the wind wrap around them in gentle gusts.

Wick closed his eyes for a moment, tuning in to the subtle rhythm of the breeze. It began as a soft murmur in the distance, rising gradually, like the land was taking a deep breath. The sound built to a crescendo, peaking as the wind brushed their faces. Neither spoke for a while, the quiet broken only by the rustling treetops and the whispering breeze. Wick allowed himself to sink into the moment, unsure how much time had passed. Eventually, he stood, stretching slightly. "Time to get you back to the farm."

Latesha sighed, pulling her hair back. "I get why John brought Sarah here now. It feels like a secret the world forgot, where cares fall away." She glanced back at the bluff. "Maybe one day, this could be our spot—a place for us to escape to when the rest of the world gets too loud." She paused, her gaze lingering on the landscape. "I'm sad to leave. Feels like we just arrived."

He pressed a palm to her shoulder. "Me too. But there's more at stake. I need to use my vision to find Nora."

They headed in the direction of the signal tree. An uneasy hush greeted them in the final stretch. Wick glanced around, but a blur collided with him, forceful as a bull. Big Mike's hulking form pinned Wick to the ground, answering Wick's startled grunt with raw strength. Wick writhed, pulse drumming in his ears.

Latesha screamed, the sound cutting through the forest like a blade.

"Run!" Wick roared. *She has to make it to the signal tree—it's her only chance. He couldn't let her hesitate.*

She froze for a breathless moment, her eyes wide, shifting between Wick and the massive figure holding him down.

Her horrified stare met Wick's. "Go!"

Her hands twitched at her sides before adrenaline—or so it seemed to Wick—kicked in. With a stumbled lurch, she turned and bolted, disappearing through the trees in a blur.

Big Mike spun Wick around, slamming him face-first into the dust. The acrid taste filled Wick's mouth as Mike's crushing weight pinned him to the ground. Wick gritted his teeth, twisting against the brute's grip, but it was futile. His mother's words rang in his ears: He shouldn't have brought Latesha. He should have been more vigilant and prepared. He knew escape wouldn't come easily—Mike's strength bore down like a slab of concrete.

Through gritted teeth, Wick hissed, "You won't keep me here." But dread pooled in his chest even as he fought against the grip. Latesha's scream echoed in his mind as Mike's hold tightened.

Chapter 32
Arrows of Revelation

Latesha had escaped. At least, Wick hoped she had—Big Mike never worked alone. The thought of her running straight into Tank hit Wick like a blow, fear gripping him as Mike's hold tightened. Wick hoped Latesha had made it to the signal tree and back home, securing her safety with his gramps and the family.

Mike shoved Wick's face into the ground. "Had enough dirt yet, kid?" Flipping Wick onto his back, Mike continued, "Are you ready to talk?"

Wick sputtered, turning his head to the side and spitting forcefully, trying to rid his mouth of the gritty paste. A cough wracked his chest, flecks of dirt flying as he ran his tongue over his teeth, wincing at the sandy texture.

"Ah, you like it, hey?" Mike said. "Thought we didn't see you in Buster's Café, did you? You may have gotten away in town, but you're not getting away this time. So where is it? Is it close? Where are the crystals? You know Vilnius is going to get what he wants. Make this easy on yourself."

Pinned down by someone twice his size, Wick looked at Mike, bold and defiant. "Get off me! Leave my family alone! Let go right now, or you're the one who will be sorry!"

Mike laughed, shaking his head with a smirk on his face. "Kid. You're in no position to bargain. I'll give you a break, alright. The question is which bone? I can start with a finger or your arm. Vilnius told us to up the ante."

Wick remained defiant. "Get off me. Last chance."

Mike made a fist, his face contorted with anger. "On second thought, I'm going to start by giving you a headache, messing up that face."

Wick grinned as Latesha stepped up behind Mike, holding a bat-sized stick.

"I like his face the way it is," Latesha said as she swung the stick with full force, clubbing Mike in the head.

Mike rolled over and lay motionless.

Latesha helped pull Wick to his feet, locking in a hug.

Wick held her out. "I told you to run, but I'm glad you didn't."

Latesha shook her head. "Don't ever ask me to promise something like that again. It's not fair."

Wick nodded, pulling Latesha back into another hug.

He wanted to linger, but reality reclaimed his attention. Wick stepped back and checked Mike to see if he was still unconscious. He reached for the stick Latesha held and prepared for the next round. As he assumed a batting stance, Kahoka and three other men came running up, bows ready.

Kahoka surveyed the scene and noted, "Looks like you have everything under control."

Latesha looked puzzled. "How did you know to come?"

Kahoka smiled. "Remember? Hear a conversation at a quarter mile? A scream like that carries even further, especially when you have wolf hearing."

Latesha nodded.

Kahoka's men stood Mike up to a big white oak, tied his hands behind the tree, and slapped him to revive him.

Kahoka looked over at Wick. "Okay, Wick. What now?"

Wick walked up to Mike. "I told you to let me go, or you'd be the one who's sorry. Now, you talk. Where is my sister? Where is Nora?"

Mike looked befuddled, like he had never been on the receiving end of a disadvantage. "Sister? Last I saw, she was at your farm."

Wick doubled down. "Spill it. Where is she?"

Mike shook his head, looking bereft.

Wick turned to Kahoka. "Can you make him talk?"

Kahoka motioned to one of his men, Yonah, seemingly conveying a command.

Yonah stepped back thirty feet, nocked an arrow, paused, and released the arrow, striking the tree about a foot above Mike's head.

Mike flinched. He swallowed hard as he looked up to see where the arrow struck the tree.

Wick thought for sure that would make Mike talk. Wick lifted his chin, gesturing for Kahoka to continue.

Kahoka made the slightest move of his hand toward Yonah.

Yonah pulled back another arrow, letting it fly closer, landing about six inches above Mike's head.

Surprisingly, Mike didn't flinch this time.

Wick felt desperate but tried not to show it. "You'd better talk, Mike, or the next one might hit you."

Mike smirked. "Kid, I don't scare easily. If they were going to shoot me, they'd have done it already."

Kahoka stepped in, touching Wick's shoulders and backing up to where Yonah stood. Kahoka took the bow from Yonah and handed it to Wick.

Wick looked puzzled. Kahoka motioned for Wick to proceed.

As Wick fumbled with how to hold the bow, Kahoka moved Wick's hand to hold the bow correctly.

"You need to practice. Here's your first lesson," Kahoka said.

Wick stared, to see whether Kahoka was serious.

Kahoka motioned for him to continue.

Wick pulled the arrow back, aimed, and released it. The arrow hit high in the tree, glancing off tree limbs before ricocheting deep into the woods. He winced as the bowstring slapped against his left forearm. Wick dropped the bow, hissing through his teeth as he rubbed the reddening skin. A welt was already forming.

Big Mike snickered, apparently humored at Wick's injury and lack of skill.

Kahoka held out Wick's left forearm, rotating it to bend outward instead of downward, and placed the bow back in Wick's hand, giving him another arrow to nock.

Wick looked at Kahoka again, searching for reassurance, and received a nod. Wick pulled the arrow back, aimed, and released it. This time, the arrow hit dirt just short of Mike.

Yonah handed Wick another arrow. The arrow whizzed to Mike's side this time, narrowly missing him.

Mike's smile seemed to disappear. "Wait a minute. I don't mind these other guys shooting, but you're faking it. You can shoot, right?"

Wick nocked another arrow, letting it fly. It pinned Mike's pants leg to the tree, narrowly missing Mike's leg.

Mike seemed to lose all composure. "Okay, okay, I'll talk. What do you want to know?"

Wick handed the bow to Yonah, walked up to Mike, and demanded, "Where is my sister?"

Mike shook his head. "Back at the farm, I guess."

Wick held out his hand for Yonah's bow.

"Kid—kid!" Mike screamed. "We don't got her."

Latesha walked up to Wick and whispered, "I don't think he knows. Maybe in his timeline, it hasn't happened yet."

Wick kicked himself internally. *Dang! Did we give him the idea?* "Okay, Mike, but you'd better give us something, or I go back to archery practice. I see ten more arrows, and there are more back at camp. Do I need to send for them?"

Mike's face looked ashen. "No, kid. What do you want to know?"

Wick turned his thoughts to his dad. "My dad has been missing. Did Vilnius have anything to do with that?"

Mike hesitated. "Kid, not that."

Wick held out his hand for the bow.

Mike quickly caved. "Okay—yes." Mike's chest heaved. "We took him."

"Why?"

"Vilnius tried to get your dad to sell out. When he wouldn't, Vilnius had us beat him up and dump him."

"Where?"

"Wrong question."

Wick's brow furrowed. "Wrong question—what do you mean?"

"Yeah, not where, but when."

"When?"

"Yeah, when?" Mike replied.

"Enough. I'm tired of asking. Just give me the details."

"He looked pretty rough after we finished working him over. Vilnius gave us the crystal, sent us back to 1922, and told us to make sure he reached a doctor in Mountain View. He wanted your dad out of the way—not dead."

The crystal! The missing piece that could tip the scales in their favor? He stepped closer, his voice sharp and commanding. "Give me the crystal, Mike."

Mike blinked, confusion flashing across his face. "I don't have it; Tank does."

Wick's chest tightened. *Of course, Tank has it.* The one person they couldn't get their hands on right now.

Kahoka tilted his head at Wick, offering assistance. Wick nodded.

Kahoka's men moved quickly, patting Mike down and checking every pocket and fold of clothing. But after an exhaustive search, they came up empty-handed.

Kahoka glanced at Wick, shaking his head.

Wick's stomach churned as he turned away, hiding his disappointment. So close—he'd been so sure. The crystal had been within reach in his mind, and now it felt even further away.

Wick's thoughts turned back to his dad. "I need to know when in 1922," he said.

Mike looked at the tree canopy. "They were working on the courthouse."

"What, like fixing the roof or something?"

"No, they were building the walls. It caught my eye because I pass the courthouse daily in Mountain View. They were starting the front walls."

The realization struck Wick like a wave, leaving him momentarily stunned. He stepped back, his gaze unfocused, the words replaying: *Did I hear that right? Could Dad be alive?* A swarm of emotions surged—relief, disbelief, anger, and the lingering pain of thinking he'd lost him.

Wick turned away abruptly, his chest tightening as emotions built within him. He held out his arm, steadying himself against the revelation. His legs felt heavy, and he walked away in silence, his steps faltering as the world around him began to blur. He stumbled to a secluded spot, his heart pounding. Dropping to his knees, he buried his face in his hands.

The sobs came unbidden, breaking free as months of sorrow clashed with this fragile spark of hope. His shoulders shook, and the forest seemed to hush, wrapping him in quiet solitude. The silence wasn't empty for the first time in months—it was a space to grieve, hope, and feel again. Wick stayed there, letting the storm pass.

Chapter 33
Embers of Determination

Wick knelt on the forest ground, tears still drying on his cheeks. His breath shuddered. Big Mike was tied firmly to the white oak. Kahoka stood nearby, arms crossed, while Latesha hovered, one hand on Wick's shoulder. Her soft sigh settled over the tense quiet.

Wick sniffed, hauling himself upright. Latesha offered a reassuring pat on his back. "Wick," she said gently, "Kahoka needs to know what to do about Mike."

Kahoka cleared his throat. "Yes, Wick. Your call. If you want my men to shoot him, we can—" He gestured at Yonah, who raised his bow and smoothly nocked an arrow. The arrow's tip pointed at Mike's chest.

Wick's chest tightened. He felt a twinge of guilt as he imagined Yonah going through with it. *I can't just—no, that's not me.* He shot Kahoka a glance and read in Kahoka's eyes that this was a bluff, meant to scare Mike. Wick inhaled shakily. "Hold on," he murmured, lifting his palm.

Yonah stayed his draw, though the arrow tip remained trained on the tree.

Wick approached Mike, heart thrumming. "Mike, I'm taking you at your word that you didn't kill my dad—and that you won't hurt my sister. You're lucky we found you before someone else did. I want Kahoka to hold you here for a day and then let you go."

The tension at the corners of Mike's mouth eased. "Fine," he said, voice gravelly.

Kahoka walked up, folding his arms over his chest. "One day," he repeated, staring Mike down. "But no promises if we see you or your buddy again."

"Understood," Mike muttered.

Wick gave Kahoka a grateful nod. A wave of exhaustion crept into his limbs as he turned toward Latesha. "Let's get you home," he said, voice wavering at the realization that the path home might not be entirely safe.

Kahoka motioned. "Yonah will see you both to the signal tree," he explained. "That should help. My wolf hearing only does so much."

Latesha nodded. "Thank you, Kahoka."

They had barely taken a few steps when Mike hollered from behind the tree, "Hey, kid—wait. You were faking it with that bow, right? No way you shot my pants leg by accident."

Wick paused, then turned, a half-smile forming. "First time I ever shot a bow. I was aiming about a foot to the right of your chest when I hit your pants leg."

A bewildered look flashed across Mike's eyes. His mouth opened, but no words emerged. Finally, he lowered his head and shook it. "You've got to be kidding me," he mumbled.

Wick shrugged. "Have a nice day, Mike."

Mike mumbled something unintelligible and looked away in disbelief.

With that, Wick turned again, and he, Latesha, and Yonah left Mike and Kahoka behind. Wick's heart lurched each time he heard a branch snap, half-expecting Tank to leap from the shadows. He glanced at Latesha more than once, guilt burning behind his eyes. This was too big a risk to bring her here. She smiled at him, like she could read his worry.

Within half an hour, they reached the signal tree. The gnarled trunk appeared unchanged—a silent witness to countless journeys. Yonah gave them a quick salute, then melted back into the woods with practiced stealth. Latesha pressed her hand against the bark, taking a last look around. Wick gently laid his palm beside hers, and they vanished.

They landed back in 2026 with a dizzying shift in perspective. The night air in Gramps's yard felt unnaturally still. Latesha powered on her phone, the screen glowing softly. A glance confirmed only fifteen minutes had passed here—two days for them, yet nearly no time at home.

Latesha exhaled, wrapping her arms around herself. "That's never going to feel normal. Time stood still here while all that drama unfolded."

Wick took a shaky step, mind swirling after Mike's revelation that Wick's dad was alive somewhere in 1922, battered but not dead. "Latesha," he said quietly, "it's not just Nora anymore. Dad too. I have to save them both."

She nodded, her voice gentle. "So—who do you go after first?"

His insides twisted. "Nora," he finally said. "She's in greater danger right now. I know Dad's living in 1922, but... hopefully recovering. Maybe with luck, I can time it so I don't lose him again. But I have to rescue Nora before any harm comes her way."

They stood there, an awkward silence thickening the air. At length, Latesha brushed her bandolier bag—her souvenir from Kahoka's camp. "I loved seeing those traditions and their family. Someday, I want to return."

Wick mustered a weak smile. "Me too." He spotted a faint glow of embers at his family's usual campfire spot, the only sign that life at home had gone on normally. "Look," he said, voice still wavering, "I need some space. Maybe I can glimpse Nora's location by sharpening my hawk vision."

Latesha gently placed her hand on his arm. "Are you going to tell your mom, gram, and gramps about your dad?"

He ran a hand through his hair, his shoulders slumping. "I don't want to raise their hopes. I'm not sure I can bring him back—not yet. If I fail, I don't want them to go through losing him again. It's better to wait until I'm certain."

She studied him a moment, concern and empathy mingling in her eyes. "I understand. But you realize they'll worry if they figure out you knew something and didn't share?"

His throat tightened. "I know. I'll tell them. Just—not now. I'll have real answers once I find Nora, rescue Dad, and bring him home."

She paused, seeming ready to say more, but nodded. A final, comforting squeeze of his arm, then she turned toward the house. Wick angled himself toward the dying embers, taking measured steps over grass that felt almost too familiar after everything he'd just endured. Dad was alive in 1922. Nora was missing—maybe in another decade altogether. The enormity pressed down on him.

He added logs to the smoldering coals, gazing at the scattered stars overhead. Safe now, yet still far from saving Dad and Nora, Wick closed his eyes and inhaled the faint woodsmoke, letting it calm him. His heart pulsed with renewed determination.

He bowed his head, thoughts turning to prayer, half hoping the hush of night might bring another precious glimpse of Nora.

Chapter 34
Echo of Twenty-One Guns

Wick settled onto the cool grass near the campfire's last embers, the moon gleaming overhead. The quiet clashed with the storm in his mind. He drew in a breath of crisp air, forcing himself to focus—Nora. If only finding her were as simple as closing his eyes and whispering her name.

Kahoka's voice echoed in his memory: Focus. Block out every stray thought. Wick pictured Nora's defiant brow and the tilt of her chin when she was determined. A pang hit him—she might be anywhere—or any when. He forced the thought aside, narrowing his mind to just her face. The wind faded—the yard seemed to vanish.

A dizzying shift overtook him. Suddenly, he soared like a hawk, the farm below shrinking to a patchwork of fields. For an instant, he glimpsed a different place—a farm bathed in hazy twilight, an old barn standing guard near the fence. Three figures walked with Nora among rows of crops. Wick's stomach twisted. He couldn't make out their faces but recognized Nora's hair in the fading sun. The scene fractured, dissolving into dappled color. He struggled to hold on—then it was gone.

His eyes snapped open. Gramps's farm returned in a rush of blurred shapes. Wick inhaled sharply, hands braced on the ground.

That flash of Nora—alive, somewhere—thrilled and unsettled him. Fields, fences—older styles of farmland, reminiscent of Billy's family property. But was it 1945, 1946, or 1947? He closed his eyes again, determined to refocus.

Seconds later, hawk vision swept him up again. He soared over a winding creek and a rutted road toward Mountain View. The small town emerged beneath a veil of amber, as though Mountain View scheduled sunrise for its convenience. He willed the hawk toward Billy's place. The bird banked left. Below, a farmhouse stood amidst trucks, two cars, and five wagons—an unusual gathering. Something significant was happening there.

Wick's heart fluttered. He recognized Billy's land, although the house appeared slightly newer, less weather-beaten. If only he could catch a glimpse of the date. He coaxed the hawk onward, pushing toward Mountain View. A modest country church came into view: Flatwoods Baptist. He glided closer, scanning the entrance. At last, a marquee sign loomed, letters bold enough for the hawk's keen sight: "In Loving Memory of John Jenkins, Funeral Service, August 21, 1944, at 2 PM."

Wick's breath caught in his chest. 1944. That was long before Billy became the teenager Wick knew. The vision jolted, his mind spinning. The next moment, everything slipped away, and he was back in Gramps's yard, blinking at the stars.

He crouched there, letting the shock settle. August 21, 1944—John's funeral. The crowd at Billy's farm must be the family paying their final respects. And Nora? She was in that timeline, too. It made no sense, yet it was the only lead he had.

With renewed urgency, Wick got to his feet and headed inside, slipping upstairs while the house lay quiet. In the attic, a musty smell drifted through the air. A dusty trunk waited in the far corner, buried beneath quilts. He eased the lid open, rummaging gently. His fingers brushed against old newspapers, black-and-white photographs, and brittle letters. He needed something from 1944—a tangible key to a specific moment.

Several minutes of searching revealed a yellowed envelope bearing the official War Department seal. Below it, "Mr. Elijah Jenkins"—John's father—was typed in crisp, unwavering letters while the 1944 postmark glared back at him. Wick's pulse quickened as he carefully slipped the letter free and scanned its contents. The stark, somber script leaped out at him: "I regret to inform you." The words were etched with the precision of a wound. He could almost sense the heartbreak of the day this letter arrived—its presence splintering the fragile hope clinging to the Jenkins household. Even the faded signature at the bottom still conveyed a sense of finality.

He exhaled, sliding the letter back into its envelope. This was a perfect anchor for 1944. Carefully, he folded the bundle. The pang of sorrow remained—John had died a hero, leaving a family forever changed—but now Wick clung to this relic as a possible lifeline for Nora, too.

Holding the letter tight, he headed to the signal tree. Its branches stretched in the moonlight, a silent sentinel of countless generations. Wick closed his eyes and pressed the letter to the trunk. The world lurched.

***

Following a dirt road beneath the blistering noonday sun, Wick soon reached the Flatwoods Baptist Church. Black-suited men and women milled around, grief etched deeply into their solemn faces. A line of trucks, cars, and horse-drawn wagons confirmed a large gathering. He caught a glimpse of Elijah and Myrtle—both looking heartbreakingly young—Myrtle's face streaked with tears she didn't bother to wipe away, and Elijah's expression set in a stoic mask, though his eyes betrayed the depth of his sorrow. Sarah sat beside them, her arm wrapped around a toddler—probably Boyd, Wick realized, seeing the familiar eyes and unruly hair. Sarah's eyes were hollow, fixed on the casket. Wick blinked hard, swiping his hand across his eyes as a tightness coiled in his chest.

As the congregation stood for prayer and to view the casket, the family gathered. Boyd clung to Myrtle's skirt, his bright eyes wide with confusion, unable to comprehend the enormity of the loss surrounding him. Beside them stood Billy, perhaps fourteen, lanky and awkward in his oversized suit, his gaze fixed on the casket draped in flowers—John's funeral.

Wick's gaze drifted to the flyer on the church pew, where he spotted it—John's obituary. February 22, 1921–August 10, 1944. The dates carved an ache deep in Wick's chest. The brief span of years served as a cruel reminder of a life cut short, in stark contrast to the memory of seeing John in his prime with his wife, Sarah, on the spring mountain, full of hope and vigor. Wick could picture them there, vibrant and carefree, untouched by the shadow of war, their laughter carrying on the gentle breeze. He rubbed his palm over his face as the ache tightened, his pulse surging at the thought of seeing those numbers etched into stone every day—a permanent testament to loss.

Wick's throat tightened. So, that's how young Billy was. He barely recognized him in that scrawny kid. The preacher spoke of John's valor, highlighting how he'd saved many in his troop and earned two Purple Hearts. "We're free because of those who serve," the preacher said gravely, and Wick recalled Gramps saying, *'Some gave all.'* Indeed, John's family had done so.

After the preacher's final words, the distinct crack of rifles shattered the air—a twenty-one-gun salute. The sharp cadence of each shot sent shivers, echoing the depth of sacrifice. Wick's pulse surged as he watched two uniformed representatives step forward. With practiced solemnity, they carefully removed the draped flag from John's casket, their movements deliberate and reverent. Then, with exacting precision, they folded it into its triangular shape. One of them presented the folded flag to Sarah, bowing slightly as he placed it in her trembling hands. Her tear-filled eyes locked onto the symbol of service, and she clutched it, her face a mixture of anguish and pride. The soldier straightened, raising his hand in a crisp salute, holding it for a measured moment before stepping back, the gesture filled with solemn respect.

The ceremony concluded with hushed prayers. Wick lingered at the crowd's edge, his eyes stinging, aware that this moment overshadowed everything. He steeled himself—he had come for Nora. But emotions roiled in his chest as he thought about how deeply John's death had affected each generation of his family.

Suddenly, movement near the cemetery gate caught his eye. Tank and Big Mike, half-concealed behind a cluster of cedars, watched him intently. Their presence here, in 1944, set alarm bells ringing in Wick's mind. He clenched his fists, heart thudding—did they follow him, or were they here for Nora? Either way, their cold gleams betrayed their intent. This timeline wasn't safe.

As the funeral ended, Wick ducked behind a small stone mausoleum to try hawk vision. He glimpsed Tank guiding Nora away from the church grounds, her face pale. They were shifting timelines again, slipping out of 1944. Wick's heart plummeted. All his planning was undone. *They've taken her away. Where are they dragging her now?*

He trembled as fury and despair washed over him. Gone. And no telling what year they'd choose next. The funeral scene faded behind him, overshadowed by one burning thought: *I have to find her. I can't let them keep playing timeline hopscotch.* If he'd tracked her here, he'd do it again—even if it meant chasing her across decades.

A single knell from the church bell resonated in the hush, marking the end of John's final tribute. Wick bowed his head, thankful for the privilege of having met his great-grandfather—Gramps's dad. The reality of it saddened. Then, with grim resolve, he set his jaw. Time might shift beneath his feet, but as long as he had hawk vision and fierce determination, he'd follow Nora through any era.

Wick lingered at the cemetery's edge until the crowd had dispersed. He wanted to keep moving, but another promise tugged at him—John's final request. Wick cut across the fields, heading toward the slow-moving creek. He hunched by the water's edge, overcome. The loss, the enormity of John's sacrifice for family and country—Wick let himself sob, voice echoing against the rocks and water.

"John, they're safe now," he whispered aloud. "You did it. You saved us all. Thank you."

When he stood, he nearly missed them—there, pushing through the weeds at the creek bottom, clusters of purple dwarf bearded iris swayed in a patch of shadow. Wick stared in disbelief. "I thought they only bloomed in spring," he muttered, then knelt, gathering a handful along with a few late grancy graybeard blossoms growing wild atop a bluff.

The trek back to Billy's house felt longer. At the porch, Wick arranged the flowers in a chipped mug, folded John's sealed note alongside, and set both just outside the front door. He ducked into the woods' edge as the family returned. Myrtle noticed first, pausing before quietly urging Elijah, Billy, and Boyd inside and leaving Sarah alone.

From the shadows, Wick watched Sarah discover the bouquet and note. She opened the letter, lips trembling, then pressed it to her heart, hugging it close. She kissed the folded paper, a smile breaking through her grief, then scooped up the flowers and carried them inside.

Satisfied he'd kept his promise, Wick turned away, walking solemnly through the trees as dusk gathered—ready once again to chase history, carrying both burden and blessing.

One thing was clear: The pursuit had only just begun.

Chapter 35
Mushrooms to Mayhem

Wick steadied himself against the signal tree, his heart pounding from the dizzying jump. The moment he landed in the night air of 2026, exhaustion hit him like a sledgehammer. His legs quivered, and black spots dotted his vision. He realized he hadn't eaten or drunk anything substantial, and he wasn't even sure how long it had been. Time blurred.

He took a few steps toward the house, determined not to wake anyone. Once inside, the kitchen rug slipped beneath his foot. He stumbled forward, colliding with a chair. A loud clatter shattered the silence.

The lights switched on. Latesha and Mom rushed into the hallway, their eyes wide with surprise. Wick struggled to stand, beads of sweat forming on his forehead.

"Wick!" Mom gasped, hurrying over to help him up. "What in the world—are you hurt?"

"No, I—just need—food—" Wick mumbled. He gripped the back of the chair to steady himself.

Latesha pressed her hand to his forehead. "You're soaked in sweat. When was the last time you ate?"

Wick forced a shaky laugh. "Uh—the squirrel feast. At Kahoka's." He swayed, wincing at the throbbing in his temples.

"Squirrel feast!" Latesha threw up her arms. "Seriously?"

At that, Gramps padded into the room, hair mussed from sleep. "Sounds like a party out here," he said gruffly. "What's going on?"

Mom shushed him. "Wick needs to sit. He nearly face-planted trying to sneak inside."

She guided Wick to the couch, where he collapsed, panting. He attempted to protest, but his limbs felt like lead. Mom disappeared into the kitchen, returning minutes later with a plate of grilled cheese sandwiches and pickles. The irresistible scent of buttery bread filled Wick's nostrils, causing his stomach to cramp with hunger. He quickly devoured both sandwiches, washing them with a tall glass of cold milk.

Mom watched with concern etched on her face. "Better now?"

Wick nodded, leaning back, color returning to his cheeks. "I—I almost found Nora," he blurted. "But Tank and Mike moved her again—to another unknown time. I have to go back."

Mom's gaze hardened. "Absolutely not. You're in no condition to chase criminals across decades. You're no match for grown men."

Wick opened his mouth, ready to argue, but Gramps raised a hand. "Laura, do you remember that story I told you about a stranger who saved me from drowning in that old hand-dug well?"

Mom frowned. "Yes. And?"

Gramps inclined his head toward Wick, a small, tired smile curling his lips. "He's that stranger."

Mom's eyes widened, darting between Wick and his gramps in disbelief. "No," she whispered. "Dad—that's not—he would've been—"

"Time travel, honey," Gramps said softly. "Stranger things have happened."

Mom stared at Wick, tears hovering at the edges of her lashes. "All right." She exhaled, composure slipping. "But he needs rest."

She pointed at Wick decisively. "You're not going back out tonight. Get rest, and you can go in the morning."

Latesha and Gramps nodded. Wick sighed, shoulders slumping. "Fine," he relented. "I'm too tired to argue." He dragged himself upstairs, sinking into bed almost immediately—but not before his thoughts spun on Nora. Tomorrow, he promised himself. Tomorrow.

***

Wick woke at dawn to the smell of sausage gravy and biscuits, courtesy of Gram. His stomach rumbled fiercely—clearly, two grilled cheese sandwiches weren't enough to erase days of borderline starvation. He hurried to the kitchen, where Mom, Latesha, Gramps, and Gram sat, with cups of coffee and a plate of crispy bacon laid out.

After the blessing, Wick heaped biscuits onto his plate, drowning them in gravy. As he devoured breakfast, he updated them on his progress: hawk vision on-demand, glimpses across time. Carefully, he avoided mentioning the more violent moments—like Big Mike's threats and the funeral standoff—knowing Mom might forbid him from leaving. He could feel her eyes lingering, so full of worry.

Once he'd finished every crumb, Wick slung his pack over his shoulder, excusing himself to check the cave for any sign of Kahoka or Kimi. He searched, but only echoes remained—crystals glittered silently in the walls. Atop the bluff, with the wind rustling cedar branches, Wick stretched out on the flat rock, determined to see if he could spot Nora again.

Hawk vision came with startling ease this time, like a surge of adrenaline. He soared over rolling fields, scanning farms. There was no sign of a funeral taking place. Instead, he caught sight of a small homestead—weathered fences and a sparse orchard. A man in a white T-shirt and overalls patrolled the yard, double-barrel breakover shotgun in hand. Nora crouched by a barn, pinned in place. A post office sign reading "September 5, 1947" flashed in the corner of his vision. Wick's heart jolted, noting the style of the trucks out front. *She is in 1947! Perfect.* He just needed an artifact from that exact date.

A week ago, finding her seemed impossible—like trying to catch a whisper in a storm. But now, across both space and time, he could finally see the way.

Wick rushed home and rummaged in old drawers until he found a local newspaper dated "September 5, 1947," something Gram had kept—he guessed—because it mentioned a relative. He clutched it tightly, marched to the signal tree, and vanished.

***

The air smelled of fresh-cut lumber as Wick materialized in 1947. He wasn't keen on strolling openly past the farm—Tank and Mike could be lurking—so he slipped downhill, headed for the sawmill.

He remembered Billy liked to hang out in the rafters after school, away from prying eyes.

After hours of dusty waiting, Billy slipped in through a side entrance. He nearly dropped his notebook when Wick waved from the shadows of the beams overhead.

"What are you doing here?" Billy hissed, climbing up to meet him.

Wick grinned, jumping straight into updates: how Nora was kidnapped, how he pinpointed her location in 1947, and how he needed help scoping out the place. Billy's eyes widened with resolve. He dashed off to pass a message to Elijah—an excuse about camping out. Then, the two boys met on a wooded trail, eventually stopping at a small campsite in a clearing.

"This is my hideout," Billy announced proudly. They pitched a battered tent, hung a lantern, and rummaged for dinner, which was—nothing.

A plump squirrel darted from a tree, eyeing them hopefully. Billy noted it was one he'd fed scraps to before. "Well, we could trap something," Billy said, half-joking. "Or—" He pointed at a patch of mushrooms sprouting from the ground, nestled among decaying leaves and twigs. The mushrooms had tall, wrinkled caps, resembling miniature honeycombs, and their earthy brown color blended almost seamlessly with the forest floor. Wick arched an eyebrow.

A comedic back-and-forth ensued, with Billy calling Wick "Mr. Science" and Wick calling Billy "Professor Fungus." They squabbled over a tattered survival guide, half-convinced the mushrooms were harmless and half afraid they would end up dead. They tested a piece on the squirrel. It ate without hesitation, its fluffy tail flicking as it scampered away.

"I'm still not sure," Wick murmured, frowning. But hunger won out. They concocted a quick stew and cooked it over a small campfire, stomachs grumbling in protest at the wait.

Just as the brew finished, the surrounding bushes erupted with commotion. Footsteps crashed through the undergrowth. Tank and Big Mike burst through. The boys froze—running wasn't an option. Within seconds, both were pinned, their arms wrenched behind their backs.

Tank sniffed at the bubbling pot. "You made dinner, kid? How thoughtful," he sneered. Mike lowered himself onto a log, eyeing the mushroom stew. Licking his lips, he helped himself.

Billy bumped Wick and nodded toward the squirrel. The boys froze as they watched the squirrel blink sluggishly, stagger in a small circle, and then tumble out the back side of the tree, landing in the underbrush.

While Tank and Mike were distracted, sniffing at the stew, Wick hissed, "Billy, look at the squirrel! We've got to say something."

Billy shook his head. "No way. They'll laugh at us—or worse. Let it go."

Wick's conscience gnawed at him as he glanced at the bubbling pot and then at the unconscious rodent. Finally, unable to hold back, he spoke up. "Hey, Tank, Mike, don't eat those mushrooms. They might be bad."

"Shut up, kid," Tank snapped, rubbing his stomach with exaggerated glee. "Smells too good to care." With a broad grin, he ladled a generous portion for himself. Tank and Mike dug into the stew without hesitation, their laughter echoing as they exchanged amused glances.

An hour later, jokes gave way to slurred words. The men's eyes drooped. Tank keeled over first, Mike not far behind. The men collapsed in a tangle of limbs, out cold.

"Whew," Billy spouted. "They must have low tolerance for fungus."

Working together, Wick and Billy freed themselves from the ropes. Wick was fueled by adrenaline. "We can't stay. If Tank and Mike come to—"

"Exactly. It's our chance," Billy interrupted. "We raid that farm, rescue Nora, finish this!"

Wick hesitated, glancing at the unconscious men sprawled on the ground. He nudged Tank's shoulder lightly, then held his breath. No reaction. He leaned closer, watching the faint rise and fall of their chests. "Still breathing," he muttered. "Just knocked out."

Billy turned, eyes widening at a rustling sound nearby. The squirrel twitched, its small body sluggishly coming back to life. "Looks like he's waking up, too," Billy noted. "Guess we didn't kill him."

Wick crouched beside Tank, quickly rifling through his pockets. Billy scoffed, crossing his arms. "Are you robbing them now?"

"No," Wick shot back, frustration lacing his voice. "Just trying to recover the crystal." But after checking both men, his search turned up nothing. He was about to stand when Tank shifted slightly, a groggy mumble escaping his lips. Wick flinched, scrambling backward.

Billy took a cautious step away. "Tie them up?" he asked.

Wick shook his head. "No time. We need to get to Nora. Besides, they might wake up if we mess with them too much." He gave Tank and Mike one last glance, then exhaled sharply. "Let them sleep it off."

"Yeah, that'll teach 'em to steal our fungus."

They bolted into the night, guided by Wick's memory of the orchard-laced homestead. Sure enough, the place lay quiet. No guards in sight—Tank and Mike must have left a skeleton crew. They peered across the yard in the pale moonlight, their breath fogging in the cool air. The barn loomed ahead, its weathered boards casting long shadows against the ground. Adjoining the barn was a hog pen, where massive hogs shifted in their sleep, their deep, rhythmic snorts blending with the faint rustle of leaves.

The barn door creaked as they slipped inside. A glowing lantern revealed stacked hay bales, a battered wheelbarrow, and the pungent smell of manure. Nora crouched in a horse stall at the far end, a chain on the latch.

"Nora!" Wick's breath caught in his throat as he lifted the latch. She sprang forward, tears welling at the corners of her eyes. They clung to each other in a trembling hug. Billy cleared his throat, an awkward grin on his face. "Guys, enough. We gotta scram before—"

A rough voice cut through the darkness. "Too late." Wick spun toward the shadows, dread slicing through him. The barn door slammed shut with a thud.

Chapter 36

Between a Hog Pen and Home

The man shoved them into the horse stall. The latch snapped shut, echoing through the barn's rafters. Wick felt Nora trembling against his arm and forced himself to stay steady so she wouldn't break. Billy crouched nearby, shooting Wick a worried glance.

Outside the stall, a gruff man leaned forward. The lantern's glow carved sharp angles along his weathered cheekbones. "You brats best get comfortable." His voice scraped low. "Word is, there's a reward for troublemakers. Tank and Mike will be pleased I found you. Enjoy your night—morning's not far off."

He smirked, then disappeared into the shadows. The barn door slammed. Wick braced his hands on the stall gate as he heard the outside latch—a sound final as a verdict.

"Wick," Nora whispered, "what's going on?" Her voice wavered.

He swallowed, turning toward her. Fear was etched deep on her face even in the weak lantern light. He forced a small, reassuring smile. "You okay? Did they hurt you?"

She shook her head, hugging herself. "No. But it's been—I don't know. Everything's a blur. Three days, maybe?"

He frowned. "Three days? You sure?"

Nora scowled. "Why wouldn't I be sure? I'm not losing it—yet."

Wick hesitated and glanced at Billy crouched near the door, testing the latch and failing. "Nora, do you have any idea what year it is?"

She rolled her eyes. "Seriously, Wick? It's 2026. Did you fall off a wagon or something?"

Wick expelled a long breath. He stepped toward her. "That's what I need to tell you. I couldn't find you, so I had to search—other times. I've been time traveling."

She stared at him, eyes widening. "Stop messing around."

"This is Uncle Billy," Wick said, nodding at Billy. "You know, from the hospital when we first reached town? Only he's my age right now."

Nora's lips quivered, tears threatening. "I—can't, Wick. I want to go home."

He inhaled slowly, drawing her gently into a hug. "Okay, okay. Let's focus on getting out of here first."

Meanwhile, Billy squinted at a rotted board in the corner, then booted it—splinters flew, and a narrow gap gaped straight into the hog pen. He grunted in frustration. "No good. The door's locked, and everything else is nailed down tight."

Nora edged closer, peering through. "I can squeeze through."

Billy looked alarmed. "Are you nuts? Those hogs don't exactly roll out a welcome mat."

Nora set her jaw. "I've been bribing them with scraps. They practically expect dessert."

Wick winced, remembering the pig incident. "Nora, you sure you're not dessert?"

She glanced from Wick to Billy, then at the gap. "Anything's better than being stuck in here."

Billy stepped aside. "Brace yourself—for mud, the smell, and a regret that stains the soul."

Wick reached out, gently grasping Nora's shoulders. His fingers barely pressed her, but the gesture stilled her. He fixed his gaze on hers, keeping his voice low and steady. "Nora, that man could still be out there. If you see him, sneak or run away. Go downhill—only downhill until you get to a creek. I'll send a hawk to guide you to the signal tree in the morning. Touch the tree and you'll go home to Mom."

Nora furrowed her brow and tilted her head, her lips parting, but no words emerged. Finally, she shook her head, her voice hesitant. "You'll... send a hawk?"

Wick nodded. "Don't think, just remember and do it. Promise?"

She blinked, clearly unsure, but nodded anyway, accepting with a look that said she'd save her questions for another time.

Nora eased through the opening. Wick winced as the stall's wood scraped her shoulder, catching the quick grimace on her face. Once she squeezed through, he heard her muffled "Ooh," followed by a gag at the stink. Wick held his breath, his nerves stretched taut. *I can't believe I'm letting Nora do this alone. If Mom knew where we were, she'd flip out—and then hunt me down herself.*

Outside, a hog snorted in surprise, but after a few tense seconds that seemed to stretch forever, Wick watched Nora climb the wood fence and vanish around the side of the barn. Listening hard, he finally caught movement in the barn's corridor. A heartbeat later, the stall's latch clicked, and the door swung wide.

Wick started to hug Nora, then recoiled at the reek. "Nora, remind me to thank you—if I ever breathe again."

They slid into the barn's shadowy passage. No one seemed to be around. A single lantern guttered on a peg, painting shadows across the walls. Wick signaled for silence. The three slipped out, the night air pressing cool and thick as they aimed for the woods.

At last, the creek shimmered through the brush—a silver escape route.

By daybreak, Billy's farmhouse appeared dewy and quiet. Wick laid a hand on Nora's shoulder. "Sis, just—yeah. We're in 1947. Billy's family's farm."

Nora blinked, beginning to process. Her breath hitched. "I need a minute. And a bath. Preferably in that order."

Wick grinned, and the tension finally broke. "That, at least, I can fix."

Outside, Wick and Billy began working on the well. The chain clattered with each heave as buckets piled up to fill a large galvanized tub on the back porch. When the tub was filled, they hung sheets as a curtain for privacy.

When it was ready, Nora stepped behind the makeshift curtain. Wick heard her gasp as the first splash of cold water landed—no mistaking that surprise. "No hot water? This place skips every century," she muttered, her voice just loud enough for him to catch. Wick had to clamp down on a laugh—clearly, his city-slicker sister was in for a real history lesson.

Billy returned with an old pair of jeans and a faded shirt and draped them over the top of the curtain for her.

Once Nora finished her bath and changed, Wick grinned and pulled her into a quick hug. "All right, much better. You did a great job saving us back there at the barn." *He couldn't believe he'd let her do that.*

Nora looked up and smiled.

Wick pointed at her hog-stained clothes. "Do you want to wash those?"

Nora shook her head and laughed. "No. Burn them."

They headed inside. In the kitchen, six-year-old Boyd zoomed a toy truck across the table.

As they entered, Billy called ahead, "Wick's sister fell in the hog pen, but she's cleaned up now."

Sarah glanced up from where she was kneading biscuit dough at the counter, flour dusting her hands. Her face softened in relief as she saw Nora cleaned up and grinning. "Glad you made it out of that hog pen in one piece, honey," she said, her voice gentle and steady. She laughed as Boyd's truck skidded past a bowl of rising dough. "Boyd, take that truck to the floor before you launch gravy into the pantry," she called, smiling.

Wick caught Nora freezing, glancing at him with wide eyes.

"That's Gramps," Wick whispered, stifling a grin as the little boy darted past. "Our Gramps."

Nora managed a shaky laugh. "This is so weird."

Wick and Billy led Nora to see the garden, the horse, the goats, the chickens, and the guineas. Myrtle opened the back door, calling them for breakfast. The aroma of sausages and biscuits teased the air. From the doorway, Wick noticed the way Nora hovered, her gaze roaming the cozy kitchen and the wood stove, so different from what she was used to. She mustered a small smile and stepped in.

They sat at the farmhouse table, crowded with home-cooked dishes. When the meal ended, Nora and Wick slipped out onto the porch. Roosters crowed as golden sunlight swept the yard.

Nora shot Wick a sideways look. "Send a hawk?"

Wick exhaled. "It's a long story. I've bounce-hopped through decades—got stuck in the 1850s, wound up in 1944, then here in 1947. I met an old mystic in a cave and got this thing called hawk vision. That's how I found you. I'll find Dad, too—just haven't yet."

She grabbed his arm, eyes sharp. "Then do it now. Bring Dad here. We'll go home together—like we're supposed to."

Wick started to protest—Mom wouldn't be thrilled with this plan.

Billy stepped up from behind and cut him off. "She might be safer here. Tank and Mike could be scouring 2026 for her. They're less likely to show up here, especially with the dogs, guineas, and my dad armed and alert."

Nora nodded, her posture finally relaxing. "I want to stay until you bring Dad here. Then we'll go home together."

He finally exhaled. "Deal—but you stick close. Billy or Elijah, everywhere."

She grinned. "Deal."

Nora helped Myrtle shell peas in the kitchen while Boyd zoomed around the table with his toy truck. Wick noticed how Nora kept watching the little boy—her curiosity was obvious. Wick lingered, content to watch Nora adapt, like stepping into a living version of their family's history.

Eventually, Wick tugged her aside. "You sure? Mom might kill me if she finds out I didn't bring you right back."

Nora's stubborn glint returned. "I'm sure. Dad, then all of us—no exceptions."

Wick nodded, unease churning in his chest. "Okay. I'll search for him, but I have to find a quiet place to concentrate."

Wick headed down the hill past the signal tree to the elephant rock. He sat and focused on his dad. Soon, he was soaring over Mountain View. Below, he saw the courthouse being constructed; the foundation started with just a few courses of stone. Across the street from the courthouse, he saw Tank and Mike dump his dad outside a doctor's office.

Heart pounding, Wick sprang to his feet and rushed back up the hill. When he reached Nora and Billy, he blurted, "I found him— Dad was there, near a half-built courthouse—but I'm not sure what year it was. I'll have to figure that out."

Billy grinned, then said, "Hold on." He disappeared briefly and reappeared with news: "My dad said it was built in 1922, though he didn't give a specific date."

Wick nodded slowly. "Off to 1922 it is," he declared.

At that very moment, Sailor Cat appeared—half white, half orange, one eye blue, the other amber. Nora's eyes lit up. "I love that cat! Can we take it with us when we leave?" she asked excitedly.

Wick chuckled. "No need—you'll see it again when we go home." Nora looked genuinely confused, her smile tinged with wonder as the surreal promise lingered. Wick couldn't blame her; if he hadn't seen Sailor across decades himself, he'd want proof too.

Nora inhaled, combing fingers through her damp hair. "Promise me you won't come back without him."

"I promise," Wick whispered, though uncertainty clenched his heart. "I just have to find something from 1922 to lock onto that date."

Nora nodded, lips pressed together, eyes brimming with hope. Billy patted Wick's arm, offering a silent "good luck."

Wick strode toward the signal tree, dread and determination tangling with every step. He had no idea where to find a 1922 artifact—just that he'd stop at nothing to rescue Dad. *No more time slipping away.*

Billy offered to accompany him to 1922. Wick shook his head. "I need you to keep an eye on Boyd and Nora. If anything happens to them while I'm gone—"

Billy squeezed his shoulder. "I'll hold down the fort, partner. Come back with your dad."

Wick pressed his hand to the storied bark. The world lurched—wind and swirling color rose around him.

Wick vanished, praying he'd make it before time finally ran out on them all.

Chapter 37
Courthouse Stones

Back at Gramps's farm, Wick steeled himself. He visualized hawk vision—floating with the clouds. He focused on the Stone County courthouse as it was taking shape. Through hawk eyes, he soared above stacked stones and the footing for the courthouse walls. The trees looked scrubby with no leaves, and the grass was brown. Dirt mixed with patches of snow. Not summer or fall. His heart sank. *What time of year? If I get there too early—*

He rifled through the attic trunk for something—anything— from 1922. He settled on a battered 1922 penny tucked in Gram's button jar—loose change, perhaps too general. Rushing back to the signal tree, he gripped the coin, braced, and touched the signal tree.

***

Color and cold consumed him. Wick landed at the signal tree in January 1922, the farm blanketed in snow. Frost crusted his lashes as he hiked the long, rutted road—it took the better part of a day to reach Mountain View, boots slipping on frozen mud the whole way. When he finally made it, the courthouse site was little more than a pit of sludge with just a few stones stacked atop each other.

He thought it was too early for his dad to arrive, but he checked the doctor's office anyway. After a quick conversation, the staff just shook their heads—no reports of anyone missing, no strangers brought in. Wick stomped for warmth as he left, hugging himself. *Way too early—I'd freeze before Dad ever showed up.*

Reluctant to spend a night shivering, he trudged the long miles back to the farm. By the time he reached the signal tree, his toes were numb. He clutched the penny, pressed his palm to the bark, and tunneled back to 2026.

***

His second try, Wick dug up an old flyer he'd seen in the courthouse archives—a yellowed broadsheet for the courthouse dedication, dated October 31, 1922. "Perfect," he muttered, hoping for a fall landing. He launched himself again through the signal tree.

Mountain View was festive—pumpkins on porches this time, and the courthouse nearly finished. Wick's heart leaped—but as he hurried to the doctor's office, he felt nagging dread. *Please, let him be here. Please.* He asked the nurse at the front, trying to sound casual. "Did anyone bring in a man—a stranger, possibly named George, maybe disoriented—earlier this year?"

The nurse's expression clouded. She didn't meet his eyes. "Yes, someone like that—months ago. Poor soul seemed mad—ranting about phones and not knowing the year. We shipped him off to the state hospital in Little Rock." She shrugged, but her gaze darted away. "It's never good for folks sent there. Most don't come back." Wick's stomach twisted. *If they committed Dad—*

He pressed again, but the answers were vague and uncomfortable. Defeated, he wandered the courthouse lawn, thinking. *I could try to spring him from Little Rock. But what if he's been suffering there for months? I've got to get back before he's taken.*

***

Back home in 2026, Wick schemed. There had to be something more precise to land him at the moment he needed. On a hunch, he visited the modern courthouse and eyed a ceremonial trowel in a glass cabinet—engraved "Stone County Courthouse—Groundbreaking Ceremony, Spring 1922." He wanted to borrow it, so he asked at the front desk, spinning a story about a class project. The clerk smiled apologetically. "Sorry, can't loan it."

"Well, could you take it out so I can look at it?"

"No, sorry, it's alarmed. When we need to open the display case, we ask the judge. You could wait around for him if you like."

Frustration threatened to choke him. He considered breaking in, but security cameras and an alarm—*what about 1947? No alarms then.*

He ported to 1947, heart pounding, and found the courthouse hall deserted late at night. The display case wasn't even locked. Wick left an apology note: "Borrowed for urgent genealogical research. Will return—" The trowel was cold and real in his hands, heavy with history. *I'll bring it back. I promise,* he told himself.

***

When Wick landed in Mountain View this time, the courthouse construction had just begun. The head mason, Bill Laroe, directed men as they hauled stone blocks into place. Wick's heart beat wildly—this was it.

Not daring to interfere immediately, Wick hurried to the doctor's office—no sign of Dad. No one had been brought in recently. *I could spend weeks hopping decades waiting for the exact moment—or maybe the best way is to stay and watch.*

Exhausted, Wick pondered where to hole up. Elijah's farm was too far. He wandered near the courthouse and spotted a blacksmith's sign across the square: "Shackleford's Forge—Repairs on Plows, Horseshoeing, Knifework."

He walked inside, heart drumming. "Need any help?" Wick tried.

The blacksmith, a thick-armed Charley, eyed him up and down. "Ever worked around steel, son?"

"Once," Wick lied. Charley chuckled.

"We'll see. Sweeping's half the job. I'll feed ya, and you can sleep on a cot in back." As Charley led him to the back and handed Wick a broom, he asked, "You know the 4 H's?"

Wick glanced up. "Yeah, they teach life skills—Health, Heart, Hands, and Home."

Charley barked a laugh, shaking his head. "Not that 4H—the 4 H's of smithin': Heat, Hammer, Harden, and Hone. Heat the steel. Hammer to shape. Harden, meaning quench her right, to strengthen. Hone/sharpen to perfection. Every step is vital. Son, when you make a knife, you hold a man's life in your hands." Charley tapped a half-finished blade for emphasis. "Never forget the trapper's motto—bad knife, bad life."

Wick nodded, trying not to look as anxious as he felt.

Charley tossed a bar of steel to Wick and grinned. "Oh, and that third step's the hardest. Remember *Goldilocks and the Three Bears*—not too hot, not too cold, just right. You'll see."

Wick was grateful—close to the courthouse, food, and a roof. The forge roared all day, the fire a living beast. He learned quickly: sweeping, fanning the bellows, fetching water, working a hand-cranked blower. Charley showed him how to heat a steel bar in the coke fire until it glowed orange, hammering it flat on the anvil, then shaping it with tongs and a hammer. Every day, Wick's palms grew tougher.

He struggled the first try with a knife—didn't heat treat it enough, and it bent on the first use. Charley grunted. "Too soft. To set the edge, you have to heat it more and quench right after the color changes." The next time, Wick left it too long; it snapped the first time it struck bone. Charley shook his head. "Not a horseshoe, boy—don't cook it to death. Like I said, she's got to be just right." On the third try, Wick watched the color closely and quenched the blade in oil. When he tested the edge, it sang on the grindstone. Charley grinned. "Best knife so far. You might have the makings for this trade." Wick's heart pounded; a knife just like the one Billy gave him, years—or nearly a century—later. *Maybe this is the knife Billy gave me.*

Wick helped Charley shoe horses and fix plows, sweat pouring, laughter sometimes breaking up the hours as Charley recounted stories about runaway mules and gossip about courthouse workers. "You're not so bad for a city fella," Charley said with a wink. Wick wondered how many lifetimes it would take to learn all these trades—and how Gramps would've laughed to see him smithin'.

On weekends, the courthouse was still a hive of activity. The head mason, Bill Laroe, called to Wick across the square. "Looking for some honest pay carrying stone, sonny?"

Wick nodded and joined in, lugging heavy blocks, mixing lime mortar, and trudging up and down wooden planks. Sometimes, he'd pause at dusk to watch the sun hitting the fresh stone. *If Gramps could see me now,* he thought, exhausted and weirdly proud.

After a few weeks, Bill grinned at Wick. "You show up every time. Would you like to try a spade for posterity? I'll let you set a stone. You'll be part of this courthouse a hundred years from now."

Wick was floored. "Seriously?"

Bill handed him a trowel and a quarried sandstone block. "Lay it true." With hands trembling—not just from the labor, but from awe—Wick pressed the stone into place, second course, just below where the placard would go. The men cheered, and for once, Wick felt connected to every story this town had to tell. *Wait till Gramps hears about this.*

Two more weeks slipped past. Bill asked if Wick could ride with the crew to pick up a new load of stone—"extra hands make light work." Wick hesitated to leave, afraid of missing his dad's arrival, but finally agreed. The trip out of town was slow, and his nerves jangled every mile. The round trip took a day and a half. When they returned, Wick helped wrestle blocks from the wagon when he noticed commotion across the street—the doctor's porch buzzing with activity.

Wick's heart jumped into his throat. He stopped unloading and sprinted over. A nurse peeked out, saw Wick, and hesitated. "You here about that patient? Disoriented fella, name of George?"

Wick nodded, pulse thundering. "He's resting. Sheriff says the state hospital's coming tomorrow. Poor soul—we couldn't find kin, and he's not right in the head. Won't stop spouting about 'time' and 'missing his family.' Sorry, son."

Wick reeled. *If they send Dad off, I might lose him for good.* He tried to sound casual. "Mind if I check on him, leave a note?"

She relented. "He's locked in that side room. We had to, for his safety—he kept trying to leave."

Wick stepped down the hall, his heartbeat whooshing in his ears. Through the wavy glass, he caught a glimpse of his dad, hollow-eyed, lost but alive. Wick swallowed. The sheriff would be there at sunrise, and he only had one night to figure out how to get his dad out without getting caught.

This is it. One chance. If I fail—

Chapter 38
Midnight Escape

Wick waited for dusk to settle. Before slipping away from the blacksmith's, he thanked Charley for shelter and honest work. Charley cracked a rare smile, his hands black with soot. "If you ever want another job, Wick, you come right back. A hand like yours—I could always use." Wick grinned, blinking fast at the sting in his chest.

He went to the courthouse yard, the walls gray under a sliver of moon. Mr. Laroe was still checking the lines of stone, lantern raised high. "Mr. Laroe? Just wanted to thank you. You let me be part of something big."

Bill Laroe sized him up, then pointed the lantern beam along the fresh wall. "Mark my words. This place'll still be here a hundred years from now. Folks will come here to debate about everything under the sun. This'll be a place for justice. You belong to it now, just like the rest of us."

Wick nodded, feeling the truth of it settle in his bones. *How right you are.*

Mr. Laroe reached behind a low crate and handed Wick a canvas satchel—inside, an original blueprint with white lines on a blue background, thick with creases, and a large hand-carved dowel, smooth as bone. "Take these. The dowels are used for the attic rafters—almost ceremonial, the way we set them. Not many would know. You're a part of history now."

Wick's mouth worked silently, unable to hide his joy. "Thank you, Mr. Laroe. Really." He decided right then that these treasures would help make up for his courthouse "borrowing spree." *If I ever make it home, I'll set things right.*

***

Wick watched the windows until dark, heart running like a squirrel. A hush covered the town. When he was sure the street was clear, he slipped around the back of the clinic and jimmied the door with a file he'd found at the forge. Wick froze as he heard a wagon approach out front—the wagon passed by.

Inside, his feet barely made a sound on the boards. He found the side room the nurse had pointed out earlier. The door was heavy but unlocked—only held closed by a stout latch. Wick held his breath, shaking as he eased the bolt back. It gave with a muted scrape. The door swung open.

His dad was huddled on a narrow cot, looking gaunt and ten years older. Dad blinked, and hope lit in his eyes—a look Wick would remember forever.

Dad scrambled up, clutched Wick in a rib-squeezing hug. "Wick! Son—oh, my—are you alright?" Wick couldn't answer for a second—his throat was thick, his head light and buzzing. He hugged back, holding on for dear life.

"No time—they'll be checking soon. Can you walk?" Wick whispered.

Dad nodded, brushing his sleeve across his eyes. "I'm beat up. Walk? No—let's run!"

Together, they slipped out the back, wound through the alley, darted behind a privy, and hustled for the woods, carefully staying off the roadways. Wick's mind churned with every step—*Don't get caught. Not now. Not this close.*

When they reached thick cover, Dad doubled over, his breath coming in hard bursts, but he laughed—a ragged but real sound. "I didn't realize those Chicago marathons would come in so handy out here."

They made camp for the night barely a mile from the edge of town, sheltering in a stand of cedars. Wick set a tiny fire, more smoke than flames. Dad shivered but finally looked at Wick and managed a crooked grin. "I missed you, son. Honestly, the past two days I've been gone have been the longest days of my life."

Wick's eyes burned. "It's been months for me, Dad." The firelight played on Dad's face—hope and relief, but a storm of sadness too. They hugged again, both shaking just a little.

Dad blinked at him. "Wait—months? It's just been two lousy days."

Wick nodded, the fire throwing flickers across his face. "Time doesn't move the same for all of us. I promise—I'll explain everything."

After they settled as much as possible, Dad's curiosity burned through the tiredness. "You know, I'm amazed at how you handled those woods out there. Where'd you learn bushcraft?"

Wick smiled through the smoke. "Gramps—and a lot of practice. Nearly froze to death." They both chuckled, a moment of levity in the dark. "I had to pick it up fast—with everything going on."

Dad sobered. "Tell me—what happened? Why am I here? How'd you get here? And what happened to Mountain View? All I remember is that Vilnius pressured me to sign over the farm. I told him where to stuff his offer—Tank and Mike roughed me up, blindfolded me, and next thing I know, I'm dumped here. No one believed me—I asked for a telephone, told them about our farm, but nobody knew what I was talking about. I learned pretty quickly to keep my mouth shut. I was sure I'd lost my mind till you came in."

Another surge of gratitude hit Wick. They embraced again, this time laughter and tears all tangled in the hug.

Wick tried to fill in the gaps—how they'd come to Arkansas, how Vilnius was after the crystals and the land, how Nora had been kidnapped but was now safe back at Billy's farm in 1947. He explained the oddities of time—how days and months passed differently, how Wick had worked as a blacksmith and even helped build the courthouse.

Dad listened, awestruck, and finally shook his head in amazement. "That's—a lot to land on a kid's shoulders. Can't believe what you've done, Wick. But you did it. Kimi picked the right man for the job."

Wick tried to laugh and cry at once. He thought his heart might burst. "I'm just glad I got you back."

Dad ran a hand through his hair, looking up at the branches above them. "Well then, I guess that's it. We get Nora, go back home to 2026, expose Vilnius, and it's over, right?"

Wick hesitated, a shadow passing over his face. "Well, not quite. Kahoka told me I have to save the land in a tribal archery shoot-out."

Dad stared. "A shoot-out? Since when do you shoot a bow?"

Wick hung his head. "I—don't."

Dad raised an eyebrow, mouth quirking. "How's that work?"

Wick rubbed the back of his neck. "Honestly, I have no clue. I've been so busy trying to save you and Nora, I haven't had a chance to practice. I guess that's the next thing on my list." He paused, then added, "Oh—almost forgot. There's still the issue with the deed."

Dad frowned. "The deed?"

Wick nodded, exasperation leaking into his voice. "Yeah. The county's file copy burned. I know, it was supposed to be fireproof—turns out, wrong. Gramps and I turned the house upside down looking for another copy. Nothing. We even saw an attorney. The Quorum Court said they might drop the condemnation if we could find a copy of the deed. I've about given up."

Dad shook his head in disbelief. "That's crazy."

Wick shrugged. "Apparently, for generations, the family just kept passing it down hand to hand. No new deeds, no probate, nothing official. They're talking about letting us keep the house and maybe forty acres, but that's not enough to protect the heritage. Sometimes I wonder if Kimi picked the right man for this."

Dad reached over, squeezing Wick's shoulder. "Son, you got this far. Don't quit now. Can't believe the stars out here—and I still can't believe you made fire with flint. Wait, you made this knife too?" He let out a low whistle. "I've got a feeling it's going to take me a long time to catch up on everything you've been through."

Wick managed a tired grin. "Yeah, when you think about it, family is more important than the land. Nora's going to be so excited to see you tomorrow."

Wick sobered. Nora was safe, hidden at Billy's farm in 1947. Tomorrow, they'd fetch her, then finally head home. "Once we have Nora, I promise—we'll return to Mom, Gramps, and Gram in 2026. All together again." For the first time in months, he had hope again.

Dad's voice was thick, his eyes shining with hope. "I can't wait. Just—let's not waste another minute."

Wick nodded, watching the thin slice of moonrise and listening to his dad's steady breathing. As he sat beside the dwindling fire, Wick stoked the embers, gratitude and relief mixing with fresh worry about what might come next. But for now, Wick rested with his dad safe, hope for morning burning bright. Whatever tomorrow brought, Wick wouldn't face it alone.

Chapter 39
Repaying Debts

Wick's mind whirled with next steps as he tucked the ceremonial trowel, dowel, and blueprint into his canvas satchel. *Reunite Nora and Dad. That's first. After that, return the trowel. Make things right before someone else notices.* He ticked them off like a mental checklist, each marked by resolve. *I can't leave a mess behind. Not if I can help it.*

They were still in 1922, the world edged with cool gray dawn. Wick led the way, picking a route that snaked up hills, dropped through hollows, and wove around bramble fence lines. They crossed creek after creek, boots slipping on wet rocks, every draw a potential hiding spot if they heard anyone coming. Dad asked about shortcuts, but Wick shook his head. "Easier to get lost than found—or spotted by the authorities. Roads are too risky."

He noticed Dad glancing at him occasionally, lips pressed tight, yet never complaining. Wick couldn't tell if it was trust or exhaustion, but Dad followed, nonetheless.

The familiar ridge near Elijah's farm appeared as the sun peaked overhead. Wick tugged at Dad's coat sleeve, exchanging a glance—Wick nervous, Dad skeptical. *How do you even start to prepare your dad for time travel?* Wick let a smile slip. "This isn't your first trip, you know," he said as they neared the signal tree. "Tank and Mike dragged you once, but you were out cold."

Dad's eyebrows shot up. "So—side effects?"

Wick grinned. "Just a little bit of nausea. Trust me."

Dad eyed the tree suspiciously, but Wick pressed his palm to the bark before he could ask more and nudged his dad's shoulder. The world spun, stomachs lurched, and Dad clutched his knees, hacking. "Whoa," he coughed, blinking at the sun-bright world of 1947. "You weren't kidding."

Wick steadied his dad. "It passes." He looked up as Nora barreled across the yard, hair flying, legs pumping.

"Dad!" Her shriek cracked as she crashed into his arms. Dad staggered under her weight—hug became grip, grip became sob. Nora buried her face in his shirt and clung to him. "I thought—I thought—" She choked on the words. Tears streamed down both their faces.

Wick stood aside, fighting a wave of exhaustion and emotion. His mind went blank, overwhelmed—no words were grand enough for this moment. He forced himself to breathe, to blink. *They're finally together. I promised Nora and Dad, and now it's real.*

Elijah stepped onto the porch, Myrtle behind him, an apron still at her waist. Sarah called for Boyd, who peeked out wide-eyed at the strangers. Billy grinned and elbowed Wick, but Wick just offered a tired half-smile. Greetings blurred—shaking hands, introductions—but the world seemed to orbit Nora and Dad.

Lunch began with Nora glued to her father, glancing up at him every few seconds. Dad clasped her shoulder, ruffled her hair, and looked down at her. Myrtle set plates in front of them, and Elijah asked about their route from town, raising his brow at muddy boots. Wick gave a tired shrug. "Just glad to be here." *Anywhere not being chased by the authorities.*

After lunch, the family stepped outside. Wick absorbed the warmth, then noticed new framing nailed to the far side of the house. Elijah explained, "We're finally putting in that well pump—decided it was time for a bathroom, laundry, and another bedroom for guests."

Dad brightened, examining the new floor joists. "Need a hand with the framing?"

Elijah flashed a grateful grin. "Wouldn't turn down the help. Here, grab the other end of this joist."

As the sun angled lower, Wick remembered what still tugged at his conscience: the courthouse trowel. He found Dad helping Elijah. "Would you be okay staying here with Elijah and everyone? I've got to run to town to return something I borrowed. It could be late before I get back."

Dad laid a reassuring hand on his shoulder. "Sure, I guess two decades is enough for them to stop searching for us." That earned a round of laughter—Billy even snorted.

Dad continued, "We're surrounded by family, Wick. We'll be fine. Do what you need to do. We'll be here."

Wick packed a sandwich, gave Nora a lopsided smile, and left the house around 2 PM. As luck would have it, when Wick reached the main road, a farmer with a tired-looking pickup offered him a ride, the road dust swirling in the heat. Wick's nerves twisted the whole way. He wished a truck could cut through time as easily as the signal tree.

He rolled into Mountain View in the early afternoon, the courthouse looming against the afternoon sky. Wick circled the area to pass time, his heart ratcheting up notch by notch. *This should be simple. Quick in, quick out. Just return the trowel without getting caught.*

Entering the courthouse, he ducked into the men's room just before closing. He waited as long as he dared for footsteps, doors, and silence. *Just a few more minutes, and I'm out of here.* At last, he crept into the hall. The display case glass caught the light. Wick pressed it open, hands sweating as he set in the trowel, the blueprint, and the dowel. He placed the note carefully atop the shelf, heart thundering:

Sorry for borrowing the trowel. Hope you forgive me. Believe it or not, here are an original blueprint and one of the original attic rafter dowels. Thank you for preserving these artifacts.

Just another minute. As he closed the glass display case door, he heard a flashlight switch on behind him, the beam reflecting off the glass door into his eyes.

A deep voice cut the hush. "Move away from that case, son."

Wick turned, blinking at the badge glinting on a thick sheriff's jacket. "I'm Sheriff Maddox. Mind telling me what you're doing here?"

Wick tried for calm, but his throat felt dry as dust. "Returning the trowel, sir. There's a note."

"Borrowed it, huh?" The sheriff didn't smile. "Borrowing without asking is theft. You're spending the night in jail until the judge can talk with you. Might be late morning."

Wick's arms felt heavy as the sheriff marched him across the square. The stone jail cell was cold—the concrete floor, the metal bars all unforgiving. Once alone, Wick slumped onto the bunk, head in his hands. *You never could break even, could you? Now, Dad and Nora will worry. This was supposed to be the easy part.*

Time dragged; his head swirled with shame and what-ifs. *Repaying debts—sure. But who's going to rescue the rescuer?*

Thirty minutes later, footsteps echoed on the stone. A silver-haired man in a sharp suit appeared outside the bars. "Hello, son. What's your name?"

"Wick," he muttered.

The man motioned to Sheriff Maddox. "Open the cell, please." The cell door opened, and Wick stepped out, wary.

The man smiled, extending a hand. "Nice to meet you, Wick. I'm the county judge. Walk with me."

As they crossed the square toward the courthouse, the judge showed no hurry. "Heard you left some items behind—blueprints, dowel, and a trowel on the shelf."

"Yes, sir," Wick said.

"How'd you come about those items?"

Wick hesitated, voice tight. "A family member worked on the original construction of the courthouse with head mason, Bill Laroe. Mr. Laroe gave him those things at the end of the job: the original blueprint and the ceremonial dowel pin for the attic rafters. The family wanted to see them preserved."

The judge paused. "They look original. Not many people know about the attic dowels. And the trowel looks undamaged. Mind telling me why you needed to borrow it?"

Wick hesitated. "I'm sorry. I can't say, sir. Just know it was important. I guess I'll have to take my lumps."

The judge studied him for a long moment. "Wick, do I know any of your relatives?"

Wick said softly, "Maybe. John Jenkins' family."

The judge's expression lit up. "John Jenkins—why, he's a war hero. He saved my brother's life at Normandy. Son, I'm sorry for your loss. John was a good man, and many in this town have him to thank for their lives and the lives of their loved ones. It's a shame he didn't make it back. You know, we need a memorial to honor men like John. Maybe I can make that happen."

Wick smiled. "That sounds great, Judge. I mean, if it honored those who paid the ultimate sacrifice of their lives in war, it might read something like, *'Our Stone County Sons.'* I'd love to see it in front of the courthouse someday—names inscribed in granite with an eagle watching over."

The judge smiled, appearing genuine and warm. "Listen. You returned the trowel. We're good. You can go. And by the way, thank you for the note and the new treasures. They are a testament to your character and integrity. I don't know why you needed the trowel, but I hope it helped you with whatever need you had. Besides, our blueprint copy had faded. Need a ride?"

Wick managed, "Could you get me to Misenheimer Road? I can walk home from there."

The judge winked and turned to Maddox. "Don't you have a patrol that way tonight?"

The sheriff nodded.

Wick settled into the front seat, the courthouse vanishing behind him. He watched shadows crawl across the fields, the satchel heavy in his lap. Somewhere back at Elijah's farm, Dad and Nora were probably laughing by the lantern glow. Just having them together seemed almost impossible—almost enough.

Maybe it's not the land or the artifacts that matter most. Not if I bring Dad and Nora home. Family is the win, even if the land slips away.

The sheriff stopped at Misenheimer Road. Wick climbed out, taking a long breath of sweet freedom, and watched the patrol car drive off.

For the first time in months, Wick felt something close to peace settle in his chest instead of dread. Home wasn't a place. It was the people you hold onto, no matter which century you find them in.

Chapter 40
The Hidey-Hole

The night at Billy's farm passed like a slow exhale. Wick lay awake, the rhythm of the evening frogs blending with his heartbeat, his brain replaying every moment since he rescued Dad and Nora. *You did it,* Wick tried to reassure himself, but even when resting, part of him scanned for what still needed doing—what threats still lingered. He was getting good at running inventory on his fears, but it never got easier.

***

Dawn brought the sound of boots scuffing dusty porch boards and the sharp *thunk* of hammers on wood. Wick found Dad and Elijah already hard at work, moving a monstrous joist beam into place to frame the new addition floor.

Wow. So, this is how they built houses before electric drills and nail guns.

"Hand me that end, Wick," Dad called, sweat already matting his brow. The board was heavier than Wick expected. He drew a breath, squared his shoulders, and forced muscle into the lift. Shoulders burning, arms shaking—*this must be what accomplishment feels like in your hands, not your head.*

In half an hour, the three of them had wrestled the last joist onto its ledger and pounded it into place. Elijah whistled and wiped his brow. "You boys finish that one, and I can handle these walls myself—all two-by-fours, nobody's getting a hernia."

Wick's dad grinned at him and shook his hand, their rough palms sticky with sawdust and effort. For one golden moment, Wick felt like he belonged—like he'd earned his spot, not by accident or time warp, but by showing up.

I can't believe I just helped with the addition to Gramps's home.

As Elijah continued to mark with a knife-sharpened pencil, Wick saw him frame up a small box—a tight rectangle, maybe a foot and a half wide and two feet long, ten inches deep—blending it between two joists. "What's that box for?" Wick asked, curiosity pulling him closer.

Elijah glanced around and pressed a finger to his lips. "*Shhh.* Hidey-hole. For valuables. Hidden right in the floor; cover's a double layer—nobody'd ever think to look. Heck, we can even keep important papers in there. Better than a bank, and nobody charges you a fee."

Wick's breath caught. *Wait. In 2026, this is the guest bedroom. The corner—thirty inches off the base molding. Could it still be there?* He fumbled for words, but his mind raced ahead, mapping every inch of the modern house as memory clicked into place. *Neither Gramps nor I ever checked that spot. Nobody would have.*

He nearly blurted it out but grinned, pulse racing instead. *If the deed and the old documents were ever truly hidden, that's where they'd be. No wonder nobody found them.*

"You all right, Wick?" Dad asked, eyebrows raised.

"I will be," Wick said, barely containing his excitement. Inside, a dozen plans spun. *If I can get us back, and if it's still there.* "I think we ought to hurry home. I'm—uh—itching to get back," he managed.

Wick drew well water. Boy, won't they be glad to get *a pump!* They cleaned up and thanked Elijah, Myrtle, Sarah, Billy, and little Boyd. Goodbyes took time—handshakes, teary hugs, reminders to visit.

Before leaving, Wick found Billy near the garden's edge, hands in his pockets. Wick pulled a cloth-wrapped bundle from his satchel—a perfectly balanced knife he'd made at the blacksmith's in 1922.

He pressed it into Billy's palm. "For you, Shooter. Made this myself. Took three tries and a lot of sweat. But Charley said a good knife can make the difference between getting lost and coming home."

Billy's eyes widened. He turned the blade over, nodding as if weighing its heft in his mind. "You just might be a blacksmith after all."

Wick smiled, choking back emotion. "For all the times you helped me find my way. Seems right you should carry it now."

Billy slipped the knife into his belt. "Thank you, Wick. You've given me more than you know."

As they made their way to the signal tree, they looked back to see Boyd waving a stick in circles.

Dad shook his head and chuckled. "Never thought I'd see my father-in-law as a six-year-old. Time travel's something else."

Nora snorted, looping her arm through Dad's. "If Gramps ever tells me to clean my room, I'm not listening to a six-year-old." They all laughed. Wick pulled them together for a last squeeze. "Ready?" They laid hands on the signal tree, and the world shivered, leaving the 1947 farm behind.

***

They landed in 2026 to shouts, tears, and the steamroller force of the Shepperd family reunion. Gram's hands flung over her mouth in relief. Mom grabbed Nora, Dad, and Wick until Wick thought she'd never let go. Latesha threw her arms around Wick, whispering into his ear, "You did it."

Even Gramps, stoic as bedrock, put his hand on Wick's shoulder and said, "You brought them home." Nora sobbed into Mom's arms, Dad laughing and crying at once, everyone in a knot of voices and hugs. Wick hung near the edge, shell-shocked and fiercely glad—not just for surviving, but for answered prayers.

He wanted to race straight to the bedroom floorboards, to check, to be sure, but forced himself to drink in the laughter and let the moment breathe. *Family first. The rest will wait. Just a little longer, I can wait.*

The celebration paused as a sheriff's cruiser rolled up, crunching gravel as it abruptly stopped. The sheriff stepped out, yellow notice in hand, face grave as he walked up to Gramps. The sheriff spoke quietly and solemnly. "Sorry, Boyd, they're giving you forty-eight hours to produce proof of ownership of the three thousand acres, or the county plans to condemn the land. Only the house and forty acres stay. Not a penny for the rest if you can't show the deed."

Gramps shook his head. "Tom, that's bad news. We haven't been able to find it. Any chance they will delay again if we ask?"

"Sorry, Boyd. They seem pretty firm. I don't see any chance of appeal without that deed."

A hush fell. Wick felt all eyes turn. He met Dad's and Gramps's gazes and didn't wait. "I'll be right back!" He grabbed the axe and sprinted past cries of "He's gone loco!" into the house.

In the guest room, he knelt, measured out from the baseboard, and knocked for a hollow sound.

He took the axe to the top vinyl layer, peeling it back to expose the flooring underneath—an older layer of milled pine with tongue-and-groove, worn with age.

Nora huffed from the doorway. "He really has gone mad."

Sweat slid down his temples. Running his fingers along the boards, he searched for an uneven seam. There, barely visible. He wedged the axe blade into the crease and levered it up, splinters cracking. The scent of musk rolled out from below. Beneath the trap door—documents wrapped in oilcloth, a sheaf of old deeds, survey maps, abstract of title, receipts with signatures fading to sepia. The original deed, with every transfer intact.

Gramps let out a low whistle. "Well, I'll be doggone. Didn't know that it was there. Son, you just uncovered history." He leaned closer, eyes narrowing at the faded ink. "This changes everything." He took the papers with trembling hands.

The sheriff smiled, relief washing over his face. He tore the court papers in half. "That ought to do."

Laughter spilled down the hallway, pure and bright as sunlight, and the whole house seemed to breathe again. Latesha squeezed Wick's hand so hard his fingers tingled. "You did it," she whispered.

Wick grinned, soaking it all in.

As the reunion drifted toward dinner, Wick pulled Latesha aside. "It's not over yet. I still have something left to do." She squeezed his arm, smile wide and proud.

Later, alone in his room, Wick tried to savor the victory, but the thrill faded fast. *I pulled off the impossible—family and land. But now I have to figure out the archery shoot. Kahoka's warning is still hanging over my head. Bow skills? There's a reason I never made the archery team in gym class. I barely know where to start!*

For a second, he wanted to curl up and forget prophecy and contests. But then he remembered how every step, creek splash, axe swing, and hug brought him here. To family, to purpose. *If I could do all this, maybe I could learn to hit a target at a hundred yards, too.*

Wick pressed a hand over his heart, feeling the beat slow and steady. Tomorrow, he'd ask Kahoka for help. Tomorrow he'd start becoming the hero Kimi and Kahoka—and his own family—believed he could be.

Chapter 41
The Gifts We Carry

The farm was at peace. The family was together. Heat shimmered over the hayfields, and the kitchen clattered with the bustle. Wick wanted to feel at rest, but one thought persisted. *You saved everyone. You found the deed—but you still have to face that prophecy. Bow shooting. The shoot-out. Guardian. I saved my family, but can I save a legacy?*

The sun filtered through thin storm clouds, painting the fields around the Jenkins farm a pale silver. Wick sat on the porch, legs dangling. The morning reunion had drifted toward chores and familiar routines. Nora and Dad were helping Gram and Gramps, and the deed was now tucked in a fireproof box.

He remembered Kahoka's warning, the shadow of prophecy, the cornstalk shoot he only half-understood. Wick stood, dusted off his jeans, grabbed his gear, and told Mom he was headed out. She just smiled and waved, like a trip to a parallel timeline was something Wick did every Saturday.

Wick stopped and held up a finger. "Wait! Mom, do we have more peppermints? I can't show up again without mints. The kids will flog me."

Mom checked the pantry and shook her head. "We're out."

Gramps chimed in. "He might appreciate a good drawknife, a wood rasp, and a file. And every outdoorsman loves another knife."

Latesha called from behind, holding her bandolier. "Bet they'd love seed beads and thread, like these."

Wick shook his head. "Really? I just wanted mints. You sure I need to take all that stuff? You know I got to lug it around."

Mom smiled. "Wick, honey. That's how you make friends. Look how much they're helping you."

Gramps motioned. "Come on, Wick, you're outnumbered."

Wick just shook his head and followed him.

Mountain View bustled—music on the square, an artisan hammering molten iron into intricate designs, sparks dancing in the air. They swung by Uncle Billy's for a visit—a rare moment for Wick to catch him up.

"Nora and Dad are safe. We found the deed. I even worked a forge and made a knife, which I gave you when we left the farm."

Billy's eyes shone. "Well, that's something, Wick." He fiddled with the worn band of his old cap. "Remember, Vilnius is like a Hydra's head—you cut one off, and two more take its place." He smiled, but there was a restlessness in it.

Wick hesitated, remembering something Gramps said earlier— that he'd thought he spotted Billy talking to one of Vilnius's guys behind the feed store, maybe Big Mike. Perhaps it was just a case of mistaken identity, but it nagged at Wick. "Gramps says Vilnius is still sniffing around town. He thought he saw you talking to one of those guys, maybe Big Mike, behind the store. Everything okay?"

Billy's smile faded, and his eyes glanced away. "Me? With those two?" He let out a low chuckle. "You know I have friends all over town, but I don't do business with villains. Sometimes stories get tangled up in crowds." He paused, then added, "That's a lot you've done, Wick. Glad you got your family through. But sometimes you have to play the long game. You'll see." For a heartbeat, Wick saw something uncertain behind Billy's eyes—guilt or worry—but Billy's smile snapped back into place before he could press. "Wish I could promise smooth sailing from here."

Afterward, they stopped at the candy store for peppermints— and, at Gramps's urging, a run to the secondhand shop and hardware store for woodworking tools, beads, and two sheath knives. Wick checked the list, laughter breaking through worry.

As they loaded the truck, Wick felt eyes on him. He turned and locked gazes with Vilnius, who watched from across the square: no words, no warning, just a cold stare. Gramps squeezed Wick's shoulder. "Don't let him get in your head, son. He's out of cards."

Wick nodded, but the unease lingered. *Even when you have what you need, danger's never far away.*

Back home, he packed everything: mints, the drawknife, rasp, file, knives, beads, and a handful of family good wishes. Mom hugged him fiercely. "Come back safe. Come back proud."

Wick hurried to the woods and the signal tree. He braced himself and touched the tree's bark, feeling his nerves churn. *No time for doubt. This is what heroes do, right?*

The woods at Kahoka's camp felt more alive than ever. Ferns brushed Wick's shins, their dew vanishing into his pant legs, and every leaf whispered stories. Up ahead, Kahoka sat with his back to Wick, a stone-bladed hatchet in hand, grinding its edge against a smooth river rock with slow, deliberate strokes. The rhythmic scrape blended with the murmur of the nearby creek, helping to mask the sound of his footsteps.

Wick hesitated, shifting his weight as he moved closer. Could he slip up unnoticed? Just once? He held his breath, careful with his steps, but before he got within reach—

"Welcome, Wick," Kahoka said, voice steady, gaze still fixed ahead.

Wick exhaled a quiet laugh. "I knew I couldn't sneak up on you, but I had to try."

Kahoka straightened, finally turning toward him, a knowing smile ghosting his lips. "Nice try. I'm glad you're here. You look like a man with too many victories and not enough rest."

Wick let a nervous laugh escape. "I don't think I've had enough of either, honestly." He hesitated, then plunged forward. "Kahoka— I need to become an expert bow shooter, and—" The words tangled. "I haven't practiced. I don't even own a bow. I can't make one, and I can't buy one like your bow."

Kahoka nodded, expression grave. "Every warrior begins without a weapon. The difference is whether he learns to wield one through sweat, pain, and discipline." He motioned for Waya, his son.

Wick tensed—he remembered the first time he'd met Waya, disdain showing in every movement of his frame, challenge in his eyes. This time was no different. Waya strode up, arms crossed, face thunderous. Kahoka spoke quietly. "My best archer, my son, will teach you."

Waya looked Wick up and down, a sneer tugging his lips. "Teach the outsider to shoot? I'd sooner lend my bow to a crow. A man must earn the right to string an arrow." Waya turned and stalked back toward the trees like the first time they met.

Wick slumped, trying not to feel small. Kahoka placed a calloused hand on Wick's shoulder. "Perhaps we need another teacher. There is someone whose skill is beyond both mine and Waya's—my father, Atsadi." Kahoka reached for a handwoven bandolier bag, its beadwork shimmering in the firelight. "Bring this. My father will know you come with my blessing. Go to the day we first parted at the cave. That is a place and time I know his camp will be near where we first met."

Wick remembered that moment perfectly. After nearly drowning, he met Kahoka and Kimi that day. "How will I recognize your father?" Wick asked.

Kahoka's eyes narrowed in gentle pride. "You will know him by his hands—thick with calluses, forever stained with Osage orange dust and sinew, each finger tracing the memory of a thousand bows shaped under his care. His eyes are keen, measuring every limb, every curve, as if the world itself were another bow waiting to be refined. His stance is steady, his shoulders strong, though age has begun to settle in his bones. When he speaks, his voice resonates with wisdom and the sharp edge of precision, as if every word were another arrow he has loosed into the air. And if you listen closely, beneath the crackling fire and rustling leaves, you will hear the rhythmic rasp of his drawknife—his signature, his heartbeat in the woods." Kahoka paused. "Tell him you are Tayen, my brother. And tell him I send my love—though he will know it already."

Wick nodded, his mouth dry. "Before I go, I brought gifts."

Kahoka studied the gifts, a slow smile breaking through his usually serious expression. "Ah, mints—the kids will devour these faster than a summer rain. Beads! Yes!" His eyes gleamed as he picked through them. "Two knives? I'll take one." He turned, already planning. "The other knife and woodworking tools—take them to my father, Atsadi. He'll put them to good use."

Wick nodded, clutching the gifts. *Now, find Atsadi and see if a kid like me can become the archer the tribe is counting on.*

Chapter 42
Practice Makes Perfect

Wick pressed his hand to the signal tree. Before porting, he tucked the bandolier bag Kahoka had given him deep in his satchel. *Find Kahoka's father, Atsadi.*

Wick arrived—nothing but woods and birds for company. He headed east, seven miles of ridges and creeks—no path, just memory and the sun slanting low. Every mile was earned: boots soaked, shoulders aching, chilled as he sloshed across shallow creeks, climbing banks with roots for handholds. The thought of family back at Gramps's—gathered, laughing—warmed him and made him lonely all the same.

Hours later, on a ridge above the White River, Wick caught sight of smoke from a distant campfire. He hiked to the river bottom. Soon, he heard voices drifting—laughter, orders, innocence, and discipline twined together. Wick adjusted the bandolier bag. *You came this far. Don't collapse at the edge.*

As he neared tents, two young men intercepted him near the edge of the camp. "Outsider, camp's off limits."

He tried to keep his voice steady. "Kahoka sent me."

The two men conversed, then one of the men held out his hands and asked, "Who is Kahoka?"

"Tsiyi, I mean Tsiyi sent me," Wick added hastily. "I'm Tayen. He said his father might help." He raised the bandolier bag.

Their expressions did not change. "We don't know you. Wait here."

Wick found a fallen log and sat. This test was patience, and maybe humility too.

A hawk circled—one sweep, another—lower and lower. Children pointed; tall warriors stared. The hawk finally settled on a bush beside Wick, seemingly waiting. This caught the attention of an older man.

"You hold my son's bag," the elder said. "Is he well?"

"Yes." Wick stood and bowed slightly. "Atsadi. Tsiyi sent me. I'm Tayen. I—" His voice broke.

Atsadi motioned for him to approach. "Come. Sit by my fire. If my son trusts you, so can I—but tell me why."

Wick sat, heart racing. He opened his satchel and spread out the gifts—a new knife, a drawknife, a wood rasp, and a file. "These are for you—from my family. Tools for working wood, for bows, for whatever is needed. And a knife for your work."

Atsadi's eyes widened at the drawknife, weighing it in his hands. He traced the blade, then ran his fingers over the rasp's teeth and the file's smooth spine. Finally, he tested the balance of the knife. "These are gifts of a craftsman, not a tourist," Atsadi said quietly. "You honor my camp, Tayen. You understand what it means to give what you value." He nodded deeply, a genuine smile breaking his dignified face. "I will use these well—and remember your hands and your journey each time."

Wick settled onto a woven mat by the fire and took a risk: the whole story, not just the need. "It started with a crystal, a gift from my uncle—a crystal that worked with a tree near our home in my time. The signal tree lets me travel across time if I have something from the right era." He pressed on: how Nora was taken, how he found Kahoka, the hawk that greeted them, how they followed it to a cave, how they met Kimi, the ancient guardian, were chosen as guardians, each for his world, and how Kimi gave both Wick and Tsiyi new names.

"He gave Kahoka wolf hearing. He gave me hawk vision. Then Vilnius—a man in my time—attacked my family, tried to take what wasn't his, and hunted my people. I fought—I saved them, but only because others helped me. Kahoka warned that my real test is yet to come: the tribal cornstalk shoot. I need to win. But—I don't know how. I barely know how to hold a bow."

Atsadi listened intently, eyes shining in firelight. "You walk a strange but honest path, Tayen."

Wick found himself choking up. "And I need help. I don't want to let my family—or yours—down."

Atsadi nodded. "Show me your hawk vision. Let me see with you."

Wick hesitated, rubbing his arms. "I can use hawk vision, but I don't know how or if I can share with others."

Atsadi smiled, moved closer to the fire, and reached out his hands. "Give me your hands. Close your eyes. Picture not the ground, but air—soaring, feeling the currents."

Wick obeyed, heart thudding, feeling Atsadi's strong hands grip his own. He imagined soaring, wind on feathers, the land mapped out below. Suddenly, his mind swooped outward, senses stretching. Atsadi's voice seemed to join his, guiding him: "Go find my son."

Wick's vision, sharpened by hawk-sight and Atsadi's steady mind, found Kahoka among another tribe, teaching children peacefully and contentedly.

Atsadi let go, smiling. "He's well, Tayen. You have much to teach—even when you don't know your way. Kimi chose well." Atsadi added softly, "Now, I will show you how to make and shoot a bow."

Atsadi led Wick to a well-worn, open-air workspace near the forest's edge, with hand-carved tools laid out on smooth logs and shavings of hickory and Osage orange scattered across the ground. "A warrior learns with his own hands," he said, handing Wick a length of seasoned Osage orange wood.

Together they worked methodically: chopping, whittling, wrapping sinew, gluing nocks, burnishing arrows, fletching with turkey and hawk feathers. On the third morning, a hawk landed at the edge of camp, clutching six bright feathers. Atsadi took them reverently. "With this, we can make four magic arrows. We will also make four regular arrows. Balance, always balance." The magic arrows went into a special case. Wick practiced only with the regular arrows.

At first, they started at a target just twenty feet away, made of tightly packed straw with a large hide stretched behind to catch stray arrows. Wick was surprised—he tried not to show his disappointment at such a short distance. "Isn't that a little close?"

Atsadi smiled. "No man builds a house of stone without laying gravel first. Master the near. We'll move the target when you're ready. That's the way of things—small to great."

Wick remembered Kahoka's trick of rotating his left elbow outward to avoid the string slap. Wick barely hit the center for days. If not for the stretched hide, he would have lost arrows. His arms ached, fingers blistered. After the first evening, Atsadi showed Wick how to make a finger tab out of hide. Atsadi's patience never faltered. "Aim small. Miss small. Respect every arrow the same."

Nights, by the fire, Wick told stories—how nearly losing Nora and Dad burned him to the core; how finding courage meant leaning on others; how land and family were saved only by others' love and faith. Atsadi listened deeply, nodded, and when Wick paused, shared stories of Kahoka's youth, ancestors' resourcefulness, and how quiet endurance wins the day.

Each time Wick began grouping his arrows on a hand-sized cloth, Atsadi quietly moved Wick back. Each time, Wick failed, missing nearly everything, muttering under his breath, but each slight improvement felt like a miracle: shoulders stronger, arms truer, mind clearer. After two moons, Wick at last stood fifty paces away. Atsadi finally said, "Try the cornstalk bundle."

The cornstalk bundle—three feet by four feet, set a hundred yards away—looked as small as hope itself. Wick's first arrow fell short. The next soared over. Sweat poured as he fired again, better, but still only grazed the edge. But the fourth shot—Wick paused, drew in, remembered Atsadi's advice, and hit the cornstalks near the top.

For two more moons, Wick practiced hours each day, each time starting at fifty paces and moving back as he hit the center.

Atsadi blindfolded Wick, spun him, and led him to a random distance. "When I take this off, you'll shoot before I count to three."

The first time, Wick hesitated, thinking too long.

Atsadi shook his head. "Too long. You're dead. A warrior can't hesitate. Assume confidence. Shoot instinctively or not at all. Draw the arrow as you raise the bow and let go. No thinking."

Each day, Atsadi repeated the drill, and each time, Wick shot a little faster. Blindfolded, unblindfolded, instinct over thought. After a few days, his arrow clipped the edge. Then, at last, one hit dead center.

On the final day, Atsadi brought out the magic arrows. "Now two at the cornstalks at a hundred yards, and one blindfolded." Wick's chest drummed. He nailed two arrows without hesitation. On the blindfolded shot, he drew, turned, and hit dead center—before Atsadi's count reached three.

"You're right, Atsadi. The arrows are magic," Wick cheered.

Atsadi laughed and pulled out six hawk feathers from behind his back and placed his hand over Wick's heart. "There's magic, Tayen, but not in the arrows—in you. That hawk's been trained to fetch stray feathers for years." He winked. "You never know what's possible until you try."

Wick tried to grin, still awed by the final shot. But doubt crept in as he looked at the bow and arrows resting in his grip. He glanced at Atsadi, his voice small. "What if I'm still not enough? What if I let everyone down?"

Atsadi fetched a tanned pouch and filled it with the arrows. "You are ready. This bow, these arrows, are yours. And I have more for you to deliver." He placed a new, finely made pair of moccasins and a second bow—worn, polished, obviously treasured—into Wick's bundle. "These are for my son, Kahoka. These moccasins will travel new trails, but the bow will remind him where he learned. Tell him he has my pride and my love. And you, Tayen—you are my son too."

Wick blinked. "But—my mother told me I'm only part Cherokee. I don't look like you or Kahoka. I've never—"

Atsadi's hand rested on Wick's chest, steady and sure. "No matter the part, you are blood of my blood. Not the tint of your skin, but the spirit in your heart. Respect for elders, family, tradition— the things that matter are earned, not given. You are the heritage and son you become."

Wick's throat closed. Atsadi hugged Wick fiercely, holding him for a long moment. "I love you, Tayen. I am proud, no matter *which* path you follow."

Wick swallowed hard. "Thank you. For everything. I hope I can be worthy." Even with bows and precious gifts slung over his shoulders, he felt lighter than when he'd arrived.

He hesitated at the camp's edge, doubts surfacing again. *I've practiced. I've learned. But am I ready? What if my best isn't enough?* He almost turned back—just one more day, one more lesson, one more story from Atsadi. But instead, Wick turned to Atsadi, placed his hand on his chest, then headed west toward the signal tree, arrows slung at his side, carrying the dawn of a new hope.

He still wasn't sure of his worthiness. But with each step through the dew, he knew: the only way to find out was to try.

Chapter 43
The Measure of Mercy

Wick felt lighter on the port home than ever before. The handmade bow and arrows from Atsadi rode against his shoulder—a reminder of all he'd learned in the last few weeks. He hurried toward the house, already rehearsing how he'd tell Gramps and Mom about Atsadi's teachings, the hawk feathers, how everyone in camp wanted to examine the tools. They would love to hear that the gifts meant something.

Before he could get a word out, Latesha nearly tackled him. Her eyes looked panicky, her hands shaking around her phone.

"Wick—Abby called. She said her dad's lost it. She doesn't have all the details, but she said Vilnius is ranting about undoing history, stopping the beginning, and winning. She thinks he's going to try something desperate."

Wick's gut dropped. "If he knows about the prophecy, maybe he wants to stop the cornstalk shoot. Or worse." He led Latesha into the house, heart pounding.

Before reaching the house, the family clustered on the porch. Wick looked back to see what had caught their attention: a white wolf at the shadowed edge of the timber, and above it, a hawk, silent in the branches, both gazing toward the house.

"That's not a coyote," Gramps muttered. He disappeared inside and returned with an old twelve-gauge leveled at the trees. "I'm firing a warning shot—cover your ears."

Wick stepped forward, gently encouraging Gramps to lower the barrel with a steady hand. "It's okay, Gramps. They're not a threat. They're a message meant for me." He glanced at the porch, where the rest of the family stood, their anxious faces carved with uncertainty. "I have to go."

He grabbed his gear, backpack, bow, and arrows. Giving a last nod, he jumped off the porch and jogged toward the cave. *This is it; I can't falter.*

At the hidden nook in the cave, Wick found a smooth stone— an artifact from Kahoka. He clutched it, stepping into the light beyond the cavern's mouth. The path to the signal tree stretched before him, each step driven by urgency.

When he reached the tree, he pressed his palm against the rough bark, feeling the gentle swirl, the dizzy certainty of time shifting.

He arrived, and—strangely—Kahoka was there. Usually patient and reserved, this time Kahoka's eyes were wide, shoulders tensed.

"Wick! It's Waya. He wants to be the hero. He took the artifact and went back for the shoot-out. I can't follow—I can't port to my lifetime. Something's wrong—history's changing; things I used to remember are fuzzy."

Wick started to explain Vilnius's threat but stopped himself. "Kahoka, I'll go. I'll protect Waya. I promise."

Kahoka grabbed his arm. "How did it go—with Atsadi?"

Even in the tension, Wick couldn't keep a proud grin off his face. "Perfect. He sent you this bow, and made me this one," Wick said, holding up the bow. "He sends his love. And I can shoot."

Kahoka eyed him, skeptical. "Show me. See that gourd?"

Wick nodded, dropped his gear, nocked an arrow, spun, and shot—dead center. The gourd leaped and split down the middle.

A smile broke through Kahoka's worry. "I knew Atsadi could get you up to speed. Now go! Find Waya. Let me know as soon as you can."

Wick picked up his things, took another artifact from Kahoka's open hand, and vanished at the signal tree—his nerves tingling, the phrase *don't hesitate* pounding with every heartbeat.

***

He arrived in a world tense with crisis—Vilnius's shadow already felt in the air. Wick switched his hawk vision high, eyes sweeping valleys and ridges until he saw a scrape of cliff with Vilnius, Kahoka, Waya, and Big Mike. Wick's pulse thundered. *They'll kill him.*

He ran, clumsily at first, through brambles and ducking under limbs, arrows bouncing at his side. Drawing closer, he assessed the scene: Big Mike holding Waya at gunpoint, Vilnius shoving a rifle at young Kahoka, both of them perilously near a ledge.

Wick stopped at a vantage point fifty yards away, drew his bow, and yelled, "Hey! Let him go—or I'll shoot!"

Big Mike scoffed. "Don't worry, Mr. V. I've seen this kid shoot. He couldn't make that shot in a hundred tries."

Wick called back, keeping the bow steady. "Mike, don't be so sure. I don't want to hurt you—but I will if I have to. Trust me."

Mike scoffed. "Not buying it. You got lucky once, but I ain't worried."

"See that pine cone above your head?" Wick challenged.

"Yeah. So what?"

Wick loosed the arrow—one clean motion. The pine cone shattered, raining fragments on Mike's head.

Mike's eyes widened, fear kicking in. "All right, all right!" He set his rifle on the dirt and stepped back, hands raised. "Kid, I'm done. I never signed up for this."

"Waya, come here," Wick called. "Mike, get out of here and don't come back."

As Waya scampered across, mouth agape, Vilnius shouted, jabbing the barrel at Kahoka, forcing him forward. "Careful! One move, and this ends. Drop your bow, or you're both finished."

Vilnius shifted his stance—just enough of his right shoulder appeared as a possible target. In a split-second decision, Wick drew, aimed, and fired.

The arrow struck Vilnius's shoulder, sending the rifle flying. Vilnius toppled over, body partly hanging off the bluff's edge. Kahoka whirled and grabbed him, keeping him from falling.

Wick rushed to help, heaving Vilnius back to safety. He kicked the gun to the side.

Waya, shaking, stared at Wick. "How—?"

Wick shrugged, fighting a grin. "Thank your grandpa, Atsadi. You'd be surprised what a little training can do."

"My grandpa, Atsadi? You met him? I want to go."

Wick turned, steadying a hand on Waya's shoulder. "Waya, he'd be proud to know he has a grandson like you. How about we go see him—when this is over?"

Waya nodded and smiled.

Kahoka, breathless, surveyed Vilnius, who was still clutching his shoulder and staring at the abyss.

Waya shook his head. "Now what?"

Wick looked at the others. "Guys," he said softly. "Those who are with us are more than those who are with them."

Kahoka frowned. "What does that mean?"

"I don't know, but I think it means we have help—more than just what we see. I don't want us to live with a stain on our conscience we can't wash off. We have to let Vilnius go."

Kahoka, still watching Vilnius with a wary grin, called out, "Let him go—as in off the ledge, or let him walk?"

Wick shrugged. "Let him walk. We're not him. If we drop him, we become him."

Kahoka nodded and pulled Vilnius away from the bluff. But as Wick and Waya started to look away, Vilnius let out a yell and lunged—flashing a knife at Kahoka, slashing his arm. Kahoka grunted and stumbled, blood seeping into his sleeve.

Wick and Waya reacted instantly, grabbing Vilnius and pinning his arms. Waya twisted the knife away and flung it. Kahoka, shaking but upright, held his wounded arm and glared.

Waya looked to Wick, jaw set. "What now? He deserves—"

Wick shook his head. "No stain. Send him on his way. Let him remember this moment whenever he tries to hurt someone again."

Vilnius, caught off guard by mercy, staggered to his feet. "You're letting me go?"

Wick nodded, voice quiet but steady. "You're outmatched, Vilnius—you always will be."

Vilnius turned and limped away, casting one last angry glance back.

Wick reached for Kahoka's arm, helping to bind the wound. Kahoka hissed but grinned. "That man's like a thistle—hard to get rid of."

Wick tried a shaky laugh. "Yeah, but even thistles can't grow everywhere forever."

Kahoka held out his bandaged arm. "The cornstalk shoot is today. With this arm, I'm out. Can you do it?"

Wick hesitated, glancing at Waya. "This is what you came for—do you want your shot?"

Waya shrugged, eyes wide. "I wanted to. Now it's obvious—destiny chose you."

Wick swallowed, hands clammy on the bow. The future of the tribe—and everything he carried—waited for him now.

He squared his shoulders. "Let's go," he said, masking the unease tightening his chest. "Time to show them how this tribe represents."

Chapter 44
The Cornstalk Shoot

As Wick, Waya, and Kahoka headed toward the cornstalk shoot, Wick's stomach churned. He wanted to represent the tribe—wanted it with everything in him—but half of him wished someone else had been chosen. Too late for that now. The day had arrived.

As the boys rounded the curve, the field stretched before them, a vast expanse thrumming with life. Nearly a hundred people gathered in clusters—talking, laughing, preparing. Wick stopped short, his pulse slamming against his ribs. He leaned over, pressing his hand to his stomach. "I thought this would just be a few people. Kahoka, what gives? Why such a crowd?"

Kahoka shrugged. "This is our harvest festival. A day of feasting, competition, and—most importantly—warriors proving themselves."

Wick straightened, forcing steadiness into his voice. "What's the prize?"

Kahoka's expression sobered. "Our families and tribes have grown too large to sustain our numbers. Some must leave. The winning warrior brings home the prize for his tribe—this land."

Wick lowered himself onto a fallen log, staring blankly at the scene before him. His limbs felt like they belonged to someone else. "You two go ahead. I need a minute."

From his perch, Wick took in the sights: kids darting, massive spreads of food tempting festivalgoers, juniors lining up for target practice, and warriors setting their sights on the looming hundred-yard cornstalk bale. The whole world bustled around him, yet he felt oddly still, trapped in the moment.

He took a slow breath and rose, joining Kahoka near the edge of the gathering.

Wick ran through what he knew. The modern cornstalk shoot had a clear set of rules. Pulling Kahoka aside, Wick asked, "Hey, Kahoka. I want to make sure I have this right. Each shot's points come from the number of cornstalks pierced—five to nine per shot. First to fifty wins. Sound right? And where do we get the steel tips?"

Kahoka blinked. "No. Where'd you hear that? We don't use steel tips, and we don't count stalks. You hit the cornstalk bale, it counts—one point, no matter where. You use the tips you have on your arrows. You start with four arrows. If you lose one, you don't get to replace it. You draw for who you shoot against. It's elimination. Last one standing wins."

Wick exhaled hard, rubbing his temple. This wasn't just a shift but a whole new set of rules. "Well. That changes things." He glanced at the throng of competitors, each sizing him up like prey. "When do we start?"

Kahoka chuckled. "Slow down. Festival first. Junior matches, lunch, wrestling matches, and grand matches. This isn't just about winning—it's about the celebration."

Wick nodded and ran his hand through his hair.

Kahoka pointed toward the range. "You'd better hurry if you want practice shots before the junior match starts."

Wick nodded. Practice. He needed that. "So, who's my competition?"

Kahoka motioned toward a warrior on the practice field. "Dusti. His name means spring frog, but you may get sick of his croaking before the match is over. He won the competition last year. Thing is, stakes are much higher now. I don't even know some of these warriors. They might be better than Dusti. We'll see."

Wick frowned. "For some reason, I thought this was a small shoot-off against just one warrior."

Kahoka grinned. "Where'd you get that idea?"

Wick leveled a stare at him. "From you, about fifteen years from now."

Kahoka laughed. "Well, maybe I forgot, or maybe I just didn't want to scare you off."

Wick sighed, shaking his head. "Nice." His laugh came easily enough. "I know that's right."

Wick headed out to practice, eyeing the cornstalk bales set up one hundred yards apart. He took a parallel stance to Dusti, studying his technique. Wick launched his first arrow—it fell short. Dusti sneered. Wick missed again but landed his third shot on the cornstalk bale.

After practice shots, Dusti turned to Kahoka. "What's this outsider doing here?"

Kahoka squared his shoulders and spoke loud enough for the nearest spectators to hear. "He is of our tribe. He is my blood brother and Atsadi's son. He bears Atsadi's bow as proof."

Dusti sneered. "He may shoot, but he won't win."

As Wick collected his arrows, the juniors took the field. Waya breezed through several rounds, knocking out competitors with clean, confident shots.

Wick clenched his jaw. *Waya's hitting great. I wish he were competing in my place.*

Waya landed two out of four arrows in the final junior match, losing just one point to his competitor. Wick and Kahoka congratulated him on a solid showing.

Wick's stomach was so knotted at lunch that he could barely eat. What he did try was incredible. *Wish I could pack this up for Gramps. He'd love it.*

As the grand competition arrived, the warriors drew lots. The coordinator's voice rang out, "First to ten points wins and moves on. Single elimination. Loser drops out."

Wick squared off with his first opponent. His first volley—two out of four—matched his competitor's. Next round, Wick landed two, his opponent three. *Down five to four. Got to do better.*

Stepping to the line, Wick fired—four direct hits. His opponent landed three. *Tied. Eight-all. This is it.*

On the final attempt, Wick struck four again to his opponent's three. He advanced.

"Nice shooting, Wick," Kahoka said, slapping Wick on the back.

Wick exhaled. "Don't congratulate me too soon. This could take four more rounds."

As he waited for the next match, movement in the sky caught his eye. A kettle of hawks soared, circling, gliding on thermal currents.

His vision shifted.

Suddenly, he saw from their vantage—how subtle wind shifts altered an arrow's course, how minute adjustments in elevation meant the difference between a hit and a miss.

Facing his next three competitors, he tapped into that insight, micro-switching his vision to track the thermals as he fired—every arrow hitting its mark, knocking out one warrior after another.

It all came down to this. One last competitor. He looked over to size up his foe—Dusti.

As Wick and Dusti faced off, each shot a perfect first volley, four out of four. Arrow for arrow, neither missed. They continued until each had five perfect rounds, totaling twenty points apiece. As they prepared to start their sixth volley, Dusti lowered his bow.

"How about we move out another twenty paces? Two arrows each?"

Wick nodded. What was one more challenge? They paced twenty steps back. Wick drew the short lot, which meant he had to shoot first.

He closed his eyes, shifting his view into hawk vision. Strong wind gusts pushed from right to left. He remembered his first failure at Atsadi's—overshooting. Would this shot play out the same?

He elevated his bow and offset it to compensate for wind gusts. He launched the arrow—it struck the center of the cornstalk bale at 120 yards.

Not bad.

He repeated the process, hitting two out of two. But it wasn't over. Dusti had yet to shoot.

Dusti hesitated, stepping up to the line. Wick caught the subtle twitch in his fingers, the way his throat bobbed as he swallowed hard. Nerves. Wick knew that look—it meant hesitation. Hesitation meant weakness. But then again, maybe it didn't. Maybe Dusti was buying time, recalibrating, preparing to surprise him. Wick swallowed, unsure.

Dusti's first shot looked on target but veered left at the last second—narrowly missing.

Kahoka and Waya whooped and tackled Wick in a bear hug.

Wick was stunned. *Was that it? Did I win? Is it over?*

Dusti turned, eyes locked on Wick. Slowly, he reached for Wick's bow and studied its craftsmanship.

"Atsadi taught you well."

Wick thanked him. Dusti nodded, then pressed his palm flat against his chest, a silent acknowledgment of honor. Several people in the crowd echoed it.

As the commotion settled, Wick found a quiet spot to sit, emotionally spent, his mind running in fragments.

Dad—Nora—deed—Waya—land—all saved.

Get Waya back home safe.

Go home—rest.

Wick and Waya bid young Kahoka adieu at the signal tree and ported back, reappearing in front of an anxious "dad" Kahoka awaiting Waya's safe return.

As they arrived, Kahoka clutched Waya, heaving a sigh. Wiping his eyes, he looked up at Wick and mouthed a silent "Thank you."

After Kahoka's embrace, Wick punched Kahoka in the arm.

"What's that for?" Kahoka asked.

"That's for keeping me in the dark on all the details about the cornstalk shoot," Wick replied.

"Well. It worked, didn't it?"

They laughed.

Wick got serious. "What about what transpired there, with Vilnius and Waya? Do you recall the details now, or is that still fuzzy?"

Kahoka pointed to a scar on his left arm. "Oh, I remember. I've replayed it over and over in my head a thousand times. I'm still not sure we did the right thing. I should have asked you and Waya to walk a short distance and say Vilnius fell over the cliff, which would have been true. Vilnius would be gone, and the two of you would have a clean conscience."

Wick opened his hands outward, eyebrows raised. "Who knows?"

Kahoka put his arm around Waya. "Wick, we'll be getting back. Waya's mom will be worried. Would you like to join us?"

"Hold on," Wick said. "Could you wait ten more minutes?"

Kahoka paused. "I guess so. What's up?"

Wick put his arm around Waya. "I made a promise to Waya. We'll be right back." Wick reached into his satchel and pulled out an artifact from Atsadi. Both he and Waya placed their hands on the signal tree.

They spent two days with Atsadi at the river encampment. Wick stood back as he watched the two bond, just as he had with Gramps after arriving in Mountain View.

As they headed back, Waya smiled and thanked Wick.

They touched the signal tree and returned to Kahoka.

"So, where'd you two go?" Kahoka asked.

The boys laughed.

Waya shared details with Kahoka as the two headed down the hill to report to Waya's mom.

Watching them leave, Wick smiled. He had reunited a family and formed a new kinship. For once, things seemed as they should.

But as dusk crept up the ridge and the wind changed, Wick couldn't shake a nagging certainty—there were always more battles to fight. Sometimes, the hardest ones came from where you least expected.

Chapter 45
Dark Night

Wick ported home with relief and triumph still singing in his veins. For the first time in months, nothing was left to be rescued, saved, or shot for. *You did it. You pulled it off. Family's whole, land is safe. Maybe now you can relax.*

He never made it past the back porch. Latesha was there—eyes red, her usual fire gone. "Wick." She swallowed hard and shook her head, unable to speak.

"What happened?" Wick said, panic squeezing his chest. "Everyone okay?"

She nodded and pointed to the house. Alarm bells blared in Wick's mind.

Inside, the family was clumped in the living room—faces pinched, all eyes glued to the TV. Mom looked at him, tear-stained, hand covering her mouth. "Wick—"

He joined the rest. The local news blared: "Local businessman Vilnius Whitmore, CEO, announced today that he has acquired the crystals needed to launch the initial public offering of Crystalis Vitalis. Construction of a new, state-of-the-art medical research lab will begin soon, employing 200 high-tech jobs, and is expected to bring much-needed economic revitalization to the county.

"In a statement, market analysts called the development 'potentially the most significant breakthrough in medical science since Genentech's licensing deal with Repertoire Immune Medicines helped reshape the landscape for next-generation T cell-targeted therapies.' If the promises hold, Crystalis Vitalis could upend cancer treatment as we know it—shifting from fighting cancer to curing it.

"Crystalis Vitalis claims its proprietary injection rewrites the body's immune system to recognize and destroy cancer cells permanently. The IPO is expected to raise over $1 billion, bringing jobs and boosting the county tax base."

Wick's blood ran cold. On-screen, a grainy video looped, showing Uncle Billy—*their* Uncle Billy—delivering a trailer load of crystals to Vilnius's company. Shaking hands. Smiling. The whole town would see it.

The world spun. Wick collapsed into the couch. Gramps moved beside him, laying a hand on his shoulder. "It's alright, Wick. You tried. This isn't your fault."

"No—it's Billy," Wick choked out. "Why? We won, and he sold out everything we fought for." Latesha and Mom squeezed Wick's shoulders, trying to anchor him, but Wick shook his head, numb. *It's over. After all that, it's over.*

Horror began to creep beneath Wick's anger—a twist of guilt and doubt sharper than grief. *I let Vilnius go. I stood on that bluff, gave mercy, and look what came of it. Did I doom our family by being soft and giving the villain a second chance? If I'd pushed and let justice win—not hope—would this be happening?* He wanted to throw something, scream, return, and undo mercy. For the first time, Wick wondered if being a "guardian" meant making the hard call—no matter the cost.

***

He stared at Billy's name on his phone, thumb hovering over decline, then let the screen go dark. The second call—he didn't even glance at it before it vanished. The third left a message: "You need to believe there's more to it, Wick. Call when you're ready." He exhaled, long and slow. He tossed the phone onto the couch and ran a hand through his hair. *Not today.*

Doubt and regret haunted every step. He paced the hall, the barn, the fields—trying not to imagine what Vilnius would do next, or how much more his family might pay for one fleeting moment of mercy on a cliff.

Days blurred. Wick drifted through chores and obligations with a sleepwalker's haze. Meals came and went; sometimes Mom put leftovers on the table, and Wick barely touched a bite. Nights were the worst—in dreams, he saw that video clip playing over and over. Billy, shaking Vilnius's hand. Smiling. Selling everything away.

Wick needed some clue to make sense out of this mess. He didn't have the stomach to visit young Billy. How could he face him? Wick struggled to find balance. *How do you tell your best friend he will betray you over seventy years later? And if you know he will, do you still consider him your friend?*

He didn't have the heart to visit Kahoka to tell him what had happened. *Let Kahoka believe it all turned out okay.* He visited Kahoka's old campsite. He didn't expect to find answers there, but he had to check anyway. As expected, trees had grown up in the campsite. He kicked the dirt and saw arrowhead flint fragments.

He went to the crystal cave, hoping Kimi or some magical answer would appear. Wick listened to the cave crickets. He sat on the bluff, staring at the old, jagged cedar tree. He recounted how supportive Billy had been, both young and old Billy. Was any of it real? He recalled how Gramps had thought he saw Billy talking to Big Mike behind the feed store. Wick pounded his fist on the ground. Bet he was planning it then. Wick replayed everything he could remember Billy saying, and how he couldn't promise "smooth sailing." He had to know.

Wick tried hawk vision, hoping soaring would lift his spirits or discover some sort of revelation. He soared over Mountain View, only to see Vilnius's men unloading crystals into the warehouse. *Forget that.*

Everywhere on the farm, the sense of victory had vanished. Whenever he wandered back from the fields, he found Gramps or Gram talking quietly in the kitchen, Nora watching him with silent questions in her eyes, Dad angry and baffled but saying nothing that Wick could answer.

One evening, Gramps made a fire in the yard. Wick joined him in silence. Above them, stars wheeled bright and cold.

"Wick, everyone's looking to you for how to feel. Lot of folks are disappointed—not just in Billy, but in what the world always seems ready to take from us."

Wick stared into the flames, nothing but emptiness inside. "I can't let it go, Gramps. He threw away everything. The farm, the cave, your house—he just let Vilnius have it."

Gramps looked at him. "All things in perspective, Wick. He may have crystals, but not the farm yet."

Wick shook his head. "Yeah, but isn't that the next step? What happens a year from now, when they need more crystals? If it's as great as they say it is, won't they just condemn the land to get more? What if they take your home?"

Gramps sighed. "Wick, this home, the farm, the cave are all Billy's. Always have been."

Wick blinked in shock. "What? I thought you and Gram owned the place."

Gramps shook his head. "Elijah was my gramps, but he was Billy's father. John died in the war. Billy was the only one left. Billy inherited it from his folks. But after his first wife died—an aneurysm, out of nowhere—he let us live here, said a man with a young family needed it more. His second wife died of cancer. He never had kids of his own. All these years, it's been in Billy's hands. He just kept it for us."

Wick struggled for words. "Why did he never say?"

"He gives in different ways than most, I guess. Been hurt in different ways, too."

Wick's anger melted into regret. "He called. Three times. I just couldn't... But what if it is my fault Vilnius came here? If I'd made a different choice—"

Gramps smiled, warmth filling his weathered features. "Sometimes forgiveness takes a while. Sometimes it takes everything you've got. Only thing harder is carrying that anger around your whole life."

Wick poked a stick into the embers, watching sparks twist skyward. "How do I even start?"

Gramps sipped his coffee, then set the mug down. "Go see him. Doesn't have to be fancy—a hug, a sit-down. Rest will work itself out."

The campfire snapped and popped. For the first time all week, Wick felt the anger in his chest soften. Maybe he was ready to try.

He watched embers float into the night. *I'm so sorry, Billy. Perhaps tomorrow I can find the words.*

Chapter 46
Echoes of Forgiveness

Wick drove his '74 blue Ford pickup to Billy's assisted living unit, hope and dread wrestling inside him. Every apology he'd rehearsed crumbled as he knocked.

Billy opened the door, looking thinner and wearier than Wick remembered—his eyes steady yet tired. For a heartbeat, they stared at each other. Then Wick stepped inside, leaving his pride at the doorstep.

"I'm sorry." The words tumbled out. "Not just for blaming you. For disappearing, shutting you out—for everything. I just—I couldn't understand."

Billy nodded and motioned Wick to sit. "Knew you'd show up. Had a feeling you wouldn't believe it till it came straight from me."

Wick hesitated. "Why, Billy? Why give Vilnius the crystals? After all we did?"

Billy leaned back and stared at the ceiling. "Because the world wanted a miracle. Not just Vilnius—everyone. People will never stop searching for fountains of youth. If not him, someone else. There'd always be a threat to the cave, the land, our family. So, I let Vilnius have his show."

Wick shook his head, voice cracking. "But won't that put us back in the crosshairs? If it works, won't they come looking?"

Billy smiled wryly. "Yes. If they were real."

Wick blinked. "Real?"

Billy grinned. "The crystals are real—just not from the cave. Picked them up from a mining outfit in Hot Springs. Plain as gravel, shiny enough."

Wick stared in disbelief. "You sold him a truckload—not one from here?"

Billy shrugged. "Never touched the cave or farm. Had those shipped, handed Vilnius the key, then watched him grin like he'd struck gold."

Wick laughed. "Did you tell him they were from Hot Springs?"

Billy sniffed. "He didn't ask, I didn't offer."

"Why would Vilnius think you would sell your family out?"

"Corrupt folks never see loyalty, only betrayal."

"But Vilnius already had the IPO. What now?"

Billy's tone softened. "Schemes like that don't last. Look at Theranos—big promises, bigger crash. Investigators catch up. Maybe not tomorrow's headlines, but trust me—truth wins. Vilnius will get what's coming."

Wick breathed easier, relief mixing with shame. "So—their cure won't work?"

Billy grinned. "They're crystals, Wick—just not Kimi cave crystals. They'll burn through every last cent chasing magic that isn't there. By the time they realize, Kimi's cave'll be yesterday's news."

Wick hesitated. "But Vilnius has one real crystal? If his scientists test it—"

Billy opened his palm, revealing the original cave crystal. "You mean this one?"

Wick gaped. The crystal that started the whole thing. "The one I traded to the clerk in Riggsville! How'd you get it?"

Billy shook his head. "I traded it as part of the deal. What's one trinket to a man with a truckload?"

Wick hugged Billy, finally letting go of the ache. "I'm sorry I doubted you. I should have trusted you."

Billy's eyes softened. "Guarding a family means knowing when to let the world burn itself out chasing shadows. We're safer this way, trust me. You've come a long way from a seventeen-year-old with a bucket full of wild mushrooms. Still making stew?"

"Naw, I picked up enough wisdom over the years to stay out of the woods—and the hospital."

They laughed.

Billy pressed the crystal into Wick's hand. "Second time I'm trusting you with this. Don't lose it."

Wick smiled, reassured. "So, I've got the only real crystals?"

Billy scooped up Sailor Cat, scratching behind the ears. "Not quite." He slipped Sailor's collar loose, showing Wick the bell with a tiny crystal hidden inside. "Sailor and I have lingered longer than we should. Having the crystal around may have stretched our days. But we can rest now. Take care of this for me."

Wick nodded, examining the collar, then buckled it back around Sailor's neck. "Nora's pretty attached. He ought to stick around. Besides, every family needs a little magic."

Billy grinned. "You did good, Wick."

Wick stood, peace welling up in his chest for the first time in weeks. "Stay at the farm sometime?"

Billy smiled. "At my age, town suits me. But I'll visit."

***

Back home, Wick stood with Gramps on the porch. Night cooled the air, and the world slowed to a hush. The two sat quietly, watching lightning bugs blink across the field.

Gramps nudged him. "Get what you needed?"

Wick nodded. "Yeah. Forgiveness. Truth. Guess I learned being a guardian means you can't fight every battle alone."

Gramps sipped his tea. "Proud of you, Wick. It's easy to do what's right when everyone's watching. But real guardians do what's right for the past, present, and future—even when no one's looking. This place is better than when you found it."

***

The next day, the family crowded the kitchen. Wick's parents beamed as Wick read a letter from the University of Illinois. "Full ride—wrestling scholarship."

Latesha and Nora shrieked with joy; Gramps hooted.

When the cheers died, Wick cleared his throat. "I'm finishing high school here, with the Mountain View Yellow Jackets. But Latesha and I plan to enroll at Illinois after graduation." Latesha flushed, grinning, and Mom squeezed his hand, eyes shining with pride.

Later, on the porch, Nora sat beside Wick, Sailor Cat on her lap. "Wick, you used hawk vision to rescue me." She paused, hugging Sailor closer. "I wish I could see hawk vision—even once."

Wick grinned, scooted closer, took her hands, and told her to close her eyes.

A heartbeat later, Nora squealed, almost launching Sailor from her lap. "I saw it! It scared me—I was flying. No ground, nothing but sky! Do it again! And you have to let my friends try on my birthday."

Wick rolled his eyes, laughing. "Maybe. With waivers signed."

***

A week later, the family stood before the "Our Stone County Sons" memorial on the courthouse lawn—an eagle keeping watch over names etched in granite. Billy traced his brother John's name with a trembling finger. Wick touched his great-grandfather's name, counting how many guardians came before him.

Before leaving, Wick guided Gramps to the placard near the corner of the courthouse, resting his hand on a stone block. "See this, Gramps? You won't believe it—Bill Laroe, the head mason, let me set this one. Hauled every stone for these two courses, week before Dad popped up."

Gramps put his hand on his forehead. "Wick, that's something! Been standing over a hundred years—and still looks more solid than I do. You do good work, kiddo."

Wick glanced to make sure Mom was out of earshot, then pointed toward the jail and smirked. "Probably shouldn't mention the time I spent there."

Gramps shook his head. "Wick, some things are better left unsaid. Your mom would croak."

***

Back home, the family gathered for a cookout.

"Let me get the campfire started," Gramps said.

"Hold up, Gramps," Wick said. "Nora and I can handle this one."

Mom and the others shot him suspicious looks.

"You're not using gasoline again, are you?" Gramps quipped.

"No, Gramps," Wick said, grinning, "Nora wants to keep her eyebrows. No shortcuts. Like you said, 'you never know when you'll need survival skills.'"

Gramps chuckled. "She'll need matches."

Wick waved him off. "She's got the flint and steel. We're training for survival, not convenience."

Dusk fell. Sailor Cat padded by, ancient magic glinting in his eyes. For a moment, Wick thought he saw a faint glow in the direction of the cave—guardianship never ends.

I guess when you're a guardian, you don't always get to pick your battles. But you do choose who you become, every step of the way. Sometimes, the battles worth fighting are the ones you walk away from—with forgiveness.

Wick and Billy camped on the back porch, night falling as embers floated to meet the stars. Wick didn't need to ask Billy if he wanted to go inside; the unspoken bond of friends across time, kindred spirits. They would camp on the porch, drifting in and out of slumber, under the open stars, watching the fire fade to coals, listening to the serenade of frogs, whippoorwills, Bob Whites, hoot owls, and the occasional yips, barks, and howls of coyotes.

As laughter from Latesha, Nora, and Dad drifted through the screen door, Wick closed his eyes, heart whole. *Family is the real treasure—no cave required.*

Where the Story Began

I wrote *The Signal Tree* to capture the wonder of a childhood lived outdoors, long before cell phones, when adventure waited in every creek bend and ridgeline. My land in the Ozark hills—where real signal trees still stand and traces of Native American history linger in the ridgelines and hollows—inspired me to share that sense of mystery, freedom, and connection with the natural world. This story grew from my desire to pass along the magic of those wide-open days and invite readers into a place where the past still whispers through the trees.

The Path We Walk

My father, Boyd Hughes, retired from the Navy in 1966 as a Master Chief Electrician's Mate. I was seven then, living with dad, my mother Betty, and my siblings Joe and Judy in San Pedro, California. Not long after we moved back to Arkansas that same year, Dad began taking Joe and me on long hikes through the hills and hollows he loved. Among the many places he showed us were the Indian Cave and the bluff where the real cedar tree still stands. Joe carved his initials into that cedar, a small mark of boyhood that time hasn't erased.

Thirty years later, in 1996, Joe and I retraced that same long hike with his two boys, Christopher and Stephen. None of us knew it would be the last time I'd walk those woods with my brother. A few weeks later, Joe and eight-year-old Christopher were killed by a drunk driver on I-40 near their home in Watertown, Tennessee.

I feel closer to Joe, to Christopher, and to Dad whenever I return to those trails. And in the quiet of those woods, I like to think I'm also brushing shoulders with forebears I never had the chance to say dinner prayers with.

This story grew from those memories—from the places that shaped us, the people we loved, and the threads that tie us to those who came before. I hope this book brings you a little closer to your own loved ones, both those still walking beside you and those whose footsteps you still hear in the leaves.

About the Author

Mike E. Hughes grew up exploring the ridgelines and hollows of the Ozark hills, a landscape that continues to shape his imagination. Many of the story's elements are drawn from his favorite hidden spots in the woods. After a career in the power industry, he turned to writing stories that blend adventure, mystery, and the quiet magic of the natural world. He lives in Arkansas, where he stewards a patch of forested land and writes at his own pace. Since the release of *The Signal Tree*, some readers have encouraged him to explore more of the cave's secrets, Kimi's origin story, and the evolving bond between Wick and Latesha—possibilities he's considering for his next project. Learn more at www.mikeehughes.com.